Robert B. Parker's

The small town of Paradise is devastated when a [...] player is found dead at the bottom of a bluff just a day after winning the team's biggest game. As Jesse Stone searches for answers about how the boy died and why, he is stonewalled at every turn, and it seems that someone is determined to keep him from digging further.

Jesse suddenly must divide his attention between two cases after the shocking murder of former Paradise police chief Charlie Farrell. Before his death, Farrell had been looking into a series of scam calls that preyed upon the elderly. But how do these "ghost calls" connect to his death? Both old and new enemies come into play during the investigation, and in the end, Jesse must find the common factor between the two deaths in order to prevent a third.

Robert B. Parker's *The Bitterest Pill*

"Exceptional . . . Faithful to the spirit of Parker's characters without sticking to the status quo."

—*Publishers Weekly* (starred review)

Robert B. Parker's *Colorblind*

"Superior . . . The impact of these events on individuals [is] palpable, giving this nuanced entry more emotional weight."

—*Publishers Weekly*

"Another well-written, fast-paced yarn from one of the acknowledged masters of crime fiction."

—Associated Press

Robert B. Parker's *The Hangman's Sonnet*

"Heartfelt . . . Coleman balances plot and character perfectly."

—*Publishers Weekly* (starred review)

"Must reading for Parker devotees."

—*Booklist* (starred review)

Robert B. Parker's *Debt to Pay*

"His best to date."

—*Kirkus Reviews*

"A complex cat and mouse game that will keep readers turning pages."

—*Publishers Weekly*

"A suspenseful, clever thriller that moves at breakneck speed."

—*Booklist*

Robert B. Parker's *The Devil Wins*

"*The Devil Wins* is such a winner of a novel that Parker's loyal fans and Coleman's new ones will be equally delighted by his skills. This series can run forever in these new capable hands and readers will eagerly await each new book about Jesse Stone. I know I will."

—*HuffPost*

"Small town, big secret, and a community's shame. In the blink of an eye, Jesse goes from worrying about potential storm damage to investigating three homicides. . . . A suspenseful, melancholy examination of loss and how sometimes, despite our best efforts, the past refuses to stay buried, and it will certainly please fans still craving more of Parker's characters."

—*Booklist*

"Coleman's solid second Jesse Stone novel finds Parker's flawed hero, now the police chief of Paradise, Mass., still having trouble separating from his ex, connecting with people emotionally, and dealing with guilt over a subordinate's near-fatal shooting. . . . Coleman succeeds in adding some needed depth to Jesse's character."

—*Publishers Weekly*

"Coleman does a remarkable job of developing the character, deepening our understanding of his struggle with the ghosts that haunt him. . . . Both a fine mystery story and a satisfying portrait of an emerging character that readers will look forward to hearing more from soon."

—Associated Press

Robert B. Parker's Blind Spot

"Fans of both Parker's Spenser and Jesse Stone series will enjoy this 13th installment. . . . Like Spenser, Jesse is a man of honor who feels he must speak for the dead. . . . It is a great, fast beach read, recommended for all detective fiction fans."

—*Library Journal*

"Coleman is continuing the Stone saga in his own crisp prose style. . . . Jesse Stone fans will be eager to discover where Coleman takes this compelling series next."

—Associated Press

THE JESSE STONE NOVELS

*For a comprehensive title list
and a preview of upcoming books,
visit PRH.com/RobertBParker or
Facebook.com/RobertBParkerAuthor.*

ROBERT B. PARKER'S
FALLOUT

A JESSE STONE NOVEL

MIKE LUPICA

G. P. PUTNAM'S SONS
New York

PUTNAM
—EST. 1838—

G. P. PUTNAM'S SONS
Publishers Since 1838
An imprint of Penguin Random House LLC
penguinrandomhouse.com

The Library of Congress has catalogued the G. P. Putnam's Sons
hardcover edition as follows:

Names: Lupica, Mike, author.
Title: Robert B. Parker's fallout: a Jesse Stone novel / Mike Lupica.
Other titles: Fallout
Description: New York: G. P. Putnam's Sons, 2022. |
Series: Jesse Stone; 21
Identifiers: LCCN 2022028050 (print) | LCCN 2022028051 (ebook) |
ISBN 9780593540275 (hardcover) | ISBN 9780593540282 (ebook)
Subjects: LCGFT: Detective and mystery fiction. | Novels.
Classification: LCC PS3562.U59 R64 2022 (print) |
LCC PS3562.U59 (ebook) | DDC 813/.54—dc23/eng/20220613
LC record available at https://lccn.loc.gov/2022028050
LC ebook record available at https://lccn.loc.gov/2022028051
p.   cm.

First G. P. Putnam's Sons hardcover edition / September 2022
First G. P. Putnam's Sons trade paperback edition / August 2023
G. P. Putnam's Sons trade paperback edition ISBN: 9780593717165

Printed in the United States of America
1st Printing

This book is for Taylor Lupica.

Not only can't I believe she married me.

All this time later, I still can't believe she talked to me.

ROBERT B. PARKER'S
FALLOUT

ONE

Jesse Stone looked out at the baseball game being played at O'Hara Field, a ballgame on an afternoon like this always a beautiful thing, at least to him, his eyes fixed at the moment on the kid playing shortstop.

Jesse felt as if he were looking at himself, back when he was a high school senior, back when he could see a whole lifetime of baseball days like this stretching out in front of him.

This kid was a little taller. Had a little more range. But not more arm. Definitely not more arm.

Nobody ever had more arm than I did.

Jesse felt himself smiling. Because even knowing what he knew about what had happened once he made it as far as Triple-A, the big leagues close enough to touch, knowing how baseball would break his goddamn heart later, he wanted to climb down out of the bleachers and be this kid's age and change places with him in a heartbeat.

Just for one more afternoon.

Have one more game like this.

"What did you think about when it was late in a game like this?" Suitcase Simpson asked.

Suit was on one side of Jesse. Molly Crane was on the other. The kid at short, Jack Carlisle, was Suit's nephew, his sister Laura's boy. About to accept a scholarship to go play college ball at Vanderbilt, unless he changed his mind at the last second. Jesse didn't follow college ball the way he did the majors. But he knew enough to know that Vanderbilt had a big-ass program, and had sent a lot of kids to the big leagues over the years.

"I wanted the ball hit to me," Jesse said.

He heard a snort from Molly.

"So you could be in control. I'm shocked. Shocked, I tell ya."

Without turning, Jesse put a finger to his lips.

"Don't you shush me, Jesse Stone," she said. "You act like we're in church."

"Baseball is better than church," Jesse said.

Molly, the good Catholic girl, stared up at the sky. "Forgive him, Father." She smiled. "And not just for that."

Jesse turned to Suit. "I feel as if I've been sitting next to fans like her at ballgames my whole life."

"You wish," Molly said.

Suit shook his head. "*I* feel like I've got a bad middle seat on a long plane ride."

The Paradise Pirates were ahead of Marshport, 2–1. League championship game. Bottom of the ninth. Jesse always wanted to laugh when he heard people calling teams "bitter" rivals in sports. Only people on the outside. They had no idea. All they had to do was watch a game like this. Every single one of these kids on this field, both teams, waiting for the ball to be put in play and so much to start happening at once, was exactly where he wanted to be.

Where I always wanted to be.

Wanting the ball to be hit to me.

He had been working with Jack Carlisle a little bit this spring, at Suit's request. Trying to teach the kid some of the things that Jesse had learned on his own. Not teach him everything he knew. Just some of it. Some of the baseball he still had in him, despite landing on his shoulder that day in Albuquerque, his dreams about making The Show crash-landing right along with him.

His father had always been more interested in being a cop than he was in baseball. Or watching his kid play baseball. Jesse could count on one hand the times the old man had actually shown up for one of his games.

Two outs now. The Marshport center fielder had just struck out swinging.

But the tying run was still at third base.

Go-ahead run at second.

"Move to your right," Jesse said quietly.

As if somehow Jack Carlisle could hear him.

"He pulled one into the hole his last time out."

Still talking to himself. But tricking himself into believing he was talking to the kid at short.

"What?" Suit asked.

"Nothing," was Jesse's reply.

The Marshport batter stepped out of the box, buying himself some time. Maybe about to win the game, and the championship, for his team with a hit, or end his season with an out.

Across the field Jesse saw Nellie Shofner, from the *Town Crier,* taking notes. She still hadn't moved on to a bigger paper, though she clearly had the talent, and the work ethic. Jesse knew she was working on a feature about Jack Carlisle, one the *Crier* was going to run as soon as he signed his letter of intent with Vandy.

Nellie saw Jesse looking over at her and waved.

"Oh, look," Molly said. "It's Gidget."

Jesse ignored his deputy chief and leaned forward, the pitcher ready to pitch and the batter ready to hit now.

Hit it to short.

He's not afraid, the way I never was.

It happened then, exactly the way Jesse had pictured it, or maybe willed it, the kid with the bat hitting a sharp grounder to Jack's right. Crack of the bat unmistakable on a ball you'd just caught clean.

But the damned ball looking like a base hit, for sure.

Except.

Except Jack Carlisle *had* moved over, the way Jesse wanted him to. Jesse had seen him do it right before the pitch, the kid reading the ball perfectly as it came off the bat. So the ball was headed into left field. But then wasn't. There was Jack Carlisle half sliding, half diving to his right, backhanding the ball. Knowing in the moment he had no chance at the kid who'd hit the ball, and was flying down the first base line behind him.

You either knew what to do next or you didn't.

Jack knew.

From his knees, he sidearmed the ball to his third baseman. Snap throw, right on the bag, something on it. *I could make that throw.* The Paradise third baseman, Finn Baker, put the tag on the runner, the runner clearly out. But if the runner heading home crossed the plate before the tag was applied at third, game was tied.

He didn't.

Game over.

Home team had won the title.

After the celebration in the middle of the field, and then the trophy presentation, Jesse stood with Jack Carlisle near second base. Suit was there, too. And Molly. Jesse knew, though, from experience, the kid really didn't want to be with them. He wanted to go be with his teammates. This was part of it, Jesse remembered, that feeling you had in the first few minutes after you won the big game, and you never got those first few minutes back.

"Party tonight," Jack told Jesse. "Over at the Bluff."

Jesse grinned. "Better not be adult beverages involved."

The kid grinned back. A younger version of Suit. Family resemblance impossible not to see. Jesse thought Jack Carlisle looked more like Suit than he did his own mother.

"Can't speak for the boys," Jack said. "But I'm not gonna blow everything by getting drunk and stupid."

Then he ran across the field to where the Paradise Pirates were already posing for pictures.

"There were guys I played with in high school who could have taught a master class in drunk and stupid," Jesse said to Suit and Molly.

"Boy, those were the days, my friend," Molly said.

"We thought they'd never end," Jesse said.

It was right before Jesse felt as if somebody had dropped a bomb on Paradise, Mass.

Two, actually.

TWO

Spike was at the Gray Gull, which he had owned for a few years now.

He was Sunny Randall's best friend but had become Jesse's friend, too. Spike also owned Spike's, on Marshall Street in Boston. He had just been spending more time in Paradise lately, primarily because his current boyfriend had a weekend place on the water.

Sunny liked to call Spike a gay superhero. Jesse had asked her one time, just in the interest of proper record-keeping, what kind of superhero she considered him.

"An inner-directed one," Sunny had said.

"Anything else?" Jesse had said.

"Hunky one," she'd said.

Back when she still considered him as such, sometimes quite enthusiastically.

"I know you want to ask me how she's doing," Spike said to Jesse when he arrived at the Gull.

Both of them knowing who "she" was.

"I'm fighting it," Jesse said. "The way I do my urge to drink."

"How about if I tell you anyway?" Spike said.

"How about I pop into the kitchen and look for possible health code violations?" Jesse said. "*Or* we could stop talking about Ms. Randall and you could show me to my table."

"Right this way, Chief Stone!" Spike said.

Charlie Farrell, who'd retired as police chief in Paradise long before Jesse had arrived from Los Angeles, was already seated at his favorite corner table, a martini in front of him. White hair, worn long, but he was able to carry off the longish hair, even at his age. Good tan. Bright red V-neck sweater. Charlie was partial to red. Said his late wife used to tell him the color "popped" when he wore it. Red golf shirt underneath it. Charlie didn't look his age, which Jesse knew to be right around eighty. It was his hands that gave him away. They always did. His hands looked older than the town lighthouse. Or the ocean beyond it.

He grinned and put his right hand out to Jesse. Jesse shook it, but lightly, knowing by now Charlie's hands were about as sturdy as leaves.

"Chief," Charlie said.

"Chief," Jesse said.

"I'd get up," Charlie said to Jesse, "but it would take too long."

"We need to get you one of those portable ski lifts you've got at the house to get you upstairs," Jesse said.

"Bite my Irish ass," the old man said.

Charlie and Maisie Farrell had finally gotten tired of the Paradise winters and moved down to Naples, Florida, after he retired. To live happily ever after in the sun. But Maisie Farrell was diagnosed with Alzheimer's two years ago, died last year from complications. Charlie had sold their condominium almost immediately after the funeral and moved back to Paradise. He told Jesse one time that he thought guys his age waiting around to die in Florida seemed like a cliché.

He pointed to his martini glass and did what he always did, no matter how many times they met for dinner, and asked if Jesse minded.

"Yeah," Jesse said. "Tonight's the night I decided to let *your* drinking finally bother me."

"Well, you never know," Charlie Farrell said.

"As long as you drink responsibly," Jesse said.

"I'm eighty years old," Charlie said. "What the hell's the point in that?"

He drank some of his drink and smacked his lips and put his glass down. He never ate the olives. Said they were more decorative than anything else.

"I never asked," Charlie said. "Were you a martini guy in your drinking days?"

"Scotch," Jesse said. "Lots and lots of scotch."

"You still miss it?"

"Only when I'm awake," Jesse said.

Spike brought Jesse an iced tea without Jesse having ordered it.

"On the house," Spike said.

"Too small to be a bribe," Jesse said.

"Gotta start somewhere," Spike said.

Charlie wanted to know how things were going with the red-haired lawyer.

Rita Fiore.

Jesse smiled. He smiled a lot when Charlie was on the other side of the table. Like he was here with his grandfather.

Or maybe a second father.

"You know how they say in sports that the legs go first?" Jesse said. "I'm starting to think they go second."

Charlie Farrell sighed.

"And the thing you're talking about that *does* go first?" he said. "It just keeps going and going. *South.*"

"So it doesn't keep going like the Energizer Bunny," Jesse said.

"A battery, maybe," Charlie said. "But a dead one."

"I'll bet Miss Emma doesn't say that," Jesse said.

Librarian emeritus in Paradise. In Charlie's demographic.

"Despite her advancing years," Charlie said, "Miss Emma continues to be aspirational, bless her heart."

Jesse laughed. Sometimes he thought the best part of being in Charlie's presence was just listening to the old man talk.

They both made small talk over filets and fully loaded baked potatoes. Jesse wanted to know how Charlie's grandson was doing. Nicholas. In his late twenties, in a wheelchair since his motorcycle spun out of control one night in the rain on the Stiles Island Bridge. Jesse was the first to the scene. The helmet Nicholas was wearing might have saved his life. But couldn't prevent the damage to the lumbar region of his spinal cord.

"He loves working at that candy store," Charlie said. "They got the kid moving up fast in sales."

It was a lot more than a store. It was the hottest new business in Paradise, Mass., the candy company owned by Hillary More. She had moved here with her teenage son the year before, opened More Chocolate, and it had almost immediately become a sensation, and not just in Paradise. Hillary More had bought the old firehouse at the edge of town, refurbished it, extended it, hired only local people to work for her, making an especially big point of hiring people with disabilities like Nicholas Farrell, who now handled talking to nonprofits using More Chocolate for fundraising. The factory where the chocolate was actually manufactured was up in Nashua, New Hampshire, just over the state line, for tax purposes.

Jesse liked her a lot. He couldn't see himself having a romantic relationship with her, as much as she kept trying to put that into play, and not just because he knew she was a single parent with a son at the high school. What he did fantasize about was her running for mayor in the next election, an idea she had already floated herself from time to time.

It was a piece of a larger fantasy for Jesse, one that involved shooting his current boss, Mayor Gary Armistead, out of a cannon.

Jesse noticed Charlie had gotten quiet when it was time for him to order dessert.

"What?" Jesse said.

"*What* what?" Charlie said.

"Unspoken thoughts have never been one of your specialties," Jesse said. "Right up there with bullshit."

"I promised myself I wouldn't bother you with my niggly problems," Charlie said.

"With you, there's no such thing," Jesse said. "You're family, Chief."

So Charlie told Jesse about the "Grandpa call" he'd gotten the day before. A female voice, young, saying it was Erin. Granddaughter. Nicholas's sister. Traveling in Europe. Telling him that one of the girls she was traveling with in Europe had been arrested with drugs, and that they both needed a lawyer, which is why Grandpa needed to wire money, like right now. Or, better yet, buy some cash cards and read her the numbers over the phone.

"Erin" said she'd call back in the morning.

"What's pissing you off so much about that?" Jesse said. "You're too smart to have gone for it. On top of that, you're a cop."

"What pisses me *off*," Charlie said, "is thinking about other geezers who do fall for this scam, and lose money they can't afford to lose. Or give the scammers an account number from their bank and get themselves good and cleaned out. Or buy into the fact that the IRS is coming after them if they don't come up with some dough, and fast."

He told Jesse then that Miss Emma had even lost a few thousand dollars to a scammer of her own the year before.

The martini was long gone. Charlie was working on an espresso now. And even though Charlie had gotten sidetracked riffing about the scam and spam calls, they both knew they weren't leaving until Charlie got his vanilla ice cream.

"I'd like to have a talk with whatever thief is behind this thing," Charlie said.

"It's the same as looking to get even with telemarketers," Jesse said. "But even if you could somehow stop one of them, it would be like whack-a-mole. There's more of them than there are of us."

Jesse turned and waved for their waiter.

"Order your ice cream," he said. "That always makes you feel better. And let this go."

"Something else that's never been one of my specialties," Charlie Farrell said. "And not one of yours, either, I might add."

"How about this?" Jesse said. "How about we put a tap on your phone? I'll put Molly on it. Next time they call, *if* they call, keep them on the line and maybe they'll slip up."

"I just want one face-to-face with these bums," Charlie said. "Maybe pistol-whip one of them."

"Focus on your next face-to-face with Miss Emma," Jesse said. "And allow your former department to serve and protect that Irish ass of yours."

Spike came over and took Charlie's dessert order.

"Two scoops tonight," Charlie said.

"Good call, Gramps," Jesse said.

"Your ass," Charlie Farrell said.

THREE

Charlie had driven to the Gull in his beloved Jetta. Despite the old man's protests, Jesse took the keys and drove him home to the small, two-story house on the west side of town that he'd kept even after he and Maisie had moved to Florida.

He had never been able to bring himself to sell it, he told Jesse one time, because there was too much history inside that house, and too much love.

"Does that make me sound like some kind of sap?" Charlie had said.

"Just makes *me* love you even more," Jesse had said.

As they were walking across the Gull's parking lot, Charlie had said, "I can drive after just one glass of vodka."

"Not as well as I can after none," Jesse had said.

"I still have seniority on you," Charlie Farrell said.

"So you do," Jesse said. "But look at me, I'm the one with the keys."

It was a little over a mile from Jesse's condo to the Gull. Jesse had walked there because he liked walking more and more, and

had been running less and less now that his knees felt as if somebody had taken a baseball bat to them. It was the shoulder injury
that had ended his career. But somehow it was his knees, both of
them, that had become arthritic over time.

You pay and you pay, Jesse thought.

For something you'd pay anything to have back.

After dropping off Charlie he walked through town, hardly
anybody on the streets tonight. The ones who recognized him
nodded. Some said hello. Some wanted to talk about the Paradise
Pirates beating Marshport.

He walked past the movie theater that Lily Cain had restored
after it had burned down. That was before Jesse found out that she
was someone other than the Queen Mum of Paradise that everybody had always thought she was, and ended up with a bullet in
her head that Jesse was sure her son, Bryce, had put there, but was
still unable to prove, to his everlasting regret.

He took a slight detour and then there were the More Chocolate buildings in front of him, upstairs lights in the old firehouse
still on. Jesse really did like Hillary More, liked her a lot, actually,
if not as much as she seemed to want him to. She was pretty and
had a good laugh and could swear like a ballplayer and could hold
her liquor.

A skill I never mastered.

But a skill, for some reason, he still found admirable, in men or
women.

Jesse kept telling himself that someday, when he was old, he
would drink again. But how old? As old as Charlie Farrell? He
stared up at the second-floor lights and wondered if Hillary might
be up there working late. Hillary. Who continued to make it crys-
tal clear that she was right here if Jesse wanted her.

"We need to keep church and state separate now that you've become a civic leader," Jesse said. "And especially if you do run for mayor."

"What about on weekends?" Hillary More said.

She reminded him a little bit of his ex-wife, Jenn. Just smarter. By a lot. With a much better sense of humor. Jenn had ultimately turned out to be a bad decision that had taken up too much of his goddamn life. Maybe Hillary was another mistake waiting to happen. But not all of his decisions, or relationships with women, had been bad. Sunny hadn't been. Things hadn't even ended bad between them. They'd just ended.

Jesse was through town and passing the house that had once belonged to Mayor Neil O'Hara, someone else who had been shot to death in Jesse's town, for the crime of getting in the way of a land deal.

Naming of the dead, Jesse thought.

The older you got, the longer you stayed on the job, the more you found yourself doing that. He wondered if Charlie Farrell did the same thing when he was alone and awake in the night. Charlie had told him one time that you developed plenty of scar tissue if you did this kind of work long enough, mostly out of necessity.

Jesse had told himself he was going to take the long walk home after he dropped off Charlie.

But now knew he was not.

So he made a right off Main Street and then another, and walked another half-mile or so, and finally stood in front of the small white cottage with the green shutters and the well-kept front lawn.

Knocked on the door.

She opened it, smiling.

"Evening, Gidget," he said to Nellie Shofner.

"Can't you get Molly to stop calling me that?" she said. "Because maybe if she does, you will."

She was actually older than Jesse had thought when she first started working at the *Crier*, thirty-two now.

She stepped forward quickly and put her arms around him and kissed him. He told himself it would have been less than gentlemanly to not kiss her back.

When they stepped back, Jesse grinned.

"First I've got to get Molly to stop calling *me* Moondoggie," he said.

"I looked it up," Nellie said. "That TV show where Sally Field played Gidget came out in 1965."

"Original movie's older than that," Jesse said. "Sandra Dee was the original Gidget."

"Who?" Nellie said.

"I basically think Molly is just making a more general cultural reference," Jesse said.

"Should I point out to Molly that calling me Gidget is a way of making *her* look old?" Nellie said.

"Sure," Jesse said. "Why don't you call her fat while you're at it."

Nellie pulled him inside, shut the door, pushed him up against it, and kissed him far more enthusiastically than she had before.

"Well, you're in luck," Nellie said. "Tomorrow's not a school day."

The next morning, Jesse awakened even earlier than he usually did, five-thirty today, dressed quietly, left Nellie sleeping soundly, was having his first cup of coffee at home, best of the day the way the first drink always had been, when he got the call about the first body.

FOUR

They found Jack Carlisle's body in the rocks and shallow water below Bluff Lookout, the most northern piece of oceanfront property in Paradise. It was a mile up the coast, maybe a little less, from The Throw, the oceanfront property that had gotten five people killed last year, Jesse nearly making it six before an old acquaintance named Wilson Cromartie, known as Crow, had saved him.

A guy jogging with his dog had found the kid's body. Had his phone with him, called 911. Suit had gotten there first, then Molly. When Jesse arrived, Molly told him that Suit was operating in a functioning state of shock, adding that she had told him it would be better for everybody for him to go home now, before he fell apart in front of everybody.

"How'd that go?" Jesse said.

"He didn't," Molly said. "Go, I mean."

"How's he doing?"

"He's not," Molly said.

Jesse looked over. "He seems to be holding it together."

"For now," Molly said.

Jesse had a total of twelve people in his department. He counted ten down on the narrow beach now, and in the water. One kid, one with potential named Jimmy Alonso, was back at the office. Another new guy, Barry Stanton, was out on patrol. Jesse knew why the rest of them were here. This was a death in the family, not just Luther (Suitcase) Simpson's.

"The kids had a party last night up on the campground," Molly said.

She pointed up at the Bluff. Highest point in Paradise. Jesse's eyes took him from up there to down here.

Dev Chadha, the medical examiner, was up the beach as the bag with Jack Carlisle's body inside it was being lifted into the off-road ambulance they sometimes used, one able to make it down the dirt path from the Bluff to the narrow beach. Jesse walked up there now. Suit tried to reach down and help the EMTs. Jesse gently put a hand on Suit's arm.

"Let them," he said to Suit.

"I need to help," Suit said.

"Let him go," Jesse said, and got between him and the ambulance as the doors closed. Suitcase Simpson. A nickname from an old-time ballplayer. Watching them load the body bag with his ballplaying nephew in it.

"He looked like he was asleep," Suit said, his voice hoarse.

Jesse nodded.

"Dev said there was bruising, other than what the fall did, that made it look like he'd been punched in the face," Suit said. "Maybe more than once."

"If he was," Jesse said, "we'll find out who did it."

They both watched the ambulance slowly grind its way up the dirt road.

"Somebody had to have done this to him," Suit said.

"Maybe it was an accident," Jesse said. "Maybe he stumbled and fell somehow."

"He said he didn't drink," Suit said.

"I used to say the same thing when I was his age," Jesse said. "And so did you."

Now Suit was the one staring up at the Bluff.

"Does your sister know?" Jesse asked.

Suit said, "I called her. Soon as I got here and saw it was him."

"Where's her husband these days?" Jesse said.

"Who gives a shit?" Suit said.

"You need to go be with her," Jesse said.

"I wanted to help," Suit said.

"I know," Jesse said.

"I'm on my way to her now," Suit said.

"You want Molly to go with you?" Jesse said.

"I'm a grown-ass man, Jesse," Suit said.

Jesse put a hand on his shoulder.

"No one in this world knows that better than me," he said.

Suit took in some ocean air, let it out slowly. Jesse watched as he gathered himself now, imagining him like a boxer getting to one knee after having just gotten tagged and knocked down. Then Suit began walking toward the dirt road. Doing the only thing you could. One foot in front of another.

Jesse and Molly began to follow him as Jesse felt his phone buzzing in the back pocket of his jeans.

Nellie

"I'm sorry about Suit's nephew," she said.

She already knew. Of course she did. She was Nellie.

Before Jesse could respond she added, "There was a fight at the party."

Jesse stopped to let Molly go ahead.

"Why are you giving that up?" he said.

"Because it's Suit's nephew," she said.

FIVE

The day Jesse's father died in the line of duty for the LAPD, died in the crossfire of a gang shoot-out in South Central, Jesse had done the only thing he knew how to do, when he was the young cop dealing with a death in the family.

He went back to work.

One way or another, there or here, drunk or sober or somewhere in between, it always came back to that for him. Only mechanism that worked for him. Like he had his own ideas about grief counseling.

Nellie still didn't have all the details on the party. Still didn't have the name of the other kid in the fight with Jack Carlisle; none of the other players would give it up, at least not yet.

"It's almost like there's some kind of code," she'd said to Jesse on the phone.

"Not almost," he said. "There *is* a code."

A fight didn't necessarily explain why Jack Carlisle had ended up in the water. But it was something. A start. One foot in front of the other.

Jesse was at Paradise High School a few minutes after the bell at nine o'clock. Jesse knew real grief counselors would be on-site before the morning was out, breaking off kids into small groups, or even working one-on-one with the ones most upset. Jesse knew the drill. There had been a suicide at the start of the school year, the girl who was vice president of the student council.

By now, Jesse was certain, the whole school knew what had happened to the star shortstop of the high school baseball team. The world of social media. Such a joy.

The principal, David Altman, told Jesse he'd need a few minutes to get the baseball team to the gym, as Jesse had requested.

Jesse was in Altman's office with him. Being there made Jesse remember all the times in high school he'd been in the principal's office. Never voluntarily.

Always with cause.

"I'll meet you there," Jesse told him. "The gym."

"I'm frankly not sure how the parents are going to feel about their children being questioned by the chief of police," Altman said. "As if the boys are suspects or something."

"If they object," Jesse said, "have them call me and I'll explain this one crucial thing to them."

"What thing?"

"That I don't give a flying fuck about their feelings," Jesse said.

Altman was short, bald, slightly overweight, favored the kind of bow tie he was wearing this morning. His face now turned the color of a cherry blossom at Jesse's word choice, which didn't surprise him, since he'd always considered the principal of the high school an officious little prig.

"I certainly hope you won't use language like that in front of the student athletes," Altman said.

"Only if one of them fucking annoys me," Jesse said.

FIFTEEN MINUTES LATER the members of the Paradise High baseball team were facing Jesse from where they all sat in the bleachers.

Jesse told Altman he could leave.

"This is my school, Chief Stone," Altman said.

"It's your school about as much as this is my town," Jesse said. "I need the boys to be able to speak freely."

"They can do that in front of me," Altman said.

"No, they can't," Jesse said. "We can do this here, or I can load up the team bus and take them all to the station and you can speak freely to their parents about that."

Altman stood his ground, but not for long, then turned and walked out of the gym as if he had important school business waiting for him somewhere else in the building.

Jesse stared up into the faces of kids he had watched win the big game the day before.

"Listen, I knew Jack Carlisle," Jesse said. "And some of you might know that. I worked with him some on playing shortstop. Won't wear you out with a trip down memory lane, but I made it as high as Triple-A when I was young. Dodgers chain. I just wasn't as good as Jack was going to be."

He was walking up and down in front of them.

"Most of you know Jack was the nephew of one of my officers," Jesse said. "So this is as personal for us as it is for you."

One of the kids raised a hand. Jesse recognized him. Kenny Simonds. The starting pitcher in yesterday's game. His father owned an auto repair shop just over the line from Paradise, in Marshport.

"Why are we here?" Simonds said. "None of us want to talk to you. And my father always says that nobody had to talk to the police if they don't want to."

Jesse nodded.

"They don't," Jesse said. "But just so you know, Kenny, I am officially treating what happened to Jack as a suspicious death."

"Thanks for the heads-up," Simonds said, his voice full of sarcasm.

"I wasn't finished," Jesse said, putting some snap into his voice. "Nobody here has to talk to me. But if you don't, if you choose not to help me investigate what happened to your friend, I'm going to look at you as hindering my investigation. And get suspicious about *that*."

He moved to his right, so he was directly in front of Kenny Simonds.

"Do I have your attention now?" Jesse said.

Simonds nodded. He wasn't the only one in the bleachers doing that. Jesse reminded himself these were high school kids, some of them or even most of them dealing with the death of a buddy for the first time in their lives.

"Were all of you at the party at Bluff Lookout?" Jesse said.

More nods.

Jesse took a closer look at the faces in front of him, noticed that the team's first baseman, Scott Ford, was wearing sunglasses.

"Now I already know one of you had some kind of beef with Jack at some point in the proceedings last night," Jesse said. "Now I need to know who with."

"Who said there was a beef?" Kenny Simonds said.

"Son," Jesse said. "I'm the one asking the questions here."

Jesse waited.

He was good at it.

Better than them.

He walked down to Scott Ford and said, "Lights too bright in here for you, Scott?"

Ford mumbled something.

"I'm sorry, son, I didn't quite catch that," Jesse said.

"I said I didn't want everybody to see I've been crying," Ford said. "Is all."

"Is all," Jesse said, nodding.

Then he quickly walked up the aisle and, before the kid could react, took off the glasses. Ford's left eye was purple, swollen, nearly closed. Maybe he hadn't known that Jesse knew about a fight before he walked into the gym. Maybe he was afraid to be the only team member not in attendance. He was a kid. Maybe he thought he could get by telling Jesse he'd been crying, as if he'd given up some crucial piece of information.

But here he was, anyway.

Jesse handed Ford back his glasses. Ford put them back on.

"Let's take a walk," Jesse said to him.

"What if I don't want to?" Scott Ford said.

"Then I can call Jack's uncle and get him over here and you can explain about the fight to him instead of me," Jesse said. "Your call."

The kid got up and began walking toward the double doors at the end of the gym. Jesse followed him. Before he was out the doors, he looked back over his shoulder. None of the other players had moved. They were just staring.

Boys to men, Jesse thought, *this fast.*

He thought: *It must already seem to them as if somebody else won the big game.*

SIX

Jesse and Molly sat with Scott Ford in Jesse's office. Jesse had asked the kid if he wanted one of his parents present, or both of them. He'd said no, his father would only find a way to make things worse than they already were, if that was even possible.

"I'll tell them later," Ford said.

"They know about the fight?" Jesse said.

"I'll tell them that later, too," he said. "I slept at Kenny's house last night. Our pitcher. The one smart-mouthing you in the gym."

"I know who he is," Jesse said.

Suit was still at his sister's house. *Thank heaven,* Jesse thought, *for small favors.* Not that he was feeling particularly religious today. This wasn't the first time he'd fantasized about getting God into an interrogation room and shining a light in His face and asking Him to explain shit like Jack Carlisle ending up dead in the water, and why He generally kept acting so pissed off at the world.

Ford sat on the other side of Jesse's desk, big hands in his lap.

He'd taken off the sunglasses. The purple around his eye seemed to have darkened just since they left the gym, the bruise spreading. Jesse also noticed the swelling in his right hand. The kid looked tired and hungover and sad. And scared being in the office of the chief of police. The only thing he'd said to Jesse on the ride over here was "Are you going to arrest me?"

"Should I?" Jesse said.

"It was just a dumb fight," Ford had said, "over nothing."

Then he had started to cry for real.

In the office now, Molly asked if Ford wanted coffee.

"Hot?" he said.

"All we got," she said.

"No."

"No, thank you," Jesse said.

The kid shifted his attention to Jesse.

"What?"

"What you meant to say to Deputy Chief Crane," Jesse said, "was 'No, thank you.'"

Oh," Ford said. "No, thank you."

"What was the fight about?" Jesse said.

"Like I told you," Ford said, "it was really about nothing."

"Scott," Jesse said in a soft, good-cop voice. "Let's not either one of us fuck around here, okay?"

The kid leaned back and stared at the ceiling with one good eye. His sunglasses were in front of him on Jesse's desk.

"Why are we even doing this?" Ford said. "I didn't knock him into the water. We were nowhere near the water when we got into it."

"I'm just trying to figure out how he ended up *in* the water," Jesse said.

"He was my teammate!" Ford said. *"He was my friend!"*

"You ever have a fistfight with your friend before?" Jesse said.

"We got into it a few times," Ford said. "My mom calls it dumb young-guy stuff."

"Not exactly what Chief Stone asked you, Scott," Molly said.

She always knew when to come in, shift the focus of the person being asked the questions. Like a pitcher changing a batter's eye angle by moving the ball up and down, in and out.

"Chief Stone asked if you and Jack ever got into a fistfight before," Molly said.

Ford was staring down at his big ballplayer's hands again.

"No," he said. "This was the first time."

But he hesitated, just slightly, before answering.

"So what was it about?" Jesse said.

"He'd had too much beer and I'd had too much beer and he accused me of something I didn't do," Ford said.

"What would that be?" Molly said.

"Messing around with his girlfriend behind his back."

He gave them a name. Ainsley Walsh. Said he'd never do anything like that, you never did that with a friend. Told them again that it wasn't anywhere near the water and that he walked back to where the other guys were and Jack had walked off in another direction.

"Toward the water?" Jesse said.

"I didn't even look," Ford said. "I just wanted to get some ice. And get away from him."

He looked up. Red eyes. Jesse thought he might cry again.

"It was the last time I saw him," he said.

He slumped into the chair, seeming to collapse inside himself. Jesse could see him starting to shut down. Finally told him he could go, but might circle back later. Asked if Ford wanted a ride back to school. Scott Ford said he'd rather walk.

When the kid got to the door, he remembered he didn't have his sunglasses, came back for them, put them back on.

"Sorry about your friend," Jesse said.

Scott Ford said, "Not as sorry as I am."

Less than a minute later, Jesse heard the shouting from the squad room.

When he came through the door he saw that Suit had Scott Ford up against a wall.

SEVEN

Five minutes later Suit was in the chair Scott Ford had just vacated, trying to get his breathing under control. Clenching and unclenching his own big hands. Molly had closed the door behind her, leaving them alone, letting them be.

"I heard about the fight between him and Jack," Suit said.

"From whom?" Jesse asked.

"My sister," Suit said. "She called me when I was on my way back here. One of the other moms called her."

"And you made a determination that the best way to process that information was to act like every cowboy asshole cop in America?" Jesse said.

Suit's face was still red. But then it never took much excitement, of any kind, for that to happen.

"I'm sorry, Jesse, I really am," Suit said. "I just lost it when I came in and saw him in those sunglasses. Like he was Joe Cool or something, after what I saw in the water a few hours ago."

"'Sorry' hardly ever fixes the lamp," Jesse said.

"It won't happen again," Suit said.

"Statement of the obvious," Jesse said.

"Please don't take me off the case," Suit said.

Jesse could see the plea in his eyes.

"He wasn't just a nephew to me, you know that," Suit said. "He was more like a son."

Jesse's son, Cole, had been accepted into the London Law Program, one approved by the American Bar Association, for second- and third-year students. It was an exclusive program, according to Cole. Its appeal might have had something to do with the English actress he had started dating before he'd applied. He and Jesse were staying in touch, but sometimes only once a month. The kid sounded happy. Leave him alone.

"You could come over," Cole had said a few days ago.

"I could become an astronaut, too," Jesse had told him.

Jesse walked over to the coffeepot and poured himself a cup. He was just buying himself time. Trying to get his own temper under control. He couldn't let Suit get away with what he'd done, not in front of the whole squad room; it was unprofessional, bullshit behavior from one of his cops. One who felt like a son to Jesse. But he had no desire to make things worse for Suit than they already were, if such a thing was even possible today. Because Jesse was certain that things had never been worse for Suitcase Simpson, his whole life, than they were right now. From the time he'd gone to work for Jesse, Suit had consistently been one of the happiest people Jesse had ever known.

It was the old Mike Tyson line. Amazing how much of life always came back to that. Everybody had a plan until they got hit.

Jesse sat back down with his coffee and drank some. Most of

the time he was the only one drinking from his pot. It was like the ballpark coffee he used to drink when he was playing ball, strong enough to fuel a small jet.

"This might be nothing more than a terrible accident," Jesse said. "He's standing there and he's hot-wired after slugging it out with the Ford kid and at least half drunk. Or more than that. We won't know that until we get the tox screen back. He's all spun around on what was supposed to be a fun night for everybody. And maybe the world started to spin around."

"I never saw him even take a single beer," Suit said.

"You're his uncle, Suit," Jesse said. "You treated him like a golden boy. Matter of fact so did I, every chance I got."

Jesse shrugged and drank some coffee.

"We'll find out how much booze he had in him," Jesse said. "Dev will do everything he can to speed this one along."

They sat there in silence. How many times had the two of them sat together in this office, working on a case, or just shooting the shit?

Just never like this.

Charlie talked about scar tissue. Jesse knew how much he'd developed on this job.

But what about Suit?

Molly came in then, quietly closed the door behind her, sat down next to Suit, took one of his hands in hers.

"Hey," she said.

"Hey," Suit said.

He turned to face her.

"I have to ask this," Molly said.

Suit waited.

"Is there any chance he could have jumped?" she said.

EIGHT

Jesse and Molly were standing near the place at Bluff Lookout where Jack Carlisle had likely spent his last moments on earth.

"Amazing view," Molly said.

"Of infinity, maybe," Jesse said.

Suit had started yelling again after Molly had raised the prospect of suicide. This time Jesse sent him home.

"Don't talk shit!" Suit had said to Molly.

"And don't you talk to Molly like that," Jesse said.

Jesse couldn't remember another time when Suit had ever done that, spoken to Molly that way.

"Jesse, you knew him," Suit said.

"Everyone thinks they know a kid suffering from depression until they don't," Jesse said.

"You're saying that's what happened?" Suit said.

He was shouting again, at both of them then.

"There is no way he killed himself!" Suit said.

"Not saying that he did," Molly said. "But we have to at least consider the possibility. We wouldn't be doing our jobs if we didn't."

"This is such BS," Suit said, shaking his head.

"You need to take the day, Suit," Jesse said.

"No," Suit said.

"Wasn't a request," Jesse said.

Molly had walked Suit to his car, then gotten into Jesse's Explorer for the ride to what was now a crime scene.

Just what kind of crime?

Jesse looked down at the waves crashing against the rocks, high tide now.

"He could have jumped," Jesse said.

"Or been pushed."

"Or gotten too close to the edge, and fallen off the end of the world," Jesse said.

"Shit shit shit," Molly said.

"We're gonna need to talk to everybody who was at that party," Jesse said. "Establish some sort of timeline. The last time anybody besides the Ford kid saw him. And no phone in his pocket, right?"

"Probably lost at sea," Molly said.

"We can still use his phone number to see who might have reached out to him in the hours after the party that night, though it's going to be the usual grind getting a subpoena for the records."

"What if we classify it as a homicide, that might speed up the process with our asshat DA."

"It's not a homicide," Jesse said. "Might not ever be. Suspicious death for now. We go by the book."

"Until we don't," Molly said.

"Shhhh," Jesse said.

"We'll start with a list of the kids at the party, get their phone numbers."

Jesse said, "And get the numbers of his other friends."

"And see if there's any we don't recognize when we get the phone records."

"Sounds like tons of fun," Molly said.

"You know what they say. Not a job. An adventure."

"Pretty sure that's the Navy," Molly said.

Jesse shrugged. "We are near the water."

Before Gabe Weathers had left the scene this morning, he'd done castings of the footprints they'd found up here, inside the crime scene tape. In addition, Gabe had taken photographs of all the prints from shoes and sneakers and sandals and whatever the hell else the ones who had come here to look at the water and the waves under what had been a full moon had been wearing. The deeper prints had enabled Gabe to pour down some of the dense liquid, Jesse forgot what it was called, that he used to make the castings.

"You gonna check everybody's shoes?" Jesse had said.

"Why the hell not?" Gabe said. "Maybe there's one print that doesn't belong. Jesus, some of these kids have big feet."

He grinned at Jesse.

"Aren't you always the one saying we need to build cases from the ground up?" Gabe said.

"Molly keeps thinking that quoting me to me is gonna get her a promotion," Jesse said.

"Wouldn't that mean your job?" Gabe said.

"She already thinks she's got it," Jesse said.

JESSE AND MOLLY walked away from the water now, over to where the party had been held. The kids had at least cleaned up after themselves, Jesse had to admit, around the fire pit. He found a couple stray cans. A few cigarette butts. That was it.

Night of fun.

Until Jack Carlisle had wandered off.

They'd find out, sooner rather than later, if there had been other witnesses to the fight. Scott Ford said he couldn't even remember exactly where they'd been when the punches had been exchanged in the night.

He said he had put Jack Carlisle on the ground. Said when he realized they'd turned the whole night into Stupidville he reached down and tried to help Jack up, but had his hand slapped away. That was when Scott Ford had walked back toward the party. They would find out eventually if Jack ever came back.

"Jack's girlfriend was at the party," Jesse said.

"Ainsley," Molly said.

"The doctors' daughter," Jesse said.

"Concierge doctors, if you please," Molly said.

"Do we know if she went looking for him?" Jesse said.

"One of the things I plan to ask her when she gets home from school," Molly said.

They were walking to where Jesse had parked his Explorer when they saw Nellie Shofner waving and heading their way.

"Weren't the two of you supposed to meet at the malt shop after your last class?" Molly said to Jesse.

"Is there no end to your dated references?"

"I try so hard to be good," Molly said.

"Try harder," Jesse said.

Nellie got right to it. Something else she always did. Something else about her that Jesse found appealing. Her not talking just to talk. Jesse had always thought small talk shortened your life.

"The fight was over a girl," Nellie said.

"We already know that," Molly said.

She smiled at Nellie.

"But no worries," Molly said, "it won't affect your final grade."

She told Jesse she'd wait in the car. Jesse and Nellie watched her go.

"You think maybe she and I can be friends?" Nellie said.

"Maybe you can get her to adopt you," Jesse said.

"You got anything I can use for my story?" Nellie said.

"No."

"Hey," she said, "I helped you out today."

Now Jesse started walking toward the Explorer.

"Okay, here's what I got for you," he said. "Ready?"

She took out her notebook.

"No comment," Jesse said.

"Wait a second," Nellie said, walking faster to keep up. "I thought the rules of engagement between us had changed."

"They haven't," Jesse said.

"So we're back to playing it that way?" she said.

"We never stopped," Jesse said.

"Wow," she said.

"We're friends with benefits," Jesse said. "Just not those kind of benefits."

NINE

Molly had pushed back her interview with Ainsley Walsh until later, as Ainsley was one of the girls organizing the candle-light memorial service scheduled for O'Hara Field at nine o'clock that night.

Jesse spent the rest of his afternoon interviewing members of the Paradise High baseball team, in his office, in fifteen-minute blocks. He'd gotten all of the phone numbers from the coach, Hal Fortin.

The stories from the kids were largely the same, making Jesse wonder if they'd gotten together and rehearsed them. They were aware that something had happened between Jack Carlisle and Scott Ford. They could see from Scott's face that at least one punch had landed when he came back. Jack never did. Everybody was lit. Nobody thought anything more of it. They were high school kids, after all, partying after the big game. All of them sure they were going to live forever.

Ainsley Walsh had left early. Len Samuels, the second baseman, said they'd just assumed that Jack and Ainsley might have gone off to talk through some stuff once Jack didn't come back, because he'd seen the two of them arguing about something earlier.

"Lot of arguments for a victory celebration," Jesse said.

"Not when there's enough beer," Samuels said.

Samuels was the last of them. When he left, Jesse sat behind his desk and opened the bottom drawer, where he used to keep his emergency scotch. His baseball glove was there now. He took it out, and his ball along with it, flicking the ball into the pocket, loving the sound of that, loving the smell of the glove, old as it was. Drinking and baseball. Baseball and drinking. He thought back to all the drinking he did, they all did, by the time they were in Triple-A. Did ballplayers still drink that much? Probably not. They went to the gym now when the game was over, not the bar. World had changed. It used to be thirty was old in baseball. Not anymore. They stayed in much better shape now. What had Mickey Mantle said that time? If I'd known I was gonna live this long, I would've taken better care of myself. Mickey stopped drinking finally, after being a legendary drunk. Went to Betty Ford. Got sober. Came out and died of cancer. Something else Jesse could ask God, he ever got alone with Him.

The ball went harder into the glove.

Baseball and drinking.

When he was young, he'd thought you couldn't have one without the other. Now he'd been sober for the longest stretch of his adult life. He'd stopped counting the days, and months, and years. He went to meetings less and less frequently. But the urge to drink was always in the room. *Not an elephant in the room,* he thought.

Just a fifth of Dewar's.

He knew the best thing was to find a meeting right now, keep the wolf away from the door. Elephants and wolves. *Mixing my metaphors now.* Such a long day. It seemed like *three* days since he'd left Nellie's house and gotten the call about Jack Carlisle.

How much did drinking have to do with the death of this kid?

I'll find out, Jesse told him.

I always have before.

He thought about Nellie Shofner now. He liked her. Liked her a lot. But he knew he didn't love her. He'd loved Jenn. He'd loved Sunny. Maybe still loved Sunny.

What he loved more than anything was being a cop.

He loved the work. Kept him sane, at least to a point. Kept the wolf away from the door.

Idle hands, Dewar's workshop, he told himself, putting the glove back in what had been the scotch drawer.

TEN

Two hours later Jesse was standing next to the bleachers alone, a few feet, no more than that, from where he'd watched the Paradise–Marshport game the day before.

Night had fallen by now, lit by candles that seemed to be everywhere at O'Hara Field.

The first speaker, a girl, said they were going to begin by playing some of Jack's favorite songs, picked out by Ainsley Walsh. Jesse saw Suit standing in the first row of the crowd, his wife, Elena, on one side of him, his sister on the other, Suit's arms around both of them.

Coach Hal Fortin spoke when the music stopped, talking about how Jack Carlisle was the most talented kid he'd ever coached, a team leader. A great kid. And a sure thing, Fortin said, to make The Show. Jesse knew it was a cliché. But it had always been Jesse's, too. He talked about The Show all the time still.

But wanted to tell Coach Hal Fortin there were never any sure things when it came to making it all the way to the big leagues.

There were more songs, none of which Jesse recognized. More speakers. Some of the kids broke down. Boys and girls. Some of them fought through, the air in the night thick with sadness. A couple volunteer firemen played "Amazing Grace" on bagpipes. Ainsley Walsh read "To an Athlete Dying Young." Jesse had heard the poem plenty of times before, once when one of his Albuquerque teammates had died of lymphoma before he turned thirty.

The only line he remembered was the one about silence being no worse than cheers.

He walked away from the field then, toward the parking lot. He would talk to Molly in the morning about what she might have learned from Ainsley Walsh, if she even talked to the kid tonight, and what her fight with Jack Carlisle had been about.

He would talk to Laura Carlisle, knowing he needed a face-to face with her, at her house, just the two of them. Suit would think he'd asked her all the right questions. Jesse knew better. Suit was too close. How the hell could he not be? But if it was suicide, Jesse needed to know, even knowing that it wasn't his job to know why the boy might have killed himself.

But he had to rule it out, in case it wasn't suicide and wasn't an accident and somebody had done this to Jack Carlisle.

Jesse thought about checking his phone and seeing if he could find a late AA meeting somewhere in the area, knowing that meetings always made him understand that whatever he had going on in his life, that first drink wasn't going to do him any good, or fix things.

He decided, just like that, to drive over to Charlie Farrell's house instead. Telling himself it would be better than a meeting, even better for the soul. Not even thinking about seeking out Nellie Shofner for comfort tonight.

Jesse felt himself smiling about that as he drove across town, feeling better just thinking about sitting with the old man, even knowing he'd just chosen an elderly man for companionship tonight over a woman in her thirties.

He'd make sure to ask Dix, his therapist, to explain that to him first chance he got. Jesse liked to give people the impression he knew everything.

Dix actually did.

ELEVEN

There were lights on in the house. A good thing. Sometimes Charlie turned in early. The Jetta was parked in the driveway. Jesse knew the old man did a lot of takeout, now that he'd proudly and successfully mastered Uber Eats.

So often when the two of them would get together, here or at the Gull or when Charlie would occasionally stop by the station when out on his morning walk, and Jesse would start some kind of bitch-a-thon about the general bullshit of being chief, Charlie would say, "Remember something: Nobody died today."

But today somebody had.

Jesse'd had experience before in dealing with a senseless death like this, plenty of times. Charlie Farrell had had more.

Before he got out of the Explorer he saw a text from Molly.

getting with Ainsley in the a.m.
wish me luck

Jesse didn't respond. Molly Crane didn't need luck, especially when the task at hand was dealing with a high school girl. She'd raised four daughters. No one knew more about talking to high school girls, or drawing them out, even getting them to reveal their secrets whether they wanted to or not, than Molly did.

She could teach a course in it.

Maybe I should take that course, Jesse thought.

Maybe it would make me smarter about women when they were all grown up.

He walked up the front steps and rang the doorbell.

Waited.

No sound from inside, not even the television in the living room, the big-boy flat screen that Charlie had bought for himself, one that was always on when Jesse would pay him a visit. If there was an old *Law & Order* on, any kind of *Law & Order—And when wasn't there one on?* Jesse thought—Charlie would be watching it.

"That Mariska Hargitay," he liked to tell Jesse, "she'd still be ringing my bell on the rare occasions when it still gets rung."

Jesse hit the doorbell again.

Still nothing.

The door was unlocked, as usual.

"Hey, Chief," Jesse called out, stepping inside. "It's me. The other chief."

He closed the door behind him and listened.

Something wrong.

Something about the air Jesse didn't like.

Not the kind of silence you got from a poem.

Jesse unholstered his Glock. On instinct. Or force of habit. Or both. Being overly cautious had never gotten anybody killed, he told Suit all the time. And Molly. And even Sunny Randall.

If Charlie came walking down the stairs now, or in from the kitchen, or from the backyard, the two of them could have themselves a good laugh about Jesse pulling a gun on him.

"Chief," Jesse said, louder this time, in case he was upstairs in the bathroom or in the yard. "You here?"

Gun at his side, he stepped into the living room.

He found him on the floor, the side of his head caved in, a spread of blood underneath him.

Charlie's own old Glock near his right hand.

Jesse knelt next to him, all the breath out of him at once, like a tire had been punctured, put a finger to Charlie Farrell's neck, knowing there was no point. Knowing he was gone.

Jesse stood and pulled his phone out of the back pocket of his jeans and dialed 911.

Swallowing hard and telling himself he wasn't going to cry in front of Charlie Farrell.

Even now.

He quickly told the operator who he was, and where he was.

"Does the victim have a name?" she said.

"Chief Charles Edward Farrell," Jesse said.

Ended the call and holstered his weapon and put his phone back in his pocket and sat down on the floor next to the body of Charlie Farrell.

"Cop," he said, his voice sounding even louder now. "Died old."

TWELVE

Jesse sat with Healy at Daisy Dyke's at eight the next morning.

Healy had been a captain with the Massachusetts State Police, homicide department, since before Jesse had arrived in Paradise from Los Angeles, back to when Charlie was still chief. He had retired as a Massachusetts legend in law enforcement a few years ago.

But he had heard about Charlie Farrell. Here they were.

"Don't take this the wrong way," Jesse said to him, "but I hope I look as good at your age as you do."

"You don't know my age," Healy said. "And ask yourself a question, by the way: What are my options?"

Neither one of them had ordered breakfast, just coffee for both of them. Daisy, whose hair this spring seemed to include most of the colors of the rainbow, said to Jesse, "The whole town heard what happened, you need to eat," when she brought the coffee to the table herself.

"I'm good," he said.

"Don't get smart with me," Daisy said, and left, at least for the time being.

"She seemed to take it personal, you not ordering food," Healy said.

"Daisy likes to play the long game," Jesse said.

He sipped some coffee. He had never asked, but was sure Daisy made up a pot special, just for him, knowing how he liked it, strong enough to take the trailer hitch off the F-100 pickup Healy had parked out front.

"Personal," Healy said, "is how you and me are going to treat Charlie's death."

"No more personal than this," Jesse said.

Healy's hair had gone completely white. There were more lines in his face than there'd been the last time Jesse had seen him. But he was as trim and hard-looking as ever. As good and hard a cop as Jesse had ever known, with the LAPD or here.

"I'm getting too old for this shit," Jesse said.

"Ought to be my line," Healy said. "All the times we've both had to deliver bad news to somebody, now we're on the other side of it, because it just happened to us."

Jesse said, "How long did you know Charlie?"

"That long," Healy said.

Two state cops, Crandall and Scoppetta, had shown up at Charlie Farrell's house not long after Suit and Molly and Dev Chadha had arrived.

"You're retired," Jesse said. "Shouldn't Lundquist be here?"

Brian Lundquist. Healy's successor with the Staties.

"He's all jammed up with some Mob thing in the city," Healy

said. "He called me soon as he heard. Asked if I wanted to take a ride over and help out a young up-and-comer like yourself. I told him that on some things you don't need to ask."

Jesse grinned. "So you cleared your schedule."

"As luck would have it," Healy said, "and by the good and enduring grace of God, my wife is out in Northern California visiting our grandchildren for a month."

He sighed.

"They were coming here for a month once school let out," he said. "But she missed them so much she decided to go there now."

"You gonna miss her?" Jesse said.

"Sure," Healy said. "Why not."

Jesse had shown him the crime scene photos by now. Told him Charlie's wallet was gone, which he thought was nothing more than a head fake from whomever did it, trying to make it look like a robbery. Cell phone nowhere to be found. Gun hadn't been fired.

"Doorbell cam?" Healy said.

"Charlie?" Jesse said.

"Had to put it out there."

Jesse told Healy now about the nuisance calls Charlie had been getting, and how he'd vowed to do something about them, take matters into his own hands, even though Jesse had tried to discourage him, telling Charlie to let the PPD handle it.

"How'd that go?" Healy said.

"Might have gotten him killed, is how it went," Jesse said.

"You believe it did?"

"Operating theory."

Healy picked up his mug, looked at it, gently placed it back on the table.

"If old cops don't die on the goddamned job," he said, "they're not supposed to go out like this."

"With all his bullets still in the chamber," Jesse said.

Daisy came and gave them refills. It was the same table Daisy used to save for Jesse and Charlie if Jesse called ahead and told her they were coming.

"Is it all right if I come in on this?" Healy said.

"Some things *you* don't have to ask," Jesse said.

He reached across the table. He and Healy knuckled each other some fist.

"How old *are* you?" Jesse asked.

"Charlie's age," Healy said.

THIRTEEN

Healy left. Jesse stayed, putting off heading over to the office a little while longer, knowing that in all the big ways, Charlie Farrell and Jack Carlisle would be waiting for him when he finally got there.

He'd had bad times on this job. Maybe never a moment as bad as this one. Hit twice like this. He was staring out the window when Daisy came back and placed a Western omelet in front of him, toast, silverware. New napkin.

"Nobody likes a bully," he said.

"Shut up and eat," she said.

He didn't feel much like smiling this morning. But Daisy got one out of him now.

"Who did your hair, van Gogh?" he said.

Daisy smiled back at him.

"You know, you might be the perfect man," she said. "For a man."

Jesse said, "You've got to set the bar higher than me."

He had finished eating and was about to leave when Hillary More slid into the booth across from him, Jesse not having seen her come in.

"You only think you don't want company," she said. "I know better. Women know things."

She was dressed as if she'd just come from the gym. Faded blue Tufts University baseball cap. Long-sleeved workout shirt, worn tight—*I'm a cop,* Jesse told himself, *trained to notice details like that*—with the Under Armour logo on the front. Her hazel eyes, Jesse had noticed before, were an amazing combination of brown and green. Even now, with very little makeup on, Hillary More was a knockout.

"Who am I to argue?" Jesse said.

"No shit, I have a sense of these things," she said.

"I'd actually love some company," Jesse said.

"Liar," she said.

Daisy brought Hillary More a mug with a tea bag hanging out the side without being asked.

"Daisy," Hillary said.

"Ms. More," Daisy said, and walked away.

"Sometimes I think she doesn't like me," Hillary said.

"Yeah," Jesse said, "but beneath that gruff exterior . . ."

"Is a pit bull," Hillary More said.

She played with the tea bag briefly and then said, "I'm so sorry."

"About the kid or about Charlie Farrell?" Jesse said.

"Both," she said. "My son, Kevin, was one of Jack's friends."

"Was he at the party that night?"

"He wasn't," she said. "He'd quit the baseball team for tennis. But he and Jack still hung out sometimes."

"We lost a great kid, and then a truly tremendous old man. But the assholes? They just keep going, and going."

"Don't they, though," she said.

"Don't tell me," Jesse said. "You found out about Charlie on your phone."

She shook her head. He knew it must be a trick of the light, but her eyes had seemed to darken just while she'd been sitting there.

"Nicholas called me," she said. "He was shattered, as you can imagine."

Nicholas Farrell and his sister were Charlie's last living family. Their parents died in the crash of a small plane owned by some friends ten years ago, a sudden and violent storm blowing in off the ocean a few minutes after takeoff.

"I'm going to get with Nicholas at my office in about an hour," Jesse said.

"So you've spoken to him?"

"He wanted to come to his grandfather's house," Jesse said. "I told him there was no point, not while it's still an active crime scene."

"Nicholas said you were the one who found Charlie," she said.

"I went over there because I wanted to talk to him about Jack Carlisle," Jesse said.

"Who could do such a thing to that old man?" Hillary said.

Jesse discreetly checked his watch, and waved for the check. Daisy gave him the finger in response.

"I'm going to find out," Jesse said. "Then I'm going to arrest whoever did it. And then be in the courtroom someday when the son of a bitch gets sent away. And live long enough to spit on his grave."

She was staring at him, eyes wide, as if seeing him for the first time.

"I don't believe I'd ever want to get on your bad side, Chief Stone," she said.

"Can't lie," Jesse said. "Few do."

FOURTEEN

From time to time Jesse would see Nicholas Farrell going up and down Main Street in his motorized wheelchair. Or driving around town in his wheelchair-adapted minivan. He'd even taken Jesse for a spin in the van one time, Jesse having to caution him not to get a speeding ticket with the chief of police inside his vehicle.

Nicholas looked like a long-haired movie star, had weightlifter's forearms, covered in tattoos that had distressed his grandfather to no end. For the past couple years he had been seriously talking about trying to qualify for the Paralympics in wheelchair tennis, because he was that good a tennis player. It was clear to Jesse in all ways that after the accident, the kid had decided to live a life instead of a concession. He was engaged to a local woman, Kelly Loughlin, whom he'd met working at More Chocolate.

He appeared to have put on another ten pounds of muscle weight since the last time he and Jesse had been in the same room together. All in all, Jesse thought he was built like The Rock.

"You know I would have been happy to come to you," Jesse said to him now in his office.

"I was happy to come here," Nicholas said. "I had to get out of the building. People are feeling sorry for me all over again."

"Can't have that," Jesse said.

"Been there, done that," Nicholas said.

Jesse had asked if he wanted coffee. It was like a default position for him when he had a visitor, unless it was a perp or suspect sitting across the desk from him. Nicholas said he'd brought his own, in one of those Yeti thermoses, in a cupholder on one of the arms of his chair.

He drank out of it, and grinned.

"Still hot," he said. "Does the same with cold."

"How *do* it know?" Jesse said.

They were both just killing a little time before getting around to the subject of his grandfather, and who might have killed him.

"I'm sure he mentioned to you how upset he was about those scam calls," Jesse said.

"His hair was on fire about it," Nicholas said. "He was still talking about it the last time I saw him." He swallowed hard. "He said he was going to find out who was behind that call if it was the last thing he did."

"I told him it was always a bad idea to take the law into his own hands," Jesse said, "even if he was still technically the law."

"Was," Nicholas said. "Past tense, goddamn it."

They sat, Nicholas's hands on the arms of the chair. Jesse noticed a wedding ring.

"Wait," he said, pointing at the ring. "You and Kelly are already married."

Nicholas's smile was sheepish.

"I usually just wear it around the house when nobody else is around," he said. "Like I'm road-testing it."

"How's it feel?" Jesse said.

"Freaking awesome," the kid said.

"Back to your grandfather," Jesse said.

"Do we have to?"

"When was the last time you spoke with him?"

"Early last night," Nicholas said. "Kelly and her friends were having a girls' night out. I offered to pick us up a couple of those flatbread pizzas from the Gull he loves . . . loved. He said he had to meet somebody and he'd call me later if it wasn't too late."

"He say who the somebody might be?" Jesse said.

"I asked," Nicholas said. "He said he'd tell me later. I told him he was sounding mysterious. He told me he didn't solve mysteries anymore, he left that to the cops on *Law & Order*. Especially that actress he liked on *SVU*."

"Mariska Hargitay."

"Sometimes called her Captain Benson, like she was a real person," Nicholas said, grinning. "Used to say she could be his superior officer anytime."

Jesse said, "Did he ever mention whether the nuisance call came on his landline or his cell?"

"Never asked."

"Whoever did this to him took his cell along with his wallet," Jesse said.

"But I thought I read somewhere that if you know the number, you can go into his records and track his calls," Nicholas said.

"We can," Jesse said. "But the bastards behind these calls do something called spoofing, so the call looks like it's coming from a legit number, sometimes a local one. Those they call neighbor spoofing."

"There must be a way to track them back to the source," Nicholas said.

Jesse said, "You just keep going deeper and deeper down the rabbit hole, all the way to hell."

Another silence between them. He saw Nicholas look down at his watch.

"Might he have said anything else on the phone that might help me out here?" Jesse said.

"We didn't talk all that long," Nicholas said. "I just finally told him that maybe I'd see him later."

He swallowed again.

"And that I loved him," he said.

"So did I," Jesse said.

"Promise me that you're going to find out who did this to my Gramps," Nicholas said.

"I promise," Jesse said.

"You're not just saying that to make me feel better?" Nicholas said.

"Let me ask you a question," Jesse said. "Anything I *could* say to make you feel better today?"

"No."

"Then get out of here," Jesse said.

"Wheels up," the kid said as he spun the chair around.

FIFTEEN

Molly and Suit sat with Ainsley Walsh in the living room of the home she shared with her parents on Stiles Island. Their office was four blocks away, closer to the bridge. The house they were in was the biggest of a gated community, one of a handful of gated communities on the island, called The Dunes, even though Molly knew that with beach erosion the way it was these days they might end up calling it The Former Dunes before much longer.

For now, she thought, *personalized medicine was being very, very good to the Walshes.*

Suit had asked if he could come along, now that Molly's interview with Ainsley had been pushed back to today, the students of Paradise High having been given the day off in Jack Carlisle's memory. Before they'd left the station Jesse had signed off on Suit accompanying Molly on the condition that he would behave himself.

"I'm not the high school kid here," Suit said. "You don't have to treat me like one."

"Prove it," Jesse had said.

"It's not like I never saw you lose your shit on the job," Suit said.

"Perk of being chief," Jesse said.

The girl looked enough like Molly's daughters to be one of them. Dark hair worn long. Great skin. *Flawless* skin, truth be told. Bright blue nails looking as if they'd been professionally done in the past couple days. Her shirt was blue with white stripes, the sleeves rolled up. Distressed jeans. Golden Goose sneakers looking distressed, too, which was apparently part of their charm.

If she isn't the prettiest girl in school, Molly decided, Ainsley had to be in the conversation. She and Jack must have gone through Paradise High looking like the perennial king and queen of the prom.

"I don't want to make this more difficult for you than it already is," Molly said.

Ainsley was at a corner of the couch, feet tucked underneath her, sneakers still very much on. The mom in Molly resisted the urge to tell her no shoes on the furniture.

"No need for you to stress," she said to them. "I'm pretty much all cried out."

"I know how you feel," Suit said.

Molly said, "The vigil last night was lovely. You all did a wonderful job putting it together."

"Thanks," the girl said. "But all's I kept thinking was that Jack should have been there to hear all the nice things people were saying about him."

She sighed. It was a gale-force sigh. Then she said, "We all should have said more of those things to him when he was alive."

"You guys went out for a long time, right?" Suit said. He smiled at her. "Is it okay to say 'went out'? Or does that make me sound older than I already am?"

"It's okay," Ainsley said. "There's really no way to say it that doesn't sound sketchy. But, yeah, we pretty much started hanging out at the beginning of junior year."

She shrugged now. Teenagers, Molly knew, were good at it. Shrugging. It usually meant boredom, sometimes a way to punctuate a thought. By the time Molly's daughters were Ainsley Walsh's age they had elevated shrugging to an art form.

"But we both knew it was going to end when we graduated," Ainsley said. "It was already starting to end."

"Happens that way a lot," Molly said. "I sent four daughters through your school. And went there myself."

"We hadn't made it official yet," Ainsley said. What came out of her next came out in an exaggerated form of what was once called a Valley Girl voice. "At least not *Insta* official."

"I did the same thing with my senior-year girlfriend," Suit said.

Molly sighed now.

"I *married* my high school boyfriend," she said.

She knew what she and Suit were doing, trying to relax the kid, maybe get her to drop her guard, having no idea at this point about what, exactly.

Suit leaned forward now, like he was kindly Uncle Suit to Ainsley, too.

"Jack hadn't said anything to me about you two breaking up," Suit said.

"Guys don't talk," Ainsley said, "even to other guys sometimes. We didn't care if everybody else knew. *We* knew."

Going in, Molly thought.

"So why did Jack think there was something going on with you and Scott Ford behind his back? Scott says that's what the fight was about the night of the party."

"*Nothing was going on!*" Ainsley said, the words coming out hot.

"I'm not suggesting that there was," Molly said. "I'm just wondering why Jack seemed to think so."

Ainsley reached forward for the plastic bottle of water on the coffee table, and drank some.

"My mom keeps telling me it's more important than ever right now for me to stay hydrated."

"Words to live by," Molly said. "But getting back to the party, why did Jack think you were cheating on him with one of his teammates?"

"He saw Scott and me coming out of Daisy's one day at lunch," she said. "I'd been there with one of my girlfriends. Scott was picking up a to-go. My friend had to leave, but I'd already ordered. Scott offered to eat his lunch there and keep me company. A few hours later Jack texted me, being sarcastic, and congratulated me on already moving on to the next guy."

High school, Molly thought.

The pandemic in high school, from the beginning of time, had been drama.

Ainsley pulled her phone out of the back pocket of her jeans, checked it, put it back.

"You have to be someplace?" Suit said.

"Kind of."

"We won't keep you much longer," Molly said. "Why were you even at the party if things were ending with you and Jack?"

Ainsley looked at Molly, eyes big suddenly, tears forming. Molly had known from the start that it was bullshit about her being all cried out.

"Because I loved him," she said. "Because he'd just had the best day he'd ever had in baseball, and when he asked me to come, I wasn't about to say no."

"When did you find out about the fight?" Suit said.

"When Scott came back."

"And he told you what happened?" Molly said.

The girl nodded. "That's when I went looking for Jack. But I couldn't find him."

Ainsley put her hands to her face and rubbed hard. Molly could never do that without ruining her makeup. Maybe Ainsley Walsh didn't need it.

"It wasn't just me who loved Jack," she said, her eyes big and red and focused on Suit now. "Everybody did."

Molly thought that it hadn't done Jack Carlisle much good on the last night of his life.

"We're still trying our best to love him now," Ainsley said. "Can you understand that?"

Molly wasn't sure she did. But telling this girl wasn't going to do anybody any good.

So they left.

SIXTEEN

S uit should be sitting where I'm sitting," Jesse said to Dix.

They were in Dix's office, in the late afternoon. Jesse had decided that he needed a visit to his therapist more than he needed an AA meeting today. Dix, who'd been a cop. Who was a recovering alcoholic himself. Dix referred to himself and Jesse as a two-man club. The Dead Drunk Society.

"Are we here to talk about Suit or talk about you?" Dix said.

Dix had bought a new house, on the west side of Paradise, an area in the process of being gentrified, maybe so it would be allowed to even remain in Paradise. It was supposed to have been a bigger development before the real estate guy who'd bought up the land—Harry Townes was his name—had run out of money, and had to flip most of the land at a loss during COVID. Before he had, Dix had bought his small house at a very good price, knowing that nothing could be built behind him because of the small land trust back there. No ocean view over on this side of town, but some spectacular sunsets, one in its early stages right now.

Dix wore his usual white shirt. Both his bald head and his nails were gleaming. Everything about him was as neat as an operating room, which, in so many ways, this really was.

He had just finished telling Dix about what Ainsley Walsh had told Molly and Suit.

"Suit wanted to drive straight over to the Ford kid's house and haul him in," Jesse said. "Fortunately I intervened."

"And I take it both of you, uh, demurred," Dix said.

Jesse grinned.

"Fuckin' ay," he said.

Dix might have grinned in return. Or perhaps it was just his lips twitching involuntarily.

"Suit made a good point the other day," Jesse said.

"He does that from time to time," Dix said.

"More often than you think," Jesse said. "He reminded me that I had done a lot of hotheaded shit on the job, especially when I was still drinking. Usually when I was hungover."

"Hangovers," Dix said, and not for the first time, "are like having a second job."

They sat in silence. Dix was better at it than anybody Jesse had ever known. Jesse sometimes thought that if you counted only the time when they were actually talking to each other, in this office or the old one, he probably would be paying half of what he actually was.

"Are you here because Charlie's death gave you the urge to drink?" Dix said.

"See," Jesse said, "this is like a meeting for me. Just with less chatter."

"Look who's talking," Dix said.

"Or not," Jesse said.

There were two overhead lights built into the ceiling, reflecting off the top of Dix's head.

"I should be feeling worse, or angrier, or something, about the boy," Jesse said. "It's Suit's family."

"But with you it's more about Charlie."

"Lot of people have died on my watch," Jesse said. "There was a lawyer I was in love with once."

"Abby."

Jesse nodded.

"But even her I didn't love the way I loved Charlie Farrell," he said.

Now Dix did smile, fully.

"That old man was supposed to die of natural causes," Dix said, "after having outlived us all."

Jesse said, "I frankly always thought *natural causes* was an oxymoron."

"Now he's gone and you felt the urge to drink."

"Occasionally northern exposure gives me the urge to drink."

"You know what I'm going to tell you now, right?" Dix said.

"That the only way to work through this is to work, period," Jesse said.

"There you go."

"Sometimes I wonder why I'm even paying you."

"Don't look at me," Dix said. "It's a rule they passed."

By now they were getting to the end of the session.

"It's not just wanting a drink," Jesse said. "It's wanting to find who did it to Charlie and putting a bullet behind his ear once I do."

"Understandable sentiment," Dix said. "But hardly productive."

"Who said anything about productive?" Jesse said.

Then he said to Dix, "You know I'm only kidding, right?"

But Jesse wasn't kidding.

Not even a little bit.

And was on his way back to the office when Molly Crane called to tell him that somebody had beaten up Scott Ford badly enough to put him in the hospital.

"Ford's the first baseman, right?" Molly said.

"What does that have to do with anything, Mols?" Jesse said.

"Because the one who did it to him is the catcher," she said.

SEVENTEEN

Molly said she was about to head over to the hospital in Marshport, telling Jesse she knew he wanted to be focusing on Charlie Farrell. Jesse told her to stay at the office and reinterview as many baseball players as she could about possible bad blood, before today, between Scott Ford and Matt Loes, the catcher.

And how it might possibly be tied in to the death of Jack Carlisle.

"I'm a master of multitasking," he said. "Want to know why?"

"I know why," Molly said. "You're the chief."

Scott Ford's injuries were serious enough that the paramedics had decided to bypass the urgent care in Paradise and take him directly to the hospital in Marshport, the facility there getting bigger and better and more modern all the time.

Scott Ford's parents were in a waiting room on the eighth floor.

Jesse had never met Shelley Ford. But her husband, Ted, ran the biggest insurance firm in Paradise and thought he was every bit the hot shit that his best friend Gary Armistead, mayor of Paradise, was. Jesse thought there should be a club for hot shits, like the Elks.

Ted Ford saw Jesse at the same time Jesse saw him.

"I assume you came over here to tell me that you've arrested the punk who did this to my son," Ted Ford said. "That *is* what you're doing here, right?"

Jesse knew Scott Ford's room number, and kept walking, having no time for Ted Ford, and even less tolerance. But Ford stepped into the hallway, cutting him off.

Grabbing Jesse's arm.

Jesse stopped, looked down at Ford's hand, then back into his eyes.

"I asked you a question," Ford said.

"Take your hand off my arm," Jesse said quietly.

"As soon as you answer my question," Ford said.

Jesse smiled, then reached down with his free hand, like he simply wanted to shake Ford's. But Jesse's right hand was a lot bigger, and stronger, and now squeezing Ted Ford's hard enough that Jesse was waiting to hear some of the small bones in it breaking.

He heard a sharp intake of breath, and maybe the tiniest of squeaks.

"Let . . . go," Ford said, his voice strained, "or I am calling your boss."

"Yikes," Jesse said.

But let go.

"So I'm assuming you haven't arrested the Loes kid?" Ford said.

"I have not," Jesse said. "I came straight here as soon as I found out that your son was in the hospital. Now I want to hear his version of what happened."

"His *version*," Ford said, "is that Matt Loes beat him to within an inch of his goddamn life."

"I want to hear about it from him," Jesse said.

"And the mayor is going to hear about all this from me," Ford said.

Jesse smiled again.

"You need to stop talking now, Ted, and let me do my job," Jesse said.

"You think I'm joking about the mayor?" Ford said.

"Still talking," Jesse said.

He took a deep breath and let it out and walked into room 821. He needed to get away from Ted Ford, and knew exactly why. Jesse wanted to hit somebody today. It had nearly been Scott Ford's asshole father.

Dix probably wouldn't see that as being very productive, either.

EIGHTEEN

Scott Ford looked the way those Ultimate Fighters looked after they lost one of those big pay-per-view fights. And sometimes after they won.

His left eye more bruised than it had been in Jesse's office. Right eye shut. Stitches above his lips. More stitches on his right cheekbone.

For a moment after Jesse walked in, he thought Ford might be sleeping. But the kid opened the only eye he could when he heard the sound of the door closing.

"Hey," Jesse said.

"I don't want to talk about it, if that's why you're here," Scott Ford said.

There was a chair against the wall. Jesse pulled it close to the bed and sat down.

"Don't have to talk about it," Jesse said. "But you need to. Your father's outside this door and fixing to organize a lynch mob for the kid did this to you."

The kid in the bed closed his left eye, and groaned, as if even that small movement had sent a spasm of pain across his face.

"Dad's probably just embarrassed I got the crap kicked out of me," Ford said.

His voice sounded raspy enough that Jesse wondered if he'd taken a shot or two to his throat. Molly had already told Jesse on the phone that there were two broken ribs.

When Jesse saw him try to lick his lips, he grabbed the water cup with the straw stuck in it from the table next to the bed, handed it to him. Ford drank and handed it back, as if even reaching over to the table might exhaust him.

"Why would you catch a beating like this from Matt Loes?" Jesse said. "I got into some beefs of my own when I was your age. Including a beauty with one of my own teammates one time. Nobody ever ended up in the hospital."

"You've probably figured out by now I've got a bad temper," Ford said, the words coming out of him slowly, as if on some kind of delay. "Matt's is worse. He and Jack were best friends. Like brothers. He's blaming me for what happened. Or for not stopping it from happening. Whatever. I think he just wanted to hit somebody. It turned out to be me."

"Know the feeling," Jesse said.

He waited a beat and said, "Who started it?"

Ford turned his head on the pillow, away from Jesse. Winced again.

"Nurse says I need to rest."

"I won't be here much longer."

The kid turned back to him. Somehow he formed a grin with his swollen lips.

"Bullshit," he said.

Jesse said, "Where did it happen?"

"Over where we had the party," Ford said.

"Anybody else there?"

Ford shook his head.

"Matt said we needed to talk about Jack, just the two of us, no-body else around," Ford said. "Get some things straight. Make sure we were on the same page."

"On the same page about what?"

The kid either didn't hear the question. Or just ignored it. Jesse thought: *He's wounded in more ways than one.*

A nurse poked her head in. "I'm sorry to interrupt, Chief Stone, but the boy's parents say you've been in here long enough."

"This is police business," Jesse said, "involving what you can see is a very serious assault. I need a few more minutes."

"Well, then, I'll be back in a few minutes."

"Call Mike Pearl while you're away," Jesse said.

The Marshport chief.

"He'll tell you I'm the good guys," Jesse said.

"Did you have any idea that Matt Loes was spoiling for a fight?" Jesse said to Scott Ford when she was gone.

"No. But it was like he'd already lost his shit before he even got there, started screaming at me that Jack would be alive if we hadn't got into it at the party."

"And it escalated from there."

"He got right up in my face," Ford said. "I told him he needed to back off. He said that maybe I should make him back off. It went like that."

He tried to clear his throat, seemed unable to do that. His voice sounded rougher as he went, and was getting weaker.

"I know," he said. "It sounds like the same dumb playground shit as with Jack and me."

"Then Loes threw the first punch?"

"Does it matter?"

"It does if you want to press charges."

"Once he got me on the ground I was afraid he was going to kill me," Ford said.

"But you're not going to press charges."

"Fuck no."

The only sound in the hospital room now was the sound of the kid's forced breathing. He told Jesse that he didn't know why Loes finally stopped swinging away, but he did, and left him there. Ford managed to get to his car and drive home. He collapsed right after he walked in the front door. His mother took one look at him and called 911.

Jesse waited.

"Is that all?" Ford said finally.

"Not quite."

"Not pressing charges," he said. "We're clear on that, right?"

"Might not be up to you," Jesse said.

"It's not up to you and it's not up to my dad," Ford said. "Now please leave me alone."

"What aren't you telling me, Scott?" Jesse asked.

And just like that, the kid snapped, rising up out of the bed, the pain of doing that written on his face, reaching for the call button, breathing hard.

"*Leave me the fuck alone!*" he yelled at Jesse then.

The nurse came through the door. She told Jesse he needed to leave, right now, or she would call security, whether he was a policeman or not.

Jesse did.

Some bedside manner, he thought.

NINETEEN

Jesse called Molly from the car and asked her how it was going with the other players. She said not one was answering a phone. He told her to forget about them for now, and go find Matt Loes and bring him in.

"What if he chooses not to, oh, I don't know, ride along?" Molly said.

"Arrest him," Jesse said.

Somehow Loes looked even bigger out of catcher's equipment than he did in it. He had a butterfly bandage over his right eye. Jesse noticed that his right hand was about a size too big. But that was it for whatever damage Scott Ford had done to him.

"I did it," Loes said as soon as he sat down.

"Aware," Jesse said. "Looking to find out what this is all about."

"You talk to Scott?"

Jesse nodded.

"Then you know what it was about," he said. "Jack."

"You've apparently decided it's Scott's fault that Jack ended up in the water that night?"

"Put it this way," Loes said. "He didn't do much to keep him out of it."

The kid had dark skin. Jesse knew his mother, Rosa, who worked at City Hall, was of Mexican descent. Matt Loes looked like her. Same dark eyes, almost black. Big all over. Hands the size of oven mitts even without the swelling on his throwing hand. His Pirates Baseball T-shirt barely contained his upper chest especially.

This kid could take me in a fair fight, no problem.

"I'm wondering if there was more going on between you and Scott besides Jack," Jesse said.

"There wasn't," Loes said.

"I saw the damage you did," Jesse said. "Why don't I believe you?"

Loes stared sullenly at him. *High school baseball star,* Jesse thought, *giving me the perp stare.*

"I don't care whether you believe me or not," Loes said.

Then he said, "I lost my head, *okay*? I should have walked away. After that, things got out of hand."

"Not exactly breaking news, kid."

"You gonna arrest me?"

"Not at the present time."

"Even though I did it."

"Even though."

The kid stood up.

"You can leave when I say you can leave," Jesse said. "Now sit your ass back down until I'm finished talking to you. Or I will throw you in a cell for my own amusement."

Loes sat.

"Was there something going on with Jack that didn't have anything at all to do with Ainsley Walsh?" Jesse said.

"I thought I was here to talk about me and Scott," Loes said.

"I'm the chief," Jesse said. "In here we talk about what I want to talk about."

There was something in the kid's eyes now. There and gone. But there. Jesse had surprised him. Or touched some kind of nerve. Or both.

Something, though.

"I don't know what you're talking about," he said.

"You sure?"

The sullen look was back. Jesse wondered if kids practiced it in the mirror.

"I'm done talking," he said.

But made no move to get out of the chair.

"Tell me what I don't know yet about your team that I'm going to find out," Jesse said.

"I don't know what you mean."

"Thinking that maybe you do."

Loes shifted in the chair now, which looked small as a barstool underneath him.

"You told us you played ball."

"So I did."

"Then you know that what happens on a team stays with the team," Matt Loes said.

"Until somebody on the team ends up dead," Jesse said.

"None of this is going to bring Jack back."

"You should have thought of that before you put Scott Ford in the hospital."

"Like I said," Loes said. "I got nothing more to say to you."

Jesse said, "For now, anyway."

"So we're done for now?"

"Get lost," Jesse said.

"Before I go," Loes said. "Can I ask you something?"

"Ask away."

"Can I get in trouble for telling you what I think?"

Jesse shook his head.

"Well, I think you don't know shit," Matt Loes said.

The kid left. Jesse let him. He took his glove out of the bottom drawer, and his ball, and began snapping the ball into the pocket of the glove. The glove and ball like his pacifiers sometimes. The sound of the ball in the glove was a signal, he knew, to everybody outside to leave him alone.

He was alone in the office for a long time. He would get with Molly and Suit in the morning, first thing, and come up with a game plan for how they were going to investigate two deaths at the same time.

Multitasking.

He was goddamn chief, after all.

He went home, reheated some of the five-alarm chili he'd cooked up for himself the night before, thought briefly, as he often did, how good an ice-cold beer would go with it, tried to make it through the Red Sox game on television, thought again how much he missed hearing the voice of Jerry Remy, who'd finally passed from cancer the year before.

He couldn't make it past the fifth inning, eyes starting to close by then, and went to bed.

His cell awakened him. Few minutes after eleven, he saw.

Nellie

"You up?" she said.

"Now I am."

"May I come over?"

"Little late," Jesse said, "for a booty call."

"*Booty* call, Jesse?" she said. "Seriously?"

"Isn't that what young people say?"

"Sure," Nellie said, "if they were young when Clinton was still president."

"What's this about?"

"Business," she said.

"Police business or yours?"

"With me," Nellie said, "it's often a distinction without much of a difference."

"Okay," Jesse said, "you've got my attention."

"Can I come over?"

"Where are you?"

"Outside," she said.

He was already putting on his jeans.

"What's this really about?" Jesse said.

"I'm starting to think that somebody might have killed that kid," Nellie Shofner said.

TWENTY

They sat at the kitchen table. As soon as they'd walked into the room Nellie had sniffed a couple times and said, "Chili night?"

"Even better the second," he said.

"Taking your word on that," she said.

"Tell me what you got," Jesse said.

"I'll tell some, but not all," she said. "Okay?"

"Okay."

He grinned, and waited.

"Learned that from the master," she said.

"Learned everything you know about the sharing of information with law enforcement," he said. "Just not everything I know."

He had made them a pot of decaf coffee. More for her than for him. If Nellie were any more wound up than she was right now, you could attach jumper cables to her heart and start a dead car.

"There's something going on with our newly crowned championship baseball team," she said.

"More than just grieving, you mean."

"Way more," she said.

She always looked like morning to Jesse, did even now. They had never spent the night together here, only at her place. Not because he was territorial.

At her place he could leave.

It was something understood by both of them, without ever having been discussed.

She wore her hair in a ponytail tonight, making her look even younger. A Brooklyn Dodgers T-shirt Jesse had given her. Apple Watch. White jeans.

"I'm here as a good citizen," she said.

"I can thank you later on behalf of the town."

"I am also here despite the fact that our relationship continues to be give and take," Nellie said. "I give, you take."

Jesse grinned. "And you don't just give when you're being a good citizen."

He drank some of the coffee. It was like his chili. Bad was better than none.

Nellie told him that the feel-good story about Jack Carlisle on which she had been reporting had turned into something quite different now.

"I'll bet," Jesse said.

"But here's the thing," she said, "and it was a thing even before he died. Even though he was the golden boy of the team, just about all of his teammates had been reluctant to open up about him."

"Suit used to say the kid didn't like to open up about anything," Jesse said.

"Gee," Nellie said. "I never run into anybody like that in my own life."

She smiled. He smiled back at her.

"We there yet?" Jesse said.

She drank some coffee.

"There was some kind of secret team meeting tonight," she said.

"Secret even from you?"

"Sad but true," she said, "I found out about it after the fact. At first I thought it might be about what happened between Scott Ford and Matt Loes, but turns out it wasn't."

"You know this how?"

"A source."

"On the team?"

"You know better than to even ask," she said.

"So what was the meeting about?"

"My source wouldn't say, said that he'd gone as far as he could."

"So it's somebody on the team."

"Stop," she said.

Jesse said, "What does a secret team meeting have to do with you thinking somebody killed Jack Carlisle?"

"They're closing ranks, Jesse," she said. "Like some sort of secret *society*. There was some event leading up to the big game, something serious, but I can't find out what it was."

"And you really think it might have gotten Jack killed."

"Yes," she said.

"Have you talked to Ainsley Walsh?" Jesse asked.

"A couple times before Jack died," Nellie said. "Just one time since."

"Molly and Suit went to her house," Jesse said.

"What did they get out of her?"

Jesse slowly shook his head.

"Give," she said, "take."

He shrugged.

Nellie said, "That girl knows a lot more than she's telling."

He asked if she wanted more coffee. Now she shook her head.

"Maybe you and Molly can help each other out on this," Jesse said, "while I'm devoting most of my attention to Charlie Farrell."

"Molly and me?" she said. "Seriously?"

"I think Molly might be more forthcoming than I am," Jesse said.

"And why is that?"

"Maybe it will be a girl thing?" Jesse said.

He stood now, took both their cups, walked them to the sink. She came up behind him and put her arms around him and kissed him below his ear.

"You ever hear about the fallacy of the predetermined outcome," Nellie whispered.

"We used to talk about it in baseball all the time," Jesse said.

"Sometimes it's not a fallacy," Nellie said.

As they walked toward the bedroom, Nellie said she was going to share one last piece of information with him, and she promised that was it.

"Our friend Ainsley," she said, "was cheating her young ass off with Scott Ford, for what it's worth. Whether either one of them will admit that or not."

"Really," Jesse said.

"Really."

"You want to stop talking about this now?"

"Very much so," Nellie said.

So they stopped talking business.

TWENTY-ONE

Jesse and Molly and Suit sat in the conference room, just past seven in the morning. They all had large coffees that Jesse had picked up at Dunkin' in front of them, along with a small box of donuts. When Molly saw the donuts she compared Jesse to Satan. Then took out a Boston Kreme and put it on the paper plate in front of her and glared at him as she took a big bite.

"You're an enabler," she said.

"The first step toward recovery is admitting you have a problem."

"The *problem* is that you keep putting donuts in front of me," she said. "*That's* the problem."

"You don't have to eat them," Jesse said.

"Like hell I don't."

Suit looked as if he hadn't gotten much sleep. Or any sleep at all.

"You okay?" Jesse said to him, regretting the question as soon as he asked it, knowing Suit wasn't okay, wasn't going to be okay for a long time.

Might never be entirely okay ever again.

"I'm not hungover, if that's what you're thinking."

"Not what I was thinking."

"Well, I'm not," Suit said.

Maybe he was so tired he didn't know how defensive he sounded.

"Listen," Molly said to him. "We're on your side, Luther. We're going to get through all of this, whatever it turns out to be, together, like we always do."

Suit took a sip of his large coffee, put the cup down much too hard, and spilled some coffee on the table.

"This isn't *like* always," he said, and mopped up the spill with his napkin.

Jesse waited until he finished with his tidying up, Suit making it look as if drying the table was the most important thing he'd do all day.

"Suit, I need to know, right here, from you, if you can work this case with a clear head. Because if you can't, I'll understand. So will Molly."

"Jesse, you know me. I *have* to be in on this. Not being in on it is what would make me lose it."

Jesse looked across the table at Suit. Even knowing his actual age, and knowing full well how long they'd worked together, what he saw was the same sweet, open-faced kid who'd been sitting outside when Jesse had first walked through the door and become his boss. Suit wanted to be a cop as much as any young guy—or young woman—Jesse had ever known, all the way back to when he was starting out as a young cop in L.A. More than that, and from that very first day, he'd wanted to make Jesse proud of him.

Suit ducked his head, then looked up at Jesse. "I promise I won't let you down."

"I believe you."

Because I know how much he wants me to.

Jesse said, "Just to reset: You two are going to run point on our investigation of Jack's death. But everything you do and anything you find out, it all runs through me."

Molly grinned.

"You being the chief," she said. "Always so easy for both of us to lose sight of that in our impulsive moments. Or any moments."

"Is that supposed to be amusing?"

"As Sunny says, if you have to ask."

"Sunny who?"

"Is *that* supposed to be amusing, *Chief*?"

"And I want to make it clear that it wouldn't hurt to keep the lines of communication open between this department and Nellie Shofner."

"Does she need another friend in the department?" Molly asked. "How many does one girl need?"

"She has this way of occasionally finding out things before we do," Jesse said.

"All due respect, Jesse?" Suit said. "The rest of the time we find out things before she does."

"If I didn't think she could help us, I wouldn't have brought it up," Jesse said. "And I think she can help us."

"I stand corrected," Molly said. "She's not Gidget. Now she's Nancy Drew."

Then Jesse told them Nellie's theory that the players on the team were hiding something, and that she had also heard that Ainsley Walsh might have been involved with Scott Ford.

"That would mean Ford lied and the girl lied," Suit said.

"To officers of the law," Jesse said. "Almost makes you question your core beliefs, doesn't it?"

"What are there, fifteen players on the team?" Molly said. "We need to talk to them one by one, see if one of them breaks ranks if Nellie is right."

"Don't take this the wrong way," Suit said, "but do you trust Nellie on this?"

"Getting things right is a thing with her, same as it is us," Jesse said. "And like I keep saying, I'll take all the help we can get."

"Too soon to give her a badge and uniform?" Molly asked.

"Only if she promises to wear it on Halloween," Jesse said.

"Pig," she said.

"No way to talk to a cop," Jesse said.

TWENTY-TWO

Jesse spent most of the afternoon in his office with Healy, going through Charlie Farrell's call records. Jesse still couldn't believe, after all these years and the times when he'd done work like this before on a case, that you could do it without the phone in your possession, just knowing the number. You could, though. They did. Incoming and outgoing calls.

They did the same with incoming and outgoing calls from his landline. Normally you needed a subpoena for landlines. Jesse could still remember the hoops through which he'd had to jump with Mayor Neil O'Hara's home phone after what appeared to be his suicide turned out to be murder. This time the district attorney's office went along with the request, even though the request for Jack Carlisle's phone records was still swimming upstream through the system. It was an election year for Ellis Munroe, and the victim was Charlie Farrell, an even more beloved figure in the town than Neil had been. When Munroe had briefly hesitated, going through the motions of citing the precedent of the O'Hara case, Jesse had mentioned that if Munroe tried to slow-walk him this time, he was going to read about it in the *Crier*.

"You remember a time when all detective work didn't run through somebody's goddamn phone?" Healy asked Jesse now. "Before people started turning phones on us like they were guns?"

"Does make the work easier sometimes, you gotta admit," Jesse said. "Gives you a better road map than GPS."

Healy looked at him over his reading glasses. "You feel that way right now with all these fake numbers?"

"There's even an app now that helps you create fake numbers," Jesse said.

"Technology," Healy said. "Truly such a freaking joy."

Jesse took off his own reading glasses, placing them on the spreadsheet in front of him. "You like cop work better when you and Charlie were young? Or with all the bells and whistles we got going with the technology now?"

"Like you keep saying," Healy said. "I'll take all the help we can get."

"Charlie used to say that the only time he was interested in an app is when it was short for *appetizer*."

Every time they thought they might have a lead, it would quickly turn into a dead end. They either couldn't place a call to a number or would find out it belonged to a dry-cleaning store in Marshport, or Salem, and had simply been ghosted. *Perfect*, Jesse thought, just because he and Healy felt like they were chasing ghosts.

They stayed at it until six o'clock. After that Jesse took Healy over to the Gull and bought him a lobster dinner. When they were finished they toasted Charlie, Healy with a Jack Daniel's, Jesse with iced tea. He always found it fascinating how tea so closely resembled the color of the booze, even if only one could try to ruin your fucking life.

Jesse drove home, called Nellie, got her voicemail, left a message for her to call if she'd come up with anything interesting across her day. Molly called and said that she and Suit had gotten nothing at all interesting out of the Paradise High baseball team, nothing they hadn't heard before, the players' answers almost sounding rehearsed.

Tonight Jesse managed to make it through the entire Red Sox game, even though it turned into one of those four-hour, nine-inning jobs that tried to challenge, mightily, his love for the game.

When it finally ended, and to his great surprise, he was still wide awake.

So he got his gun, the keys to the Explorer, put on a RELAX cap that Sunny had given him as a joke, then did the same thing he'd done one time already this week.

Took a ride over to Charlie Farrell's house.

TWENTY-THREE

They were still treating it as an active crime scene. But Jesse still had the key to the house that Charlie had given him a long time ago.

"Why do I need a key when you insist on leaving your door unlocked?" Jesse had asked him once.

"I want you to have it in case it is locked the night the Messenger of Death beats you here one night."

"Messenger of *Death*?" Jesse had said.

"You never had a tarot card reading?" the old man had said.

"Wait, *you* did?"

Charlie had winked. "Miss Emma made me."

Now Jesse stood just inside the door, in a darkness so profound, a quiet that made it difficult for Jesse to get enough air into him once he was inside. All he could think of was that, son of a bitch, the Messenger of Death *had* beaten him here the other night.

But which messenger?

Jesse wondered, not for the first time since Charlie's death, what he might do if he ever got his hands on the killer, and there was nobody else around.

Could I kill him?

Or her?

Jesse knew the answer to that one. What did they say in the lawyer shows on TV? Never ask a question to which you don't already know the answer.

Jesse knew.

He *knew.*

Turned on some lamps now, and overhead lights. The place, as always, was military neat. No surprise there. Charlie had been a Marine as a kid, sure he was going to be shipped out during the Cuban Missile Crisis, having no idea back in the early sixties that he might have been enlisting to go fight a war.

Kitchen counter spotless. Everything in the silverware drawer neatly arranged. Refrigerator was still well stocked. Cans and spices, also neatly arranged, in the cupboard. Jesse pulled open the freezer drawer and smiled at the half-full bottle of Grey Goose.

Jesse went up the stairs and into his bathroom. Opened the cabinet over the sink. Heart pills there, cholesterol meds. Bottle of Viagra, the prescription recently filled. Jesse smiled again. Maybe it wasn't just Miss Emma who had been aspirational.

"Charlie," Jesse said out loud. "You dog."

He thought about the night he went to Neil O'Hara's house, after Neil had been shot in the head at The Throw. Going through his things. It was always the same, no matter who the vic was, whether it was a friend or not. No matter how much it hurt. He was looking for something he had missed. Something they'd all missed. Something that didn't belong. Something that should have been here, and wasn't. Something that would open a door for him, get him out of what so often felt like a locked room when he was looking for clues.

Looking for something that would help him find out who had done something like this to a wonderful old man. What did people always say when someone around Charlie's age would die? Eighty's a good, long life.

Not if you were looking for eighty-one, it wasn't.

Past midnight now.

Jesse went to the top of the stairs, looked down at the chairlift Nicholas had gotten for Charlie, one the old man said he refused to use. "It'll be there when you need it, Gramps," Nicholas had told him, and Charlie had said, "When I'm dead."

It was at the bottom of the stairs. Maybe Charlie was secretly using it. And just never made it back to the second floor the night he died.

Jesse walked into Charlie's bedroom now. He was sure he could still pick up the faint scent of the sandalwood cologne that had been a Christmas gift from Miss Emma, what she said was the sweet smell for her sweet man.

There was a small writing desk on one side of the room. Jesse went through the drawers. The top middle drawer had a stack of phone bills on it. Jesse opened the envelopes and saw all the numbers circled. "Scam" he'd written in the margins.

Charlie's laptop was on top of the desk. Whoever had done it to Charlie had left the laptop. But why not take it along with the cell? Maybe the guy was in a rush after he did it, and never made it up the stairs. Maybe something outside spooked him. Voices, perhaps. The lights from a car. Or a car horn. Maybe he grabbed what he could grab and ran, like the bitch that he was.

Gabe hadn't even taken the laptop to the station. He'd gone

through it here, after Nicholas had given him Charlie's password. Before Gabe had backed everything up, he told Nicholas he was worried that he might find something embarrassing.

"Not unless you count getting his ass kicked online in rummy," Nicholas had told Gabe.

Jesse sat down at the desk, opened the laptop, typed in the password. He saw how much Amazon shopping Charlie did. He'd told Jesse that online shopping had become his guilty pleasure. When Jesse reminded Charlie that he was always talking about how much better he liked the world when there were only three TV networks, Charlie said, well, yeah, that was before he found out Amazon would deliver groceries to his door.

Jesse saw that Charlie bought a lot of audiobooks. He loved to read and hated to admit it, but his eyes were going, even with the special, oversized reading glasses he wore, at least when Miss Emma wasn't around.

There were a lot of baseball websites in his browsing history, most of them involving old-time ballplayers. Jesse even saw that a week or so ago Charlie had accessed the site for the Albuquerque Dukes, the team Jesse had played for until the Dodgers had moved them to Portland twenty years earlier. Maybe he was trying to find out just how good Jesse had been in his last season of organized ball.

Charlie had also visited "Minor League Stats and History" at Baseball-Reference.com. Jesse never did. He never went back and looked at his stats, mostly because he knew them as well as he knew his Social Security.

Somehow he felt like a peeper more than ever, invading Charlie's privacy, learning his secrets, as innocent as they were. He was the one afraid that he might find something embarrassing.

But thankfully did not.

Jesse had been searching the browsing history on Google Chrome. He switched over to Safari now, the history quite limited. Maybe Charlie had just started using it, and Jesse found it impossible to believe Charlie had any reason to clear it.

Every single item on his Safari history involved the same subject, including a *Los Angeles Times* article on this particular subject.

"You have got to be shitting me," Jesse said out loud.

He copied all of the links, forwarded them to his own email address, closed the laptop, left.

When he got home he found Suit on the floor outside the door to his condominium.

Not dead.

But probably wishing he was.

TWENTY-FOUR

He was passed out drunk until he wasn't because Jesse was slapping him away, then hoisting the big man to his feet and half-dragging, half-carrying him inside.

"Elena know where you are?" Jesse asked him.

Suit mumbled something Jesse couldn't understand.

"Does your wife know where you are, Suit?"

"No."

"Why did you come here instead of home?"

"No good options," Suit said. "Shape I was in, I figured even you were a better option than she was."

Jesse walked Suit over to the couch in the living room, sat him down, Suit slumping to the side like he wanted to curl up there and try to sleep.

"You gonna be sick?"

"Don't think so."

"Hold the thought."

Jesse called Elena then, told her that Suit was with him, he'd just had too much to drink, and was going to sleep it off here.

Elena didn't react to the news with anger. Molly often described Elena as the five best things that had ever happened to Suitcase Simpson.

"He's hurting so much, Jesse. You have to know that."

"I do."

"I guess drinking was his way of dealing with it tonight."

"That was always my first option," Jesse said. "And second. And third. But no matter how many times I tried, it never seemed to work."

There was a pause at her end.

"He didn't get into any fights, did he?"

"Just with himself," Jesse said. "Spoiler alert? He lost."

Jesse told Suit he needed sleep. Suit said not yet. Jesse asked where he'd been drinking. Suit said the Scupper, a place in the Swap whose general state had improved the way that whole section of town had, which had transformed into "The Scupper: An Eating and Drinking Saloon." To Jesse that just meant better food, slightly less sawdust on the floor, fewer fights, inside or out.

Jesse asked with whom he'd been drinking.

"Max."

"Who's Max."

"Bartender. I used to play football with him."

Jesse nodded. Of course. Sometimes he got the idea that Suit had played ball at one time or another with everybody except Tom Brady.

"I hope you Ubered here."

"Walked."

"From the Swap? You know how far that is on foot?"

"Do now."

He went into Jesse's bathroom and took a shower. Jesse left some sweatpants that were too long for him but probably would fit Suit just fine, and an old hoodie that had ROBBERY HOMICIDE on the front, one Jenn had given him as a birthday present when they were still married.

Suit still looked wobbly when he came out of the bedroom. Like he had been tagged a few times tonight.

But closer, incrementally, to being Suit.

"I finally knew enough to get out of there," he said. "Drunk as I was, I knew that if somebody made me for being shit-faced in public, you'd fire me."

His hair was still wet. Eyes bloodshot. Jesse nodded at the kitchen, sat him down at the table, handed him a mug of coffee. Suit's hand was shaking as he brought it to his lips. Jesse knew this feeling. He knew Suit's *face*, he'd seen it often enough in the old days staring back at him from the mirror. Jesse had ended up like this at Molly's house more than a few times when he didn't know where else to go. When he didn't want to be alone as drunk as *he* was.

Even though she still called him the alonest man she'd ever met in her life.

"Nobody ever fired me when I was like this," Jesse said, "at least not once I got here."

Somehow Suit managed to build a small smile. "But they sure tried."

"And nearly succeeded a few times."

"What you really needed was a boss like you."

"Got one," Jesse said. "Name of Molly Crane. Maybe you've heard of her."

Jesse asked if he wanted to try to eat something. Slightly bigger smile from him. "Maybe next month."

"Was gonna have you stay here," Jesse said. "But I should take you home."

"Face the music?"

"You know that's not your bride."

"And tonight's not me."

"Aware."

"It just hurts so bad, Jesse."

"I feel the same way about Charlie."

"You didn't go to the bar."

"No longer an option for me," Jesse said. "At least not so far today."

They sat in silence at the kitchen table, the only sound the ticking of an old Seth Thomas clock that had belonged to Jesse's mom, and had survived the cross-country ride when he'd left Los Angeles. In the hoodie, Suit looked like a kid again. Just one who'd had a very bad night, in the middle of a far worse time for him.

"*I don't know how to do this!*" Suit said, the words coming out hot.

"Nobody does, Suit. Till they have to."

"I know I'm supposed to be strong for my sister," Suit said. "The problem is, I don't feel strong." He ran a big hand through his wet hair. "I feel like I'm the one who's falling."

Jesse asked if he wanted more coffee. Suit shook his head. Jesse took his mug and put it in the sink. Past one by now. Suit wasn't the only one who needed sleep. Jesse wanted to get with Nicholas first thing in the morning, see if he had an explanation for what Jesse had found on Charlie's computer. Then pay a visit to Miss Emma. He'd talked to her already, on the phone earlier. He wanted to see if she could remember in better detail her last few phone conversations with Charlie. And to learn more about how she'd been ripped off.

"Jack didn't kill himself," Suit said, staring down at the table-top. "I know that boy." He paused. "*Knew* that boy. He would never do something like that, not with everything ahead of him."

"Suit. Look at me."

Suit did.

"Every teenage kid who ever did something to themselves had it all in front of *them*."

"*No!*"

All of the hurt in his voice now.

Jesse said, "I'm not saying he did. But at this point in our investigation, we can't rule it out. Okay?"

"Okay."

"But what I know for sure is that you're no good to Jack like this. Or your sister. Or me. We clear on that?"

Suit nodded.

"Gonna take you home to Elena now," Jesse said.

And did.

TWENTY-FIVE

Jesse had never been inside More Chocolate before. But his first reaction, seeing the big space on the ground floor, was that it had been designed to make the staff feel as if they were just hanging out, and not working, like this was the student union.

But even at nine in the morning, there was enough energy in the place to power the whole town if the grid went down.

There were four-desk pods scattered around the room. Pastel colors dominated. Track lighting, soft. Jazz music playing softly. Nicholas Farrell's wheelchair, Jesse saw, wasn't the only one at More Chocolate. He saw a young woman with a prosthetic leg. A ping-pong table at the far end from where you entered. A regulation basketball hoop, a small hard court in front of it, that included a free-throw line. To Jesse's right was a coffee station, and a menu board above it that seemed to have more options than Starbucks.

"This looks like camp," Jesse said to Nicholas.

Nicholas grinned. He was in a black Metallica T-shirt today. Black jeans. Broken-in biker boots. Jesse idly wondered if he'd been wearing the same boots the night of the accident on his Harley.

"I gave Gramps a tour here one time," Nicholas said, "and he said pretty much the same thing. Except he called it a playdate."

Nicholas pulled over a chair for Jesse from the empty desk next to his.

"You said you found something," he said.

Jesse told him about the crypto sites that his grandfather had accessed recently.

"Was he into that stuff?" Jesse asked.

Nicholas laughed.

"My *Gramps?* The only currency that interested him was at Bank of America. Or maybe under his bed, for all I know."

"So why was your grandfather, at his age, suddenly so interested in learning about cryptocurrency?"

"Do you know what it really is?" Nicholas asked.

Jesse looked over his shoulder. "Wait, you were asking me that?"

Jesse tried to follow then as Nicholas gave him a crash course on digital assets, even though Nicholas predicted that there was a crypto crash coming, even on the legitimate market. Then he was on to Bitcoin and secure trading and ownership.

When Nicholas got around to talking about public blockchains, Jesse held up a hand.

"But is it real money?"

"It is and it isn't," Nicholas said.

"So why are people so hot for it?"

"Why? Because there's no real central authority overseeing it, no bank or government agency acting like the crypto chief of police, if you want to think of it that way. But it's much more mainstream recently."

"Sounds to me like a different way to launder money."

"Not for everybody," Nicholas Farrell said. "Some of it is completely legit. And maybe most of it, far as I can tell. But money laundering does come up a lot when people are talking about crypto crime-ing. Guys on the wrong side of the law generally try to use the currency to launder dough from other crimes, cyber-crimes a lot of the time."

Jesse said, "You seem to know a lot about it. Why didn't Charlie just go to you instead of the Internet?"

Nicholas grinned. "I'm young and looking for ways to make easy money. But it didn't take me long to figure out it's a little bit like casinos, even though they want you to think it's a sure thing. The house always wins. It's just that nobody is quite sure who the house *is*."

"Why do you think your grandfather might have been trying to give himself a crash course?"

"Maybe he heard some of the boys talking about it at the club."

Paradise Country Club. Charlie had been a member for more than fifty years, which meant when a civil servant himself didn't have to rob Bank of America as a way of coming up with the money, real money, to join.

"Any of the old boys in particular?"

"Any of them or all of them," Nicholas said. "You really think this is important?"

"To be determined."

Hillary More was behind Jesse then.

"What's to be determined? Our first date, Chief Stone?"

"Morning, boss," Nicholas said. "Jesse and I are trying to figure out why my grandfather had taken an interest in cryptocurrency before he died."

Hillary sat down on the edge of Nicholas's desk. She was wearing a short leather skirt, which, to Jesse's trained policeman's eyes, went very well with long, tanned legs. He knew the thought police would come after him if they found out he was still thinking thoughts like these. But sometimes he couldn't help himself.

"If Charlie figured out how it all works," she said, "I wish he'd explained it to me."

She smiled at Jesse. He smiled back. It was a good smile. Went with the rest of her.

"Might this be something that helps you find out who did this awful thing to Charlie?" she asked.

"Ever hopeful."

"One thing about my Gramps," Nicholas said. "He generally didn't spend a lot of time cruising the Net. He used to say he wasn't going to take up a whole hell of a lot of the time he had left on this earth staring at a little screen. So whatever he was doing, there was a purpose behind it."

"To make easy money himself?" Jesse said.

Nicholas shook his head. "He thought easy money was an oxymoron."

Jesse knew that Nicholas had begun to take care of Charlie's finances the past few years. He asked him now to check all of his accounts, checking and savings and IRA, just to make sure that Charlie hadn't made any odd transactions lately on his own. Nicholas said he'd get right on it, but first he needed to be wheels-up for some coffee.

"Where you off to next?" Nicholas said.

"To see Miss Emma, and ask her about her boyfriend."

When Nicholas was gone, Hillary said, "At least Miss Emma *had* a boyfriend."

"Be careful what you wish for," Jesse said to her.

"I'm *never* careful, Jesse," she said.

He had no snappy response to that, so he left her and her legs sitting there.

TWENTY-SIX

Emma Cleary said she'd never been in a police station in her life, not one single time. So she asked Jesse if they could meet for lunch at the Gull.

"You would be the prettiest lunch date I've had in a long time," Jesse said.

"Shut it," Miss Emma said.

Jesse knew she lived with her daughter, Maryanne, an English teacher at Paradise High, over on the west side of town, maybe four or five blocks from Charlie's house. Before he ended the call, he asked if Miss Emma needed him to pick her up.

"I'll be walking, thank you."

"All the way to the Gull?"

"I'm a senior citizen, young man, not a goddamn invalid."

She was waiting for Jesse at the Gull when he arrived, the lunch crowd there as loud and brisk and busy as usual. She gave him a wave from the window table. Jesse didn't know her well, but well enough, from the times he'd run into Charlie and Miss Emma—he had difficulty thinking of her any other way—around town. She reminded him a little of Betty White, not that he was going to share that observation with her, especially not after Betty White had passed away the previous year at the age of ninety-nine.

Fluffy white hair, bright blue eyes, not much more than five feet tall by now, if that, shrinking the way old people did. She stood to greet him and he saw that she was wearing khaki pants, a pink sweater, shoes to match the sweater. Jesse noticed that she slipped easily out of her booth when she rose to greet him. He recalled Charlie telling him that Miss Emma still rocked yoga classes a couple days a week. He should have known better than to offer her a ride. Something else Charlie had told him. She liked to walk everywhere, even though she still drove herself when she needed to in a Jetta of her own.

Jesse waited until after they ordered their salads to say, "I'm truly sorry for your loss, Emma."

"Shouldn't that be my line, too?" was her reply.

She had hearing aids, both ears. It appeared to be her only concession to her age, which was the same as Charlie's; they'd graduated Paradise High the same year. She married her high school sweetheart and Charlie married Maisie. Then after both high school sweethearts were gone, they somehow found their way back to each other.

And were supposed to live happily ever after.

"How are you doing?" Jesse asked.

"I'm pissed off, is how I'm doing. I wasn't supposed to fall in love again. Neither was he. But we did. Now he's gone and I'm still here, and I'm just going to have to call bullshit on that."

The blue eyes were flashing now. *I could put them on top of one of our patrol cars,* Jesse thought.

"So just what am I supposed to *do* about bullshit like that, Jesse?"

He grinned. "Have lunch with me."

"I want you to promise me you're going to find who did this to my Charlie."

"I don't make promises I'm not sure I can keep," Jesse said. "But my plan is to catch him."

"The fucker."

Jesse tried not to smile. He knew from Charlie that the petite old lady across from him could swear like Samuel L. Jackson.

"You'll really do that for me?" she said.

"All due respect?" Jesse said. "I'll be doing it for me."

He told her then about what he'd found on Charlie's laptop, asked if he had mentioned anything at all to her about a sudden interest in cryptocurrency or Bitcoin or anything like that. Emma Cleary said that he was more likely to have been discussing kryptonite. All she knew, she said, was that his hair had been on fire over the past month about the scam calls. She kept telling Charlie to let them go. But he'd gotten more and more fixed on them.

"Dog with a bone," she said. "Old dog."

"Tell me about it."

"It was like he'd decided that he was, by God, going to crack one more case. I'm sure he told you that I lost a fair amount of money I really couldn't afford to lose a while back and felt like an old fool after I did. Gave somebody my Medicare ID number during COVID, and paid a heavy price for it." She gave a vigorous shake to her head. "Don't want to talk about it."

"Agree to disagree on the old fool part, Emma. Calls like those cleaned out people of all ages to the tune of about thirty billion dollars last year. Billion with a *b*. Pretty sure all of that money didn't come from your age grouping."

"I still felt like a dumb shit afterward. It's why I was cheering him on while he tried to find out who was at least behind some of these goddamned calls."

She drank some water, her hand shaking, put her glass back down. Jesse noticed that she had barely touched her salad. But he hadn't done much better. Nothing about this felt social.

"The last time I spoke with my Charlie was the night it happened," she said. "I could tell he was preoccupied. I always could. I asked him what was bothering him. He said nothing was bothering him. I told him something was bothering him. He told me I didn't know everything. I said, 'About you I do, old-timer.' Then he laughed and told me he loved me and said he'd call me later, he thought he might have caught the bastards."

"That was all?"

"Like he had all the time in the world," she said. "Like the two of us, old as we were, had all the time in the world."

She started to cry now. She was one tough old broad, in all the good, old-fashioned definitions of that, from the old days, when you could call someone as terrific as Miss Emma a great broad and not get flogged in the public square.

She didn't make a sound as the tears fell over her cheeks. She just sat there, looking at him across the table, until she finally reached up and dried them with her napkin.

"Still an old fool," she said.

"Still agreeing to disagree."

Jesse paid the check. Miss Emma pointed at both their salad bowls and said the next time they met up to *not* eat, lunch was on her. Jesse told her he never passed up a free meal, especially when it was with a pretty girl.

"Shut it," Miss Emma said.

TWENTY-SEVEN

Molly followed Matt Loes once he pulled out of the students' parking lot at Paradise High after school let out. She had told Suit what she planned to do. He wanted to go with her. But Jesse had told him to take the day and Molly told him the same thing, because Jesse had told her *why* he wanted Suit to take the day.

"Suit always says he wants you to teach him everything you know," Molly told Jesse. "But I'd always assumed he already knew how to drink. Or, in your case, how *not* to drink."

"I can't believe I've lived in Paradise this long and was never married to you," Jesse said.

"You know why. I pledged my love to another a long time ago."

"Poor bastard."

Molly knew she was following a basic Sunny Randall rule of detecting: When you're uncertain of what your next move should be, follow somebody.

Or annoy somebody.

Or both.

Matt Loes drove an Audi that appeared to have some miles on it. He stopped at the Dunkin' drive-thru, then made his way out of Paradise before getting on Route 32 and heading for Marshport. Molly managed to stay a car or two behind him, but really was unconcerned that the kid would even dream he was being followed, much less being followed by a cop.

Sunny swore up and down that following people, for no good reason, often worked like a charm for her.

Molly still spoke to Sunny on the phone from time to time, but they had drifted apart, primarily because she and Jesse were no longer seeing each other. Molly missed her, though. Just not as much as Jesse did, whether he'd ever admit that to Molly, or himself, or not.

Molly knew from Jesse that Nellie Shofner had it in her head that Molly didn't like her.

Not true.

She just didn't like her for Jesse.

Big difference.

Molly knew it bothered Nellie, thinking Jesse's best friend didn't like her. But she was young. Plenty of time for her to recover from a case of hurt feelings.

Eventually Matt Loes arrived at his destination at Silver Lake, up in the northwest section of Marshport, an area Molly knew well from her high school days.

There was a small dock there for locals who couldn't afford the dock prices over in Paradise. If you didn't want to battle the ocean waves, it was as nice a place to swim as there was in the area. The beach wasn't very wide, and too rocky in most places to suit Molly. But it was big enough on which to party, as long as you cleaned up afterward, because Mike Pearl, the Marshport chief of police, was well known for handing out littering tickets that rivaled anything you could get for speeding.

Matt Loes pulled up and stopped in front of the small white house with bright red trim that served as the dockmaster's office. Even from where she'd parked her old Cherokee on a dirt road just past the Silver Lake lot, Molly could see the big sign on the door that read GONE FISHING.

There was another car, a blue Range Rover, parked in front of the office. Molly could see the big PARADISE BEACH sticker on the back window. No shocker there. There were so many Range Rovers back in Paradise, Molly sometimes imagined them reproducing like rabbits.

When Matt Loes got out of his car, Ainsley Walsh got out on the driver's side of the Range Rover.

Scott Ford got out on the passenger side. He was moving gingerly. But obviously well enough to be riding around in a car. Maybe he was a fast healer, even after getting the crap kicked out of him.

Molly quietly closed the door to the Cherokee, grabbed her Nikon from the backseat, walked up through a small patch of woods to give herself a better view of the kids, using some trees for cover.

Matt Loes, Ainsley Walsh, Scott Ford.

Apparently Loes and Ford had patched up their differences, fairly quickly.

They all sat down on the front steps to the dockmaster's office. Ainsley lit a cigarette.

Bad girl, Molly thought.

But how bad?

The three of them sat there for ten minutes before a third car pulled up next to Ainsley Walsh's Range Rover. A newer model Cherokee, by a lot, than Molly's, and in much better shape.

Coach Hal Fortin got out.

Molly leaned against the closest tree, and began shooting pictures.

Fortin walked over to the kids, said something, immediately slapped Matt Loes hard across the face. Snapped the kid's head to the side. Loes took it. Molly just kept shooting. Fortin now pointed toward the water in the distance. The three kids started walking. Fortin walked behind them until they were out of sight.

Molly put down her camera, then said something Sunny used to say when a clue presented itself.

"Oh, ho," Deputy Chief Molly Crane said.

TWENTY-EIGHT

J esse and Molly and Suit were waiting for Hal Fortin when he arrived at Jesse's office. Suit had brought in an extra chair from the squad room, and placed it between his and Molly's.

Fortin was a big man, six-four at least, had been a star first baseman at Paradise High when he was a kid, the kind of prospect Jack Carlisle was. But halfway through his senior year he took a fastball to the face, and even with the flap on his batting helmet, the pitch did so much damage to his right eye that his career was over in that moment, just like that.

Jesse knew the feeling. He noticed now, this close to Fortin, that the eye still drooped slightly.

"You better have a good reason for wasting my time like this," Fortin said as he took his seat. "We've still got a state tournament that we're going to try to win without our best player."

"Show must go on," Jesse said.

"What's that supposed to mean?"

"Another way of saying that we're all moving forward from Jack's death."

"Like I don't know that?" Fortin said.

Jesse wondered how long it would take for Fortin to annoy him even more than he did when he was coaching a game. Now he had his answer. He wasn't just too goddamn loud on a ballfield.

"So what's this all about?" Fortin asked.

Jesse said, "I wanted to ask you what you were doing at Silver Lake last night with two of your players and Ainsley Walsh."

"The boss means he wants to know what you were doing with Matt Loes and Scott Ford and Ainsley after you slapped Loes, who, as I'm sure know, just beat up Ford bad enough to put him in the hospital," Suit said. "Sounds like their friendship survived, huh?"

Fortin turned toward Suit, looking surprised, as if he'd just remembered he was still in the room.

"I don't have to answer any of this," Fortin said.

"Pretty sure slapping around one of your student athletes, as coaches like to call them, could get you fired," Molly said.

"This is bullshit," Fortin said.

"Which part?" Jesse said.

"First of all," Fortin said, "what gives you the right to follow me."

"Well, Hal, as chief of police, I can follow anybody I goddamn well please."

"And Jesse technically wasn't following anybody," Molly said. "I was the one following Matt Loes to the lake, and then you showed up."

"I wasn't talking to you," Fortin said.

"But we're all talking to you, aren't we, Coach?"

Jesse idly noted that for Fortin's hair to be as dark as it was, his age, he had to be coloring it. Maybe to make himself more relatable to the kids.

Or maybe there wasn't enough dye in the world for Hal Fortin to do that.

"I didn't slap anybody," he said.

Jesse reached forward and opened the manila folder on his desk and slid out the pictures Molly had taken at the lake. He had already told her she might be a better photographer than Nellie. Molly had said, "I'm better at a lot of things than she is."

He pushed the pictures closer to Fortin. He picked up one, looked at it, tossed it back down on Jesse's desk.

"Okay, you got me," Fortin said. "I slapped him because of what he did to Scott. You're telling me you never had a coach who gave you a little tough love from time to time?"

"If they did," Jesse said, "it was always just the one time."

"What were you really doing with those kids at the lake?" Molly asked.

"I don't need to tell you anything," Fortin said.

"You're right, you don't," Suit said. "And we don't need to take these photographs to your boss, even though we could."

"Or to Nellie Shofner at the *Crier*," Jesse said.

"That snoopy little bitch," Hal Fortin said. "She's the one who needs a good . . ."

He managed to stop himself.

Molly smiled.

"Down, boy," she said.

"For the last time," Jesse said, "tell us what you *were* doing with two of your players and the girlfriend of your dead star at Silver Lake last night."

Fortin started to speak. Jesse held up a hand. "And if you did need to talk to them, why do it one town over? Why the secrecy, Coach?"

The chair underneath him looked as small as the one underneath Matt Loes had. It was fascinating to Jesse watching a guy, Fortin, to whom being in charge was probably like some powerful narcotic, deal with being on the wrong side of power. Jesse's, in this case. But trying to figure out a way to somehow take back the room.

"Okay," he said finally. "*Okay.* I just needed to get with the three kids I thought had been closest to Jack as anybody at that school and remind them that the whole town is watching them. Watching *us.* While everybody is talking about Jack and speculating about Jack, and what might have happened to him. I wanted to tell them not to become part of the noise themselves."

"What noise?" Suit said.

"The noise about whether or not it might have been suicide, for chrissakes," Fortin said. "Or drugs. Or booze." Fortin reached over now and slapped Jesse's desk hard and said, "Or if somebody might have thrown the kid into the water."

His face was a clenched fist now. Jesse had seen it before when somebody on his team made a big out, or a big mistake.

Fortin lowered his voice.

"I told the guys who are supposed to be my team leaders that they can't do stupid shit like getting into a fight," he said. "More than anything, I told them that we need to take care of Jack dead as much as we did when he was alive."

"Not your job," Suit said.

"Says who?" Fortin said.

"Says his uncle," Jesse said.

"So we're clear," Suit said to Fortin, his voice quiet, "he thought you were a raging asshole."

"I don't have to take this," Fortin said, "whether you're his uncle or not."

Fortin stood.

"Sit the fuck down," Jesse said, in the same tone he'd used on Matt Loes.

Fortin hesitated briefly, but then sat.

"What are you all hiding about Jack Carlisle?" Jesse asked.

"Nobody's hiding anything."

"I think you are," Jesse said. "And when I find out what, because I will find out what, it will likely be just the two of us having a chat."

"Are you threatening me?" Fortin said.

"Not even close," Jesse said.

Fortin opened his mouth and closed it and finally said, "I got nothing to say to any of you."

This time he got up and out of the chair too quickly and the chair tipped over behind him. He left it there and walked out, leaving the door open behind him, and then was gone.

"Good talk," Jesse said.

Jesse was alone in his office about twenty minutes later when Jimmy came in without knocking, out of breath, to tell him about the 911 call that came in from Nicholas Farrell's house.

"Shots fired," Jimmy said.

Jesse closed his eyes, but could only see Charlie dead on the floor.

"By whom?" he said.

"Nicholas."

"Is he okay?" Jesse said.

"He's the one made the call."

"Tell me exactly what he said."

"He just said that we needed to get over there, because he shot the son of a bitch," Jimmy said.

TWENTY-NINE

Nicholas lived even closer to where Charlie Farrell had lived than Miss Emma did. Usually Jesse could make it there by car in five minutes. He used the siren now, made it in two.

Nicholas was in his wheelchair when Jesse came running up the walk and through the front door. Back in the chair, as he pointed out to Jesse. He held an icepack to the right side of his face. There was dried blood over his right eye.

His .38 was on the coffee table.

"I walked . . . I *wheeled* in on the guy," Nicholas said.

"Then what?"

"He swung the tire iron in his hand and did his level best to separate my head from my shoulders," Nicholas said. "Maybe it was the same thing he used on Gramps. The tire iron."

"You get a look at him?"

Nicholas shook his head. "Some kind of ski mask."

Jesse said, "We need to get *you* looked at."

"Later."

"What happened after he clobbered you?"

"I went with the blow and slowly rolled out of my chair, like the blow had knocked me out," Nicholas said. "But I had time to grab my gun from the little pouch under the right armrest."

"He didn't notice you go for it?"

"He was leaning over to swing at me again. Maybe for the fences this time. That was when I rolled over and shot him."

"Where?"

Nicholas grinned. "I was trying to aim for center mass, like Gramps taught me at the range. But I fired too quickly, and got him in the hand instead. He screamed, picked up the tire iron, and ran like a bitch."

"Sounds like calling him that is insulting to all the other bitches in the world."

Jesse took the icepack away, saw how bad the bruising was on that side of Nicholas Farrell's head, took out his phone, called his own doctor: Jim Frazier. Told the nurse it was Chief Stone and he was bringing somebody over.

Jesse grinned and said to Jim's nurse, "Tell him he needs to see this kid right away, or else."

After he'd put his phone away Nicholas said, "Or *else*? Or else what?"

"You know, I've always wondered about that myself," Jesse said.

He took another look around the room, which had been tossed, and not in any kind of professional way. The desk on the other side of the room was not dissimilar to Charlie Farrell's. The drawers were on the floor. Papers scattered everywhere.

"Charlie told me you handled his money," Jesse said. "Were you still doing that when he died?"

"He took great pride in the fact that he hadn't balanced a check-book properly since my grandmother passed," he said.

"Is there anything in the books that somebody could be worried about?"

"If there is," Nicholas said, "it beats the shit out of me what it might be."

Jesse put the sofa cushions back in place, and sat down.

"Odd that the guy broke in in the middle of the day," he said.

"Maybe not so much. I was supposed to be at work. But I left some files here that it turned out I needed there. From the looks of the place, he must've been almost finished when I came through the door."

"You didn't drive?"

"Figured I'd get some exercise, over and back. Kill two birds with one stone. Except then I nearly got killed myself."

"This had to have something to do with Charlie."

"Nothing else makes sense, right?"

"Somehow this guy, whoever he is, thought you might know something your grandfather knew. Something that has somebody scared."

"But what?" Nicholas said. "You think somebody killed Gramps and might have been willing to kill me over cryptocurrency?"

There was a ping then.

Incoming text, to Nicholas.

He took his phone out of his pocket, looked down at it.

His eyes got very big.

"What the fuck," he said.

"Who's it from?" Jesse asked.

"Gramps."

THIRTY

Nicholas wordlessly handed his phone over to Jesse.

There was a text, from what had been Charlie Farrell's number. All the letters in lowercase. Some words running together. Jesse recognized his old friend's distinctive style. Charlie had been a thumb user. Jesse had never gotten the hang of that. But the older he got, and as much dexterity as he had lost, he was happy he could still properly grip a baseball.

> troubleinparadise.
> maybe roosterin henhouse
> about to cockblock them
> think i know whoitis
> talk later, gramps

Jesse copied the text, sent it as a message to himself, handed the phone back to Nicholas.

"Where's this been?" Jesse said. "You get texts stacked up like planes waiting to land at Logan?"

"I actually think I might know," Nicholas said. "A few months ago my girlfriend and I were in a group chat, a bunch of couples making a plan to go away for the weekend. And while that was going on, some texts just got lost to the ether. I did some research. It's more common than you think, texts coming to you late, or just getting lost, even if they say 'delivered.'"

"Gives you the creeps," Jesse said. "Like Charlie talking to us from the other side."

"Trying to tell us something," Nicholas said. "Just after the fact."

Jesse felt himself smiling.

"Not just a cop to the end," he said. "After the end."

"Is *any* of this making sense to you?" Nicholas said.

"Just this," Jesse said. "We know the guy who killed Charlie took his phone. Maybe he got around to reading his text messages, and saw what he wrote to you, and decided you had to know something."

"We just have no idea about what."

Jesse said, "Maybe your grandfather figured out where the scam and spam calls were coming from, and who was behind them."

"And that was worth killing him over?"

"What I'm going to find out," Jesse said. "Something else you can take to the bank."

Nicholas looked down at his phone again.

"Trouble in Paradise," he said.

"Not the first," Jesse said.

THIRTY-ONE

There was one race about which Michael Crane had talked, what he called his white whale, the Clipper Round the World Yacht Race, starting up again after being paused for the past two years because of the pandemic.

He'd explained it to Molly by showing the course to her on the huge wall map in his study, how you ended up crossing six oceans over ten or eleven months, depending on how good your boat was, and the men crewing it. You could sign up for some of the legs or all of them. Michael always said he'd be in for all if he ever got his chance, a chance to participate in what he called the Olympics of yacht racing, because you were up against people from all walks of life and all corners of the world.

Now he had gotten his chance, because of Teddy Altman, the billionaire for whom he'd crewed before in big races, because Teddy's new yacht had finally been finished during the Clipper's two-year hiatus. Teddy asked Michael to captain the crew, offering him more money than Michael would normally make in five years. Michael accepted.

"I have to do this," Michael told Molly.

"I know."

But they *both* knew it wasn't just about the Clipper Round the World Yacht Race, that this was a way for them to separate without legally or officially declaring that, or telling their children, for them to be separated by six oceans, for nearly a year.

It was because Michael now knew about Molly and Crow.

She had finally confessed to her husband about her one-night stand—did people even still call it that?—with an Apache whose real name was Wilson Cromartie, a career criminal at the time Molly slept with him, but now one who had, for all Molly and Jesse knew, gone straight. Or as straight as he could manage, being Crow. Molly would eventually be shot in their investigation of Neil O'Hara's death. Crow would save Jesse's life shooting a hired gun named Darnell Woodson. That was how Crow ended up back in Paradise.

And back, at least temporarily, in Molly's life.

Just not all the way back, the way he wanted to be.

Molly didn't know whether it was Catholic guilt that finally caught up with her, about something that she'd told only Jesse and her priest, just the one time, in real Confession. Whatever brought her to the moment, and realizing what the consequences might be and how it would hurt him, Molly told the man she had loved since high school about Crow.

She only left out the part about how fully aware she'd been last year that her attraction to Crow was as powerful as ever, like it was part of her goddamn DNA now.

Bless me, Father, for once again taking your name in vain.

Michael didn't get angry. Did not ask for a lot of details.

"Just the one time?" is what he said.

"Yes."

"But once was enough, wasn't it?"

He said he would need to get a place of his own, and then they'd figure out how to tell their girls. But then Teddy Altman had called. Michael told Molly that it would be like a story from another time, and that he was going off to sea. He told her he would update her on his progress occasionally. He showed her an app that enabled her to track Teddy's boat, which would eventually end up in London next year, hopefully ahead of everybody else.

"I love you," Molly told him on the day he left for Teddy Altman's private plane.

"I know," he said, and then was gone.

That was a month ago. She still hadn't heard from him, but Michael had told her that it might be a while before she did, and that might not be a bad thing.

Molly had always told Jesse that he was the alonest person she'd ever known. Now, on nights like this one, on *most* nights, she at least had a sense of what it was like to be him.

Like she was now the deputy chief of aloneness in Paradise, Mass.

Someday, maybe even soon, she would tell Jesse the truth about Michael the way she'd once told him the truth about her and Crow.

Just not tonight.

Tonight she was working, sitting at the kitchen table, trying to find out other people's secrets, even in a place that was pretty much, far as Molly could tell, the opposite of secrets.

Instagram.

THIRTY-TWO

Molly was on Instagram herself only to keep up with her daughters, as well as any mother could keep up with her daughters on social media, especially now that they were all out of college and, blessedly, supporting themselves.

That meant keeping up on them without drone tracking or twenty-four-hour surveillance, both of which Molly had occasionally considered when they were college students, one after another.

Her youngest was now living in New York City, in the West Village, with three of her college roommates.

All things considered, Molly had liked it much better when they were in a dorm.

By now Molly felt as if she were well schooled, mostly by her kids, in the basics, the protocols, of proper Instagram behavior. It had become the platform of choice for kids, more than Facebook or Meta or whatever Marky Mark Zuckerberg was calling it these days.

Just about all of the boys on the Paradise High baseball team were on Instagram. So were the girls that Molly and Suit knew by now were hanging out with—or hooking up with—the players.

Tonight she was continuing to look for any relevant posts about Jack Carlisle, something or anything that might give her a better idea about what had happened to the kid that night, when he basically wandered away from the campfire and never came back.

She wasn't really looking for deep, dark secrets, because only an idiot teenager would post those. Or even put them in a story knowing they'd be gone tomorrow. This was, after all, the public square for the modern world. One of them, anyway. Molly liked the old world better, when high school kids like the one she'd been a thousand years ago actually got by passing notes to each other.

This wasn't the first time Molly had speculated about exactly when having an unspoken thought—or having an untaken snapshot—turned out to be against the law.

Jimmy Alonso had told her that she should look into TikTok, too, but Molly was certain that might be above her pay grade—let her try becoming the queen of Insta first.

She poured herself a glass of wine. Her one and only for the night. She wasn't going to start drinking alone, at least not in excess, with her husband gone. Molly hated clichés, and wasn't about to become one.

She went through the accounts randomly, not alphabetically, jumping back and forth between the boys and the girls. She had a list of names on the table next to her, and kept checking them off, one by one.

Tonight she had begun with the three kids she considered her headliners: Ainsley Walsh and Scott Ford and Matt Loes. Scott Ford posted hardly any pictures of himself away from baseball.

Some included him posing with Jack Carlisle, sometimes in a goofy way. But there were just as many with other players. The last post, from him, about Jack had come the day after the accident:

Not the way the story was supposed to end

Accompanying that was a picture of what Molly assumed to be Jack's baseball glove, his bat, his PHS cap, sweat-stained and looking well worn.

Matt Loes hadn't posted a picture in months.

Miss Ainsley Walsh, though, she was so active on Instagram, hyperactive really, posting so many shots of herself, that Molly wondered how much time she had left to actually live her life once she stopped posing.

There were a lot of pictures of her and Jack Carlisle, at least up until a couple weeks before the accident. *The accident.* Molly was still thinking of it that way, while waiting for new information to come in. Or bring the information in her own damned self. It wasn't even summer yet, but it had been an unusually warm spring, so there were a lot of bikini shots of Ainsley, the bikinis amazingly skimpy. Molly was suddenly feeling the urge to call her daughters and apologize for the comments she'd always made about their bikinis.

There was a picture of Ainsley and Jack at Fenway Park, mugging for somebody's phone, the Green Monster in the background.

There were pictures of them at an Ed Sheeran concert at the Garden, for which they had great seats near the stage.

Once again looking ridiculously happy.

Impossibly young.

Michael and I looked that way once, just at a Stones concert.

Something else Molly wondered as she sat at the table: How in the world she would have survived high school if there had been social media then, and cell phones, and everybody knew every single move everybody else was making?

Or would she have been Ainsley, turning her life into one long photo op?

Not Ainsley, she told herself.

Not even the teenage me.

Definitely not.

Molly had liked having secrets, until there came the secret that might end her marriage.

She sipped wine. Kris. Her new favorite white. A generous pour, no doubt. But just the one.

So much of what she was reading, and seeing, made her sad, the desperation for some of these kids, even the boys she knew to be the stars of the team, to be noticed, looking for validation or approval or something under the guise of likes they were getting. As if they needed to be told that they Mattered.

But not all of it made her sad.

Some of it made Molly envy these kids, especially the girls who simply seemed to be having a blast, as if they got the joke and if you didn't, that was on you.

Some had mourned Jack Carlisle in a touching way. Some were overwrought.

Molly looked up and realized she had been at this for more than two hours. It didn't bother her. It had shortened another long night here alone.

There was a lot going on at her old school, so much of it making her feel older than the fight song. But nothing on her night of Instagram that resembled a clue.

She was about to close her laptop and head to bed when she decided to visit Ainsley Walsh's page one last time, to see if anything new had shown up.

A new comment had shown up five minutes earlier.

Promises to keep.

It had come from someone calling themselves Pepsquad1234.

It made Molly think of the old Robert Frost poem about the woods dark and deep, and promises to keep, and miles to go before sleep. She didn't remember many poems from when she was in high school. But felt as if everybody remembered that one.

She reached for her wine.

When she looked back at her screen, Pepsquad's comment was gone.

THIRTY-THREE

Jesse decided that the best thing to do, so as not to get the chattering class in Paradise—it was a bigger party than Republicans and Democrats combined—chattering about Nellie Shofner's relationship with the PPD, was for them to meet at Molly's for coffee the next morning.

Jesse. Molly. Nellie.

"We could have done this at the office," Molly said, "unless you were afraid the rest of our department would have thought they missed the memo on Take Your Daughter to Work Day."

Jesse said, "I am going to point out again that you're not as funny as you think you are."

"Am too," Molly said.

Jesse asked her to play nice with Nellie today and Molly said she'd try her hardest.

"Do more than try. Or else."

"Not for nothing, Chief," Molly said, Jesse hearing the smile in her voice over the phone, "but that or-else shit may work with other people. But not me."

When they were all there Jesse had coffee. Molly decided to have tea after Nellie asked for some. If Molly had any idea that Jesse and Nellie had spent the previous night together, or how many nights they were spending together, she didn't let on. But she probably knew. Jesse sometimes couldn't figure out how Molly Crane knew all the things she knew about him.

But she did.

They sat in the living room. Molly's laptop was open on the coffee table. When she told Nellie what she'd seen last night, the comment on Ainsley's page there and gone, Nellie said, "Pepsquad1234, right?"

"You saw the same one?"

Jesse could see how hard Molly was trying not to look, or act, surprised.

"I've seen it pop up a couple times before," she said. "Once on Scott Ford's page. Once on the Loes kid's page. Promises to keep."

"Then disappear?" Molly asked her.

Nellie nodded.

"Why put it up and then take it right down?" Jesse said.

"We'll be sure to ask Pepsquad when we find him," Molly said. "Or her."

"We need to find out what promise," Jesse said.

"We," Molly said. "Like the Three Musketeers?"

She was smiling at Jesse over her cup, but it was the kind of smile you got when you were the one being trolled.

"Technically," Nellie said, "there were four, if you count D'Artagnan."

"You did study for the final!" Molly said, but at least she put out her fist and let Nellie bump it after she did.

Nellie ate some of the biscotti Molly had put out for them.

"Why isn't Suit here?" Nellie asked Jesse. "Shouldn't he be the fourth Musketeer?"

"I want him in the game. But I'm still easing him into it. Right now, I feel as if Nellie is more dialed in to these kids than we are, just because she was working on that piece about Jack."

"Working with you guys doesn't mean I'll compromise my standards," Nellie said. "But for now we have the same goal, which means getting the story right, whatever it takes."

Jesse went into the kitchen, poured himself another cup of coffee. Molly had made a pot.

When he came back he said, "Even when I was just starting out with the cops in L.A., we knew which reporters we could trust. And knew it cut both ways. The reporters knew which guys on the street had the best intel." He shrugged. "It's all as old as both jobs."

Molly grinned. "Says the guy who has mostly no-commented his way through life."

"I've evolved," Jesse said.

"Apparently so," Molly said.

"What happened to playing nice?"

"This *is* playing nice."

Jesse wondered if they sounded as much like an old married couple to Nellie as they did to his own ears.

"Be nice to know who Pepsquad is," Jesse said. "But I have this feeling it will be about as easy as these ghost scam numbers Healy and I are chasing with Charlie."

"It can be done," Nellie said. "But it ain't easy."

"I know this cop," Molly said, "who's always saying that if this shit were easy, everybody would do it."

"Gee," Nellie said, "I never heard that one."

She smiled at Molly. Molly smiled back.

More progress.

"I think the best thing for us, going forward, is for Nellie to keep working the kids," Jesse said. "Starting with girlfriends. Mols, maybe you could talk to some teachers today. We haven't talked to any of Jack's teachers yet. There wasn't a star jock I ever knew who didn't need a little boost from at least one of his teachers."

"What about Suit?" Molly said.

"I want him to get with Ford and Loes, the two hotheads. Maybe individually, then the two of them together. Eventually we'll make another run at the coach, just not yet. But there has to be a good reason why he met up with them in Marshport."

Nellie stood. "Can't say it hasn't been fun. But I gotta get to my real job."

Jesse said that he was going to hang with Molly here before they both went to the office, he had some other police matters to discuss with her.

"Oooh," Nellie said. "*Po-lice* matters."

"Talk later," Jesse said.

Nellie was about to walk out the door when she turned around.

"Thanks for the tea, Aunt Molly," she said, and then was through the door and closing it behind her before Molly could come up with a good comeback.

"What are you smiling at?" Molly said to Jesse.

"She got you good there."

She asked if he wanted more coffee.

"*I'm* good," he said.

"What's this police business?"

"I lied," he said. "I just wanted to ask how Michael's doing."

"Doing the South Ocean Leg, I believe it's called."

"You talk to him?"

"Next week," she said. "I'm updating our seafaring cellular plan."

She grabbed the mugs off the table. Jesse picked up the plate with the biscotti on it. He wasn't much for biscotti, not even to dunk in his coffee. It always tasted like stale cake to him. And wasn't a damn Dunkin' donut, all anybody needed in the morning.

When Molly turned back from rinsing the mugs, she threw her chin out at Jesse.

"What?"

"*What* what?" he said.

"You've got that look."

"Do not."

"I didn't tell you which look."

"No idea what you're talking about."

"It's the look where you think you're me, knowing things about me the way I always know them about you," she said. "Well, you don't."

"Whatever you say."

"Okay."

"*You* okay?"

"Even better than that," Molly said. "And look at me, I've practically got a new partner."

"Ish."

Molly asked what Jesse had planned for his own day. He told her he was going to talk to a man about funny money.

"Just not ha-ha funny, I'll bet."

"Not even close," he said.

She walked him to the door. As he was walking down her front walk he looked over his shoulder.

"Have a nice day, Aunt Molly," he said.

Then he was running toward the car as she yelled something after him about how far she wanted to get her foot up him.

Or something along those lines.

THIRTY-FOUR

Sandy Lipton, retired hedge-fund guy, might not have been the richest man in Paradise, Mass. But Jesse knew that Sandy at least had to be in the conversation.

But what set him apart from the others, at least in Jesse's mind, was that he was far and away the richest guy in town who Jesse liked this much.

He had cashed out of his fund a few years earlier, before COVID. Now all he wanted to do was have fun, travel the world with his wife, Rose, before the next goddamn variant came along, and play enough golf to finally lower his handicap. It was an endless mystery to Jesse, the fascination guys like Sandy Lipton had with a sport that had them all talking as much as they did about handicaps. There it was, anyway.

They met in the dining room at Paradise Country Club, still flying the flag in front of the clubhouse at half-mast in Charlie Farrell's honor.

Sandy was waiting for Jesse at a table overlooking the eighteenth green. He was around sixty, curly hair still more brown than gray, wire-rimmed glasses. Smiling. But then he was almost always smiling. He had once told Jesse that while it was true that money might not buy happiness, it could sure as blue-chip stocks put down a sizable down payment.

"Still playing a lot of golf?" Jesse said after he had sat down and the waitress had taken their orders for iced tea, Sandy's with lemonade.

"Only when it's light out," Sandy said.

When they'd set up the lunch, Jesse had explained to Sandy that his sudden interest in crypto and Bitcoin and NFTs was because of what he'd discovered on Charlie's laptop, and could think of no better person to ask.

"You blowing smoke up my ass?" Sandy said.

"Totally."

"Never hoits," Sandy said.

He ate some of a breadstick. "Sounds like you don't have much to go on, other than websites and supposition. Like blue smoke and mirrors."

"And scam calls making Charlie as angry as I'd ever seen him."

"You obviously believe the two might be connected."

"I wouldn't necessarily bet on that yet," Jesse said. "My old man always told me never to bet the way you're rooting."

"Happens to me all the time on the golf course," Sandy said.

"Charlie was looking into crypto, something I *would* have bet he'd previously had zero interest in," Jesse said. "And I know he was trying to track those calls. It's not a great leap to think that whatever he found out poked a bear. And then had somebody go after his grandson after Charlie was gone."

"You think it's the same person?"

"You're an analytics guy," Jesse said. "What do you think?"

"I agree with you," Sandy said. "I think maybe a nice old man somehow got sideways with bad men."

"Tell me about crypto."

"Invisible money that's real, if you can wrap your mind around a concept like that," Sandy said. "But it's like crack to bad guys, to the point where they probably wish they'd invented it themselves. Put it this way: If you've stolen something of value, converting it to crypto not only keeps your profit safe, it makes it undetectable to the government."

Jesse told Sandy Lipton that all he really knew about it came from the brief crash course Nicholas Farrell had given him.

"Sounds to me," Jesse said, "as if crypto and all that other shit is a way for bad guys to launder money without going through the process to do it the old-fashioned way."

Sandy gave Jesse a crisp two-fingered salute.

"Well done, soldier," he said. He grinned. "I'm assuming you don't want *my* tutorial to include digital wallets and the cloud and blockchains."

"Not unless you want me to arrest you," Jesse said.

Their club sandwiches arrived. When the waitress had walked away Sandy said, "The first crooks to embrace crypto were your basic drug dealers and porn dudes. People who really were used to being old-school money launderers, no matter how young they were. Move the money around, leave no tracks or fingerprints, everybody was living scummily ever after."

"Sounds like the Wild West."

"Before the sheriff showed up in town."

"Meaning the government."

"Realizing it still needs to build a better mousetrap for the rats," Sandy said. "Listen to me: Crypto isn't going away, even if the bubble seems to have burst for now. There's still a war going on between good guys and bad guys over there on the dark side, with the good guys hoping the bad guys stay greedy, keep looking for creative ways to make the value of their ill-gotten gains go up while they wait for a market adjustment they know will come. Because trust me on this: Anybody who thinks that crypto ain't gonna rise from the ashes again is bananas."

He grinned again. "You following this?"

"Somewhat," Jesse said.

"Bottom line?" Sandy said. "There's a shitload of profit to be made if you can manage not to get caught. All you need is a computer and a low moral compass."

"Could we be talking about enough money to kill over?" Jesse said.

"Everybody's got a different price, Chief. Except you, pretty sure."

Sandy Lipton talked more about crypto then, marveling at how it had gone from the dark web to television commercials with big stars doing them.

Finally the waitress brought Sandy the check, telling him there was no rush.

"You got a final piece of advice for me?" Jesse asked him.

"Yeah," Sandy Lipton said. "Follow the funny money."

THIRTY-FIVE

Jesse went back to his office after lunch, spent the rest of the afternoon researching crypto and people that various governments around the world were starting to catch, trying to get a sense of how the ones who had been caught had messed up.

And could not shake the feeling that he was out of his depth here.

He rarely felt that way when working a case, even when he was in the place he sometimes thought of as the deep, dark forest. It was because the subject, or at least a part of it, was money. Jesse had never cared about money, even when he was married to Jenn. Maybe there had been a time in his life, before he'd ruined his shoulder that day in Albuquerque, when he thought about being rich as a ballplayer, and famous. But then that was gone. And he was a cop. Cops didn't make much money, in L.A. or here. Or anywhere. The job wasn't about that. The job was about the J-O-B. He had some money in the bank. Jenn, at least until she had quit television—or television had quit her—had always had money of her own, and had asked for nothing when they got divorced and before she had finally become rich by marrying a rich guy.

Her shit, Jesse liked to tell himself, had finally come in.

Jesse knew the basics. How much he made, what his annual bump in salary was going to be, what he had in his savings account, what his pension would look like someday, if he ever made it that far. He'd made some money on the old man's house when he'd died, and invested it in some long-term bond funds that the late Abby Taylor, the lawyer with whom he'd once been in love, had suggested. The returns were steady enough that Jesse rarely checked them these days.

He knew enough about hedge funds from Sandy Lipton, and because Sunny had gotten herself involved in a case about a dead hedge-fund guy who had nearly walked away with Spike's restaurant in Boston during the first siege of COVID. But even that subject was above what Jesse considered his pay grade. And was fine with that.

Only now along came crypto.

And Charlie's interest in it.

Who's the rooster in the henhouse? Jesse asked himself, for maybe the fiftieth time since he and Nicholas had read Charlie's text.

He was after a murderer here, that made him feel as if he were on solid ground. Whoever it was, and whatever Charlie had found out about him, Jesse knew this:

He was smarter.

He'd never believed the old line about jails housing only dumb guys. Some very smart guys had ended up getting themselves locked up. But even the smart ones finally slipped up, somewhere along the way.

This guy would slip up. It was what Jesse kept telling himself. Whoever did it to Charlie was the one who was out of his depth.

Because I'm the one after him.

Neither Molly nor Suit was around when he decided to leave for home. He thought about calling Nellie and asking her if she wanted to order dinner in at her place, but decided he would just go home instead, order in there. He did, from Sushi Moto, let Delivery Dudes do their thing, ate General Tao's chicken, extra-crispy, and fried rice, and some dumplings.

He thought about calling his son, Cole, in London for a month after falling hard for an English actress he'd met in L.A. They hadn't spoken in a couple of weeks. But it was late there. He'd call him when all the craziness ended. If it ever did.

What henhouse had Charlie been talking about?

There was no ballgame tonight. He looked at his channel guide and saw that *Unforgiven* had started on Turner Classic Movies while he'd been eating, turned it on, stayed with it until the frontier justice when Eastwood caught up with Gene Hackman and put one in his head.

Jesse went to bed after that.

IT WAS RIGHT before dawn the next morning, about the time when Jesse was first opening his eyes, when Suit called. Never good at this time of the morning.

Ever.

Kind of call that couldn't wait.

"Somebody just called in another body from the water over there at Bluff Lookout," Suit said. "Five minutes ago."

"ID."

"Jesse, I called you as soon as we got the call. I'm on my way over there now."

There was a pause at Suit's end.

"What else?" Jesse said.

"There's a wheelchair down there, too," Suit said.

THIRTY-SIX

Nicholas Farrell's voice was thick with sleep when he finally answered his phone.

"Jesse," he said. "You know what time it is, right?"

"I do."

"Is everything okay?"

"Now it is."

He then told Nicholas about a body being discovered not far from where they'd found Jack Carlisle. And about the wheelchair discovered along with it.

"You have an ID yet? The wheelchair community in Paradise isn't exactly the size of the Junior League."

"There may already be one as we speak."

"Can you call me back when you have a name?"

Jesse said he would.

"Somebody in a wheelchair going over the Bluff?" Nicholas said. "Would somebody do something like that?"

"Only in the movies," Jesse said, thinking about a famous old black-and-white film, he couldn't remember the name, the crazy bad guy pushing an old woman in a wheelchair down a flight of stairs.

When Jesse got to the Bluff he walked past a couple of his squad cars to the edge and looked down at the water, the wheelchair still in the rocks, looking as small as a kid's tricycle from up here.

The smaller ME van they'd used for Jack Carlisle was back down there. So were Molly and Suit. Molly turned and looked up and saw Jesse and gave him a small wave. Jesse waved back. He was certain she was Suit's second call, after Jesse; that was the locked-in drill.

For the second time in a week, which had now become an even shittier week, Jesse made his way down the trail to the narrow strip of beach at the water's edge. Suit had waited to touch the wheelchair. He was already wearing his blue nitrile gloves. Jesse reached into the side pocket of his windbreaker now and put on his own and the two of them lifted up a wheelchair that looked a lot like Nicholas's onto the second off-road vehicle down here, this one with a flatbed in back. Then the two of them secured it with rope.

"Evidence," Jesse said.

Suit smiled, and for a moment he was Suit again, and things were the same as they always were between them.

"Why you're chief," Suit said. "Never would have figured that out on my own."

Jesse walked over to where Molly was standing with Dev Chadha. Molly had her notebook out. Without Jesse asking she said, "Vic's name is Sam Waterfield."

"Wallet?"

"Soggy as hell. But still in the pocket of his jeans," Molly said.

"Phone?"

She shook her head.

"The only Waterfield I ever heard of played for the Rams a thousand years ago," Jesse said.

"Good to know," Molly said.

"Nicholas Farrell told me the wheelchair population in our town is small."

"Just got smaller," Molly said.

"Tell me about it."

"So how'd he end up down here?" she said.

"He had help," Jesse said, "if you want to call it that."

"And you know this how?"

He pointed up to where he'd been standing a few minutes ago.

"The wheel tracks stopped about ten feet from the edge," he said.

"Not like he got out of the chair and tossed it and then jumped," Molly said.

"Not only do I think somebody did this," Jesse said, "I think somebody wanted to send a message with the chair. But what do I know?"

"Everything?" Molly said, and grinned.

Suit was still talking to Dev Chadha.

"You think there's any way this is connected to Suit's nephew?" Molly asked.

Jesse was staring again up at the Bluff.

"A police spokesman," he told Molly, "said they're not ruling anything out at this point."

"I'm not your girlfriend," Molly said.

"You can say that again," he replied.

THIRTY-SEVEN

I sent everybody home," Hillary More said to Jesse. "Everybody who works for me, that is."

He had offered to come to her office. She said she'd prefer to come to his, she didn't want to be in either of her buildings today. Or anywhere near her own company.

Where Sam Waterfield had worked.

She sat across from Jesse's desk now. Jesse had called her from the scene to tell her about Sam Waterfield. He had already called Nicholas Farrell, and asked how well he knew Sam Waterfield. He said hardly at all, actually, that Sam was one of the sales and marketing whiz kids. One of the upstairs cool kids, he said.

After Hillary More's shock had worn off, she asked how she could help. Now here they were, coffee mugs in front of them. Jesse hadn't told her about the wheel tracks. They'd get to that.

"Tell me about him," he said.

"Terrific kid," she said. "Good with people. It didn't take long for me to move him up to sales and marketing, one of our second-floor hotshots. And strategies, figuring out what worked for other chocolate companies, what didn't, stuff like that. Some of them sell love. Some sell to young women. He told me our goal had to be checking the most boxes."

"Background?" Jesse said. "Waterfield's, I mean."

She took a deep breath.

"This won't be the short version," she said. "There was just this spark to Sam. A foster kid who ended up with a full ride to Northeastern. Then ended up in the chair because of a summer party at the Cape before his senior year, too much beer, jumping off a balcony into a swimming pool. Wrong end. Still graduated with high honors. He was working at the Apple Store on Boylston Street when we started up. He heard we were hiring people with disabilities and applied. He told me when I interviewed him that he only had a question for me: Did I hate to lose as much as he did. I told him he was hired. Then I asked him where he saw himself in five years. He told me he wanted to be running his own company. I asked, 'How about this one?' and he said, 'If you say so.'"

Without asking, Hillary got up and walked over and poured herself more coffee. She said that it was too early for her to be drinking what she really wanted to be drinking.

"Never was too early for me," Jesse said.

"I've heard stories," she said.

"All true," Jesse said.

"Why would Sam do something like this?" she said.

"Like what?"

"Drive himself off a cliff, basically," she said.

Jesse drank some of his own coffee. Ballpark coffee today,

strong as he could make it. If it bothered Hillary, she hadn't let on. Or just liked it the way Jesse did. Until she could have something stronger.

"I don't believe he did it to himself," Jesse said.

"You're saying you don't think he killed himself? I've been wondering since you called if I'd missed the signs that he may have had a dark or sad or depressed side to him that nobody knew about."

He told her about the tracks then, no reason not to, how there were pronounced tracks in the grass and dirt until there weren't, no overnight rain to wash them away.

Told her what he'd told Molly, that this might be a message killing of some kind.

"A message about *what*?" she asked. "And to whom?"

"I was hoping you might be able to point me in the right direction."

She slammed her mug down on his desk, somehow managing not to spill coffee on it.

"*He was helping me sell candy!*" she said, in a voice loud enough to be heard in the squad room. "I mean, for God's sake, Jesse."

He made a calming gesture with the palms of his hands. She nodded and took in more air.

"Were there any problems with anybody at work?"

"From everything I know, he was one of the most popular people in the place," she said, "whether they were selling the chocolate or making it or getting it distributed. I know this sounds like a cliché. But he was a total team player."

"Was he involved with anybody I could speak to?" Jesse said. "Girlfriend? Boyfriend?"

"He had a roommate," she said. "Steve Marin. He worked with

Sam. The only reason I know is that I happened to see them one night having dinner at the Gull. Sam told me he'd found a wheelchair-accessible apartment over in Marshport, and they'd moved in a few months before."

"Have you spoken to Marin?"

"Tried," she said. "First thing. No answer. Landline or cell. Left messages on both."

"Was he at work yesterday?"

"No," she said. "Turns out he took a couple of vacation days this week. Didn't tell anybody where he was going."

"I appreciate that," Jesse said. "And you calling when you do hear from him. And he hears about his roommate."

"I'll do anything to help you get to the bottom of this."

When Hillary More realized what she'd just said, she smiled, as if embarrassed.

"Bottom. Poor choice of words."

"Go easy on yourself. It's like you had a death in the family."

"Like Nicholas," she said.

"And Suit. And me."

"Because of Charlie."

Jesse said, "I've had bad weeks around here. This has been turning into one of the worst."

"Could this possibly be connected to Jack Carlisle? Or Charlie?"

Jesse spared her his theories about coincidence.

"Two deaths at the Bluff. One of them involving one of your employees."

"When you put it like that."

"I'm going to find out what happened to all of them," Jesse said.

"Because it all happened in your town."

"Not mine. I just work here."

"Even you don't believe that, Jesse," she said.

He asked her for Sam Waterfield's address, and Marin's phone numbers. She wrote them down on the pad in front of her, ripped off the page, handed it to him. He placed it next to the phone on his desk.

"I don't believe I'd ever want to get on your bad side, Chief," Hillary More said.

"Few ever have," Jesse said.

THIRTY-EIGHT

Molly and Suit sat with Jack Carlisle's English teacher in the faculty lounge at Paradise High School, a half-hour or so after the end of the school day.

By then both Matt Loes and Scott Ford had declined their invitation to meet before baseball practice, even after Suit pointed out that if they didn't want to talk with them now, they were going to end up talking with Chief Stone later, and nobody ever really wanted that.

"My father says that if any of you have anything to say, you can say it to him," Scott Ford said.

"From what I hear, talking to your father would truly be a blessing," Molly said. She'd always told Jesse and Suit she came by her sarcasm naturally.

Molly knew that she didn't need Suit to be a part of her interview with Paul Connolly. But knowing Luther Simpson as long as she had, which meant longer than Jesse had, she understood, mostly in her heart, how much he needed to be a part of this investigation, every chance he got.

Needed to be needed, mostly.

The three of them sat in a corner of an otherwise empty lounge. Connolly had already told Suit how deeply sorry he was for his family's loss. He had longish gray hair, gray beard to match, wore a leather vest over a plaid shirt, jeans, old-school black Converse canvas sneakers.

"My sister says that you and Jack had a great relationship," Suit said.

Connolly smiled, and casually stroked his beard. *Maybe what it was there for,* Molly thought.

"*Great* might be a bit of a stretch," he said. "Kids open up to teachers they like, but you always know they're holding back more of themselves than they're actually sharing. He was a senior, he was the star athlete of the whole school. He liked English more than any of the other jocks I teach." He shrugged. "Basically, we were good, which was enough for me."

Connolly kept stroking his beard, somehow managing not to look pretentious as he did. *No mean feat,* Molly thought.

"He was a great student," he said. "I sometimes think he liked writing almost as much as being a ballplayer, not that he was going to share that with any of his teammates. Or classmates."

Molly watched him. She couldn't tell how old he was, but thought his face was younger than the gray in his hair. A nice face.

A kind face.

Would've had a huge crush on him when I was a senior.

Totally.

"If he could write like he could play, he must have been some writer," Suit said. "You a baseball fan?"

Connolly grinned. "Casual, at best. But when I would catch a game, I knew enough to know that what Jack was doing out there was different from what everybody else was doing."

"When I played sports here a hundred years ago," Suit said, "my favorite teachers were just the ones who kept me eligible."

Keep them talking.

Suit knew the drill as well as Molly did. Jesse had drummed it into both of them.

"That wasn't Jack," Connolly said. "He didn't need my help for that, or help from anybody else who passes through this lounge, as far as I could tell. He just liked my class better because he liked writing. If there was one thing I nagged him about, it was that I wanted him to get into a good writing program when he got to Vanderbilt."

Molly noticed a teacher, an older woman, come into the other end of the lounge, open the refrigerator, grab an apple, and leave.

"Did you notice any sort of change in Jack recently?" Molly asked. "Get the sense that something might have been bothering him?"

"What are you really asking me?" Connolly said. "If he was acting depressed, and possibly suicidal? Because I want you to know how vigilant all of us who do what I do for a living are about that subject in the modern world of teenagers."

Suit leaned forward in his chair. "Molly didn't mean anything by it. These are questions that need to be asked, and I'm talking as Jack's uncle here as much as a cop."

"I apologize if I offended you, Deputy Chief," Connolly said to Molly. "Or sounded as if I was the one who'd been offended. That wasn't my intent."

"Nor was there any intent to offend on my part," Molly said.

"The truth is, baseball season was the time of year when I spent far less time with Jack than usual," he said. "Maybe even less time this year than in the past years, because it's senior year. I guess the last time I saw him was a week before he died. And he just seemed like Jack to me. Maybe a little more anxious because it was coming to an end. Baseball, high school, all of it. But that was pretty normal, in my experience."

"Nothing out of the ordinary, though," Suit said.

Connolly shook his head. "I told him that the prospect of college had scared the hell out of me when I was his age. It's why I gave everybody in the class one grand final senior writing project."

"You mean like for a term paper?" Molly said.

"An autobiographical play," he said. "One act. One in which you were the main character. Maybe the only character, speaking directly to an imaginary audience. More than anything, I wanted them to try to capture this moment in their lives theatrically."

"Had you seen it?" Molly said.

Connolly shook his head.

"As far as I know," he said, "no one had."

Stroked his beard again.

"I wish I had," Connolly said. "Maybe I would really have gotten to know him."

In a quiet voice Suit said, "I'm starting to feel the same way."

THIRTY-NINE

Suit told Jesse later that his sister, Laura, his only sibling, didn't know anything about a play Jack had been writing. Gabe hadn't found any document like it in the files on Jack's laptop.

"So where is it?" Jesse asked Suit.

"You're asking me? Maybe he hadn't started it yet. There's still a few weeks before graduation. Maybe he'd just been outlining it, or taking notes."

"Gabe said he didn't find anything like that in his desk at home."

"The kid kept to himself, Jesse," Suit said. "As much as the other kids liked him, he really only had a few people he was really close friends with. And the girlfriend. As much as Ainsley Walsh said everybody loved the guy."

"By the way? She ever mention why she took down that comment about promises to keep?"

"I asked her," Molly said. "She said it had popped up before and just made her more sad than she already was."

"Back to Jack," Jesse said, "He had to be working on that assignment somewhere."

"If he was."

"Let's assume he was, for the sake of conversation."

"So where?" Suit said.

"I've been meaning to pay a visit to your sister," Jesse said to him. "Maybe now's as good a time as any. Maybe everybody who went to the house missed something."

They were in the conference room. Molly was with them. Gabe had just left.

"I thought you wanted us to concentrate on Jack's case," Molly said. "Or is this one of those fluid-type situations you like to talk about."

"It is," Jesse said. "And as I am currently doing a rather shit job on finding out who killed Charlie Farrell, I thought I might help out on Jack."

He stood now. It meant they were done in here for now. Molly grinned. "Who asked for your help?"

"See how she talks to me?" Jesse said to Suit.

"Wish I could get away with that," Suit said.

"I need to get to know this kid as more than a shortstop. And maybe just put a new set of eyes on it," Jesse said.

"You were a lot less controlling when you were still drinking," Molly said.

"No way for me to be a good judge of that."

"Why is that?"

Jesse put out his hands in a helpless gesture. "I was drunk."

An hour later Laura Carlisle was walking him up the stairs to her son's bedroom, in their house on Earl Avenue. Laura said that she'd spent enough time in the room, at least for now. And maybe forever. Every time she went back in she felt as if she couldn't breathe.

"I thought it would be a comfort," she said. "Being in there, I mean, with all of his stuff, being able to feel his presence. But it just made me sadder and angrier and hurt more than it already did, if such things are even possible."

The door to the bedroom was closed. They were standing in the hall.

"Thank you for not being the latest person to tell me it will get easier with time," she said.

"Haven't said it to Suit," Jesse said. "Certainly not going to say it to you."

He could see the family resemblance. Laura had a softer, feminine version of Suit's face. Nearly six feet tall. The air inside the house, before he was even inside the kid's room, was so heavy with sadness Jesse felt the urge to go around opening windows.

"Thank you for that," she said.

She'd already given them permission to go through Jack's MacBook Air. Gabe had done what Gabe did with searches like this, treated the laptop like a crime scene. When he was done he told Jesse that it seemed like the usual mess you'd find with a high school boy, much of it sports stuff on Safari, which seemed to be his primary browser. But when he'd switched over to Google Chrome, Gabe had said, the kid may have used something called Incognito.

"The kid knew his way around Safari's privacy mode," Gabe said. "And if he was using that deal called Incognito, which doesn't record anything you do, there's no way for us to know that." Gabe had grinned at Jesse. "Why they call it 'Incognito' chief."

"So we're talking about an extremely private kid," Jesse had said to Gabe.

"Hell, yeah."

Before Jesse entered Jack's bedroom, Jesse had asked Laura Carlisle why she thought her son might have been using something like Incognito.

"Well, he wasn't afraid of me spying on him," she said. "I'm not that mom. I mean, I know kids use Snapchat to send texts these days, because they disappear almost before you've finished reading them, the way I understand it."

"Like they're all trafficking in state secrets."

"Exactly."

"But does it make sense to you, the Incognito thing?"

"Have you ever heard the expression *interior self*?" Laura Carlisle asked.

"It's often applied to me by Molly Crane, among others."

"That was my son," she said. "I'm not surprised to find out that he might be a budding playwright and not mention that to his mother."

"I know you've been asked this," Jesse said. "But did he seem depressed lately?"

"No. Maybe a little quieter than normal, which is saying plenty, believe me. But he had a lot going on with baseball and school. The only way I can explain it is that he was just being a slightly more interior version of Jack."

She put a hand to her mouth. Jesse could see tears forming. She said she had things to do downstairs, and to take as much time as he needed.

Jesse opened the door and walked into Jack's bedroom and remembered what it was like when he'd been in his own room in the small house in Culver City they'd moved to when he was in high school, when he could close the door and keep the world out, before the world could come find you because of the phone in your pocket and the laptop on your desk.

He'd told Laura he was looking for a hard copy of the play he might have printed. She told him she'd already looked through his room, come up empty, but to have at it, maybe she hadn't looked in all the right places.

Jesse made a meticulous search of the room, which featured a huge color poster of Red Sox shortstop Xander Bogaerts over the desk. Jesse liked watching Bogaerts play. He was good, didn't go out of his way to be flashy, made all the plays you were supposed to make and plenty you weren't. He just wasn't Ozzie Smith, Jesse's guy, because nobody was, because Ozzie was the best who ever was.

He should have seen my poster of the Wizard of Oz, stretched out in midair, body parallel to the ground, glove extended.

Jesse went through the desk and the dresser. He checked under the mattress and under the bed. The only thing he found beneath the mattress was a new glove the kid had obviously been breaking in, a ball in the pocket, a string around all of it. A sight that squeezed Jesse's heart

The way kids playing ball had done it from the beginning of time.

Still no app that could do that if you wanted to get a glove broken in right.

He went through the books in the small standing bookcase. A lot of baseball books on the top shelf. And *Playwriting: Structure, Character, How and What to Write,* by Stephen Jeffreys. There was *A Separate Peace,* too, Jesse's one true favorite, above all others, when he was in high school. He'd even named the one dog he had in high school Phineas, after one of the main characters.

If he had finished his play, why hide it, even if he was his mother's secret boy?

Say the kid had taken his own life, and knew he was going to do it, would he have written about that, like a last will and testament, even for a high school senior?

His mother was right about one thing.

This room was a very sad place. Like the saddest place in the whole town. Jesse understood why Laura Carlisle didn't want to be in here any longer, even though Jesse knew she would come back, again and again. And again. He wondered how long she would keep things the way they were in here. Or if she was already thinking about selling the house and moving to another one in Paradise. Or just moving out of town for good, even though Suit was all the family she had left.

Jesse went to the door, which Laura had closed behind him.

Turned around.

Something wasn't right.

Didn't fit.

He went back and sat down at the swivel chair at Jack's desk and went through the drawers again.

Then knew what was bothering him.

Too neat.

Way, way too neat.

Jack Carlisle was a high school senior. He was a *guy.* Even if he'd been neater than most guys his age, no one was *this* neat, or this organized. He could be wrong. But didn't think he was. Jesse was sure the mother had neatened things up before he came. Or had done that in the days after Jack was found in the water.

But everything in these drawers was too neat and too organized.

Would his mother have done that?

Or would she have just cleaned up the room, and not the inside of the desk?

Go ask her.

Jesse went back downstairs and found Laura Carlisle at the kitchen table, writing in a journal of her own. She smiled up at Jesse. "Like mother, like son."

"Need to ask you something," Jesse said. "Other than you and my people, has anybody else been alone in Jack's room lately?"

She shook her head. "Sorry, no."

"I'm sorry to have intruded," Jesse said.

"Take care of Luther."

"I will."

She started to get up. Jesse told her to stay where she was, he could see himself out. He was already outside when Laura Carlisle opened the front door and called out to him.

"There was one other person," she said.

FORTY

Before Jesse left the office for the day, Molly came in and sat down and said, "You need to listen to me."

"When have I not?" he said.

"When you do whatever you want to do without caring what anybody else thinks," she said. "That's when."

He waited, knowing she was just getting started. Because he knew her. Jesse wondered if Michael Crane knew her this well, even being married to her. Wondered at the same time if anybody would ever know him as well as Molly Crane knew her boss.

"I know how well you are at compartmentalizing," she said. "Maybe as good at it as anybody I've ever met. And I know how you want to be the one to find out who killed Charlie—you're on one of your missions."

"Wouldn't you be?"

"Hush and listen," she said.

He did.

"But we've got three bodies now," she said. "And we are a team.

And there is no reason on God's earth why we all shouldn't be working together on everything, the way we always have. So if you can help us with Jack Carlisle's death, we can also help you with Charlie's. And we all have enough time to work together to find out who put that guy in the wheelchair in the water."

She blew out some air.

"All I got."

Jesse felt himself smiling.

"You're right," he said.

Molly smiled.

"Excuse me?"

"I said, you're right."

"Would you mind putting that in writing?" she said. "Then I could take a picture of it and use it as my screen saver."

"You've made your point."

"I know."

Jesse said, "You and Suit head over to that apartment Water-field shared with this guy Marin, and see what you can find."

She stood. "On it."

"Hey, Mols? Thank you."

"You never have to thank me."

"Yeah," Jesse said. "I do. Because sometimes I forget."

She asked what he was up to. He told her where he was going, and why.

"You gonna tell the mom?"

Jesse shook his head.

"I don't have to ask for her permission."

Molly slapped her forehead. "I forgot! You're the chief!"

"Fuck, yeah."

He got into the Explorer and made the short drive to one of the older sections of Paradise, near where the Strand Theater used to be on Washington Street. Over the last few years, a lot of town houses like this had gone up in Paradise for people who didn't require a view of the water.

Jesse parked on the street and walked up to the door. There was an old silver Cherokee parked in the driveway, with a Paradise High sticker on the back bumper.

Jesse walked up and rang the doorbell and the blond kid answered the door, still dressed in tennis shorts and a gray PHS T-shirt, a head taller than Jesse at least. When Jesse would occasionally watch tennis on television, it struck him that the star players were getting bigger. Men and women.

"Kevin," Jesse said, "I'm Chief Stone."

"I know who you are," Hillary More's son said.

"May I come in?" Jesse said.

"Am I in trouble?"

"You're not," Jesse said. "But I might be for not calling your mom before I came over here."

"What do you want to talk to me about?" Kevin More said.

"What you were doing in Jack Carlisle's room the other day," Jesse said.

FORTY-ONE

They sat in the living room. Kevin More stretched out long legs from an antique chair, and from his teenage slouch. Jesse took the sofa. Somehow the kid managed to look even taller sitting down. He reminded Jesse a little bit of a young Brad Pitt, but then most really good-looking young blond guys did, even though Pitt wasn't a young guy anymore.

"You on the tennis team at the high school?" Jesse said.

He wasn't sure the kid was going to relax with the chief of police in his living room, but he had to try to break the ice, now that he'd essentially ambushed him by showing up here.

"I finally realized I wasn't ever going to be more than Jack's backup in baseball, and gave it up," he said. "I really only went out for the team because so many of my friends were on it."

"Like Jack."

"Not just Jack," Kevin More said. "It was my last year of high school, and I just wanted another excuse to hang with them. But Coach finally told me I was wasting my time, and his."

"A sweetheart, your coach."

"You've met him, then."

Jesse nodded.

"It pissed me off, but he was right," Kevin said.

He took out his phone as if it were some kind of lifeline.

"My mom *is* gonna be mad," he said. "Us talking, I mean."

"She likes me," Jesse said.

The kid almost smiled. "She's actually mentioned that a few times."

"Were you close with Jack?" Jesse said.

Kevin More ran his hand through his hair, more of it on top than on the sides, which were nearly shaved down to the skin. Jesse saw a lot of that these days. Molly would know what the style was called.

"Jack was a great teammate, but only close with a few of the guys on the team," Kevin said. "Matt and Scott, mostly. But the thing about him was that he treated everybody the same. That probably brought us closer, because he was a star and I wasn't. Made me think he was even cooler than he already was."

He took in some air. "Makes everybody miss him even more."

"Your mom said you weren't at the party that night."

"It was for the team," he said, "even if some girls went. I just would have felt weird."

"Gotta ask this," Jesse said. "Did you reach out to Jack that night, maybe after the party?"

"No. Like I said. He was at his team party."

"You're sure?"

"One hundred percent."

Jesse waited, one small beat.

"So why were you at Jack's house the other day?" Jesse said. "I asked his mom, and she said you were the only one of his friends who stopped by."

Now he looked past Jesse, as if hoping his mother would come through the door.

"Shouldn't I have an adult present to be talking to you like this?"

Jesse smiled. Kindly old Uncle Jesse.

"How old are you, son?"

"Eighteen."

"You're old enough to vote in this state," Jesse said. "And if you're old enough to do that, you're old enough to answer a few questions that might help us find out how Jack died. And why."

He cleared his throat, and swallowed. Hard.

"Okay."

"Did you and Jack hang out a lot at his house?"

"I don't know if it was a lot," Kevin More said. "We both liked writing. I was better at that than baseball. He was good at both."

"Were you in Paul Connolly's English class?"

He shook his head. "Mrs. Burton's."

"Did you know anything about the play he was writing for Mr. Connolly?"

"He told me about it. But why does that matter?"

"In my business," Jesse said, "you don't know what's important until it is. It's not a glamorous job, mine. You just keep pulling on strings."

Then Jesse paused and said, "So he didn't show it to you?"

"He hadn't shown it to anybody yet, as far as I know. All he told me was that he thought it was really good. But he never showed it to anybody . . . until."

"You sure about that, Kevin?"

"I'm just telling you what Jack told me. He said it wasn't ready to be seen yet." Kevin More shook his head. "And why does it even matter? Why does any of this even matter? It's not going to bring him back."

"It matters to me, why what happened to him did. If you're his friend, seems as if it should matter to you."

Kevin closed his eyes and shook his head again. "It still won't bring Jack back."

"Why were you in his room?"

"Maybe because I wanted to pretend that he was on his way home from practice and things were going to be the way they used to be, that's why." He swallowed hard, and squeezed his eyes shut. Jesse thought he might be about to cry. "Maybe it was my way of saying goodbye to him. Who the fuck knows?" He shook his head again. "*This sucks so much!*"

Like the words had exploded out of his heart.

Finally Jesse said, "Why'd you go through his desk?"

The kid had been looking down. That snapped his head back up. "Wait . . . *what?*"

"The things in his drawer were too neat. His mother said they were never that neat. But she didn't touch anything in there. My people know how to search a desk like that, but leave things as close to the way they found them as possible. They even took photographs of the contents of his desk. Now Jack's mom says the only other person who was in there before I showed up today was you."

Before he could answer, Jesse said, "Were you looking for something?"

Kevin More shook his head.

"The play maybe?" Jesse said.

"No!" Kevin said. "I told you he was keeping that private until it was time to hand it in. And the way I see it, if it was private when he was alive, it should stay that way now that he's gone."

He did start to cry now. Old enough to vote. But still a kid.

"So you weren't looking for anything in his desk?"

Kevin More wiped the back of his hand across his face. Jesse thought he might be buying himself some time, assessing what would happen if he lied to a policeman and got found out later.

"There was maybe just this note I wrote him a couple weeks ago. We were getting near graduation, and it wasn't something I wanted to put in an email. I wrote a few others lately, just telling people that just because we were all going off to college, I hoped we could stay friends. It was just between Jack and me and I didn't want anybody else to see it. Not even his mom." He let out air. "Just the kind of stuff that friends should tell each other more often. Now I'm glad I wrote it, if you want to know the truth."

"Did you find it?"

"No," the kid said.

He stood.

"Now you know everything I know," Kevin said. "Can you leave me alone now? And maybe leave Jack alone at the same time?"

There was no need for Jesse to tell the kid that wasn't happening. Kevin More rose up out of his chair now. "I need to study."

"I just want to find out how your friend died," Jesse said.

"Maybe even that shouldn't be anybody's business," Kevin said.

"It's my business," Jesse said.

He walked out of the house and got into his car and drove back to the station. Molly and Suit called from Molly's car when he was back in his office.

Molly had them on speaker.

"Steve Marin's gone," Molly said.

"I assume you don't mean dead and gone."

"Like packed up and cleared out and gone," Suit said.

"See you when you get back."

"There's one more thing," Molly said. "Just for fun, and because I try to spend my time productively, I ran his name through the system."

"And he's got a record," Jesse said.

"Does he ever," Molly said.

Two hours later Jesse was back in his car, having canceled his dinner plans with Nellie Shofner, and made another, this one in Boston.

"What can I tell you?" he said to Molly before he left. "Strange bedfellows."

"Sweet Jesus," she said. "I hope not."

"Figure of speech," Jesse said.

FORTY-TWO

They met at a mom-and-pop Italian restaurant in the North End called Tony and Elaine's. Wine bottles in baskets. Red-and-white checked tablecloths. The whole place smelled like red sauce. Jesse felt that if he looked hard enough, he could find a framed photograph of the Pope on one of the walls. Right next to a signed one from Sinatra.

"You can imagine my surprise when I got your call," Richie Burke said.

Ex-husband to Sunny Randall. Son of Desmond Burke, which meant son of the Irish Mob in Boston. Father, Jesse knew, to Richard Burke, the product of Richie's second marriage, long since over, the way his marriage to Sunny was, despite Richie's best and continued efforts for a second trip up the altar with Sunny. Or Round Two, the way Jesse used to describe it.

Owner of his own saloon, a legitimate business by all accounts, a few blocks from here.

"Imagine my surprise at placing the call," Jesse said.

They had been in each other's company only a handful of times, usually by accident. It was always awkward between them, but cordial. Or perhaps wary. The only thing they had in common, apart from Richie's family connection to the kind of bad guys it was Jesse's sworn duty to put away, was that they both loved Sunny Randall.

"Before we get to it," Richie said, "are we gonna talk about the elephant in the room?"

They had each ordered pasta with Bolognese sauce. When in Rome. Richie had a glass of Chianti in front of him, Jesse a Coke.

"Pretty sure Ms. Randall would be resistant to that reference," Jesse said. "I assume she's the elephant to which you're referring."

"You talk to her lately?"

"No."

"Even though you two were broken up," Richie said, "she was less than pleased when she found out you were with Rita Fiore."

"It didn't last."

"Never does with Rita."

"Fun while it *did* last, though."

"So I've heard," Richie said.

"Sunny with anybody these days?"

Richie said, "She was going around with some newspaper guy last I heard from her."

"No standards."

"I still see her for lunch or dinner sometimes," Richie said.

"How does that go?"

"I'm now of the opinion she likes my son better than she likes me."

Richie broke off a piece of the warm Italian bread in the basket in front of him, dipped it in olive oil, and ate it.

"So tell me about this guy Marin," Richie said. "You say he worked for my father when he was a kid."

"Only briefly, according to Healy. Your father never mentioned him?" Jesse said.

Richie grinned. "You'd probably be amazed about how little I talk to my father about his business. And how many Steve Marins he's employed in various capacities."

"According to Healy," Jesse continued, "Marin didn't last long with your father because he was too much of a hothead. Liked beating up people who didn't pay more than he should have. When your father let him go, he moved on to Jackie DeMarco's old crew, under new management by then. When he was still a kid, not even out of high school. All-around headbanging. They even clipped him for arson before he ended at the youth center in Roslindale from there."

"I thought juvie records are supposed to be sealed."

"Not to Healy, they're not."

Richie drank wine. "How'd he end up working at a chocolate company in Paradise, Mass.?"

"Not sure yet," Jesse said. "But I'm going to find out tomorrow."

Hillary More had tried to call Jesse a few times, but hadn't left a message. He was sure it was about his visit to her house, and conversation with her son. Lots for them to talk about tomorrow.

The food was delicious. No shocker there. They were in the North End of Boston, which considered itself to be a capital of Italian food the way Fenway Park considered itself to be the capital of big league baseball.

"Jackie DeMarco died, right?" Jesse asked Richie.

"So he did. But this guy named Roarke had been the new management you mentioned even when Jackie was still with us."

"What can you tell me about Roarke that might be useful?"

"Not as much as my father can."

Richie pulled out his phone, punched out a number, waited.

"Need some intel on Roarke," Richie said.

He listened, nodding, for what felt like a couple minutes to Jesse, or even more. Then he said, "Just asking for a friend."

Listened again. "Jesse Stone, Dad."

Richie Burke grinned then.

"Yes, Dad. Sunny's *copper* friend."

"Wait, while I've got you," Richie finally said into his phone. "You know where Jesse might find Roarke if he were so inclined?"

Nodded one last time and put the phone back in his pocket.

"The gentleman's full name, though my father clearly considers him something less than a gentleman, is Liam Roarke."

"Irish," Jesse said. "That can't be good."

"Never," Richie said. "He says that their interests haven't yet collided in any meaningful way, mostly because Roarke, at least up to now, has had a different area of interest."

"That being?"

"My father called Roarke the king of crypto," Richie said.

Jesse put down his fork and stared at Richie Burke.

"Oh, ho," he said softly.

"Haven't heard that one in a while," Richie said.

"Oldie but goodie."

"My father says that if Roarke is sideways with anybody these days, it's Tony Marcus."

"Because of crypto?"

"And the fun-filled world of money laundering in general."

Jesse explained then about Charlie's laptop and crypto to Richie.

"Could be a coincidence," Richie said.

"And the earth could be flat," Jesse said.

Richie grinned. "Prove that it's not."

"If your father knows where Roarke is, that must mean he keeps an eye on him from time to time."

"There's a reason why Desmond Burke has lasted this long," Richie said.

Jesse called for the check, then paid it.

"Wait, no dessert?" Richie said.

"You interested in taking a ride with me?" Jesse said.

"I've got the babysitter until eleven."

"Who knows," Jesse said. "Could be the beginning of a beautiful friendship."

"Somehow I doubt that," Richie Burke said.

Then he said, "You sure you want to do this?"

"Hell, no," Jesse said.

FORTY-THREE

Molly told herself that if Jesse could go have dinner with Richie Burke, she could have dinner with Nellie Shofner.

"I accept," Nellie had said when Molly called to make the offer. "Can I call you partner?"

"Only because it's better than that Aunt Molly crap."

"I take that back."

"Too late," Molly said.

They met at the Gull. Spike was once again working as his own host tonight. He didn't have to do it. He owned the place. But Molly knew he did it because he liked it. She had never encountered anybody who enjoyed being in the restaurant business more than Spike did. He clearly never saw what he did as a job. More a performance. Like it was a role he was born to play.

When he saw Molly and Nellie come in together he said, "One of you lose a bet?"

"Girls' night," Molly said.

"And neither one of you called me?" Spike said, and showed them to a corner booth.

They both ordered white wine. When their drinks came Nellie asked, "What should we drink to?"

"Jesse."

"Who brings people together, even when he's not around."

"Yeah," Molly said, "he is a giver."

They sipped wine and talked about how neither of them had much to report from Paradise High even as they kept canvassing more students and teachers. The only real news of the day had come from Jesse, because of what he'd found out about Hillary More's son. And how it was Jesse's firm belief that he hadn't been there looking for a note he'd written, but what Paul Connolly, the English teacher, had described as an autobiographical play Jack had written.

"And whatever secrets it might contain," Nellie said. "Or truths."

"Promises to keep," Molly said.

"Theirs," Nellie said, "or ours?"

Molly watched as Nellie's eyes swept across the rest of the room. Molly knew how old she was. She couldn't escape the fact that Nellie looked younger than that. She just did. Molly wondered if it might have something to do with Molly's own age, and how the whole world, male and female, was starting to look younger to her. Jesse often said the same thing.

Nellie's hair was shorter than it had been a couple days ago.

A younger version of Sunny.

Hundred percent.

The waiter came over and asked if they were ready to order. Molly told him they were going to need a few minutes.

"Say the boy did kill himself," she said, "even though Suit doesn't want to hear that and none of us really want to believe it. You ever think that if he wanted people to know why, he would have left a note?"

"I'd still like to know that," Nellie said.

"So would my boss."

"You don't?"

"It would solve the mystery, no doubt," Molly said. "But what does that get us?"

"Closure?"

"For us," Molly said. "The boy already has his. I've actually always thought the whole notion of closure, at least for the living, is a bunch of shit."

They sat in silence. The dining room began to fill up. The bar area was already full of people and noise. The Gull had been the most popular restaurant in Paradise for as long as Molly could remember. Spike had just made it better, and even more popular than it had been before. Maybe because he was its face, and upfront star. And the food had gotten a whole hell of a lot better on his watch.

"What I can't figure out," Nellie said, "is why these boys on the team, even now, are so fearful of pissing off their asshat of a coach."

"And pissing him off royally by talking to you."

"He called me a bitch," Nellie said, "if I'm not mistaken."

"Were I you," Molly said, "I'd wear that one like a merit badge."

They both ordered lobster rolls, with fries. The plates came out of the kitchen at warp speed. Spike brought them to the table himself, and asked if they wanted more wine.

"Nellie's parents told her to be home by eleven," Molly said, "or she loses her car privileges."

"I had that coming," Nellie said.

"Where's the chief tonight?" Spike asked.

"He is dining in Boston tonight with Mr. Richie Burke himself," Molly said.

"Sure he is."

"I'm serious."

"Care to explain how such a thing came to be?"

"No," Molly said, "I do not."

"I thought the policeman was supposed to be my friend," Spike said.

"Live and learn, pal," Molly said.

They happily ate the best lobster rolls in town, maybe the entire North Shore. Every time Molly felt an urge to ask Nellie about Jesse, she stopped herself, telling herself it was none of her business. Even knowing in her heart that Jesse's business would always be hers as well.

"The tox screen said no drugs," Molly said. "But none of us really expected there to be."

"So maybe somebody pushed Jack into the water," Nellie said.

"A good-sized kid."

"Maybe the other guy was bigger."

"But who would do something like that? And why?"

Molly drank wine.

"Shit," she said.

"My sentiment exactly," Nellie said.

"A truly shitty sentiment at this point."

"We need to catch a break here."

Molly had the better view of the front door, so she was the one who saw Hal Fortin come walking into the Gull before Nellie did.

"Check it out," Molly said.

Nellie smiled. "Coach Asshat himself."

Spike showed Fortin to a window table on the other side of the crowded room.

"My friend Sunny Randall has a saying," Molly said.

"I think I've heard most of them by now, sadly enough."

Molly said, "When all else fails, annoy someone."

"Yup," Nellie said. "Definitely heard that one from the chief."

"Shall we?" Molly said.

Nellie told her to lead the way.

FORTY-FOUR

You want to know where Roarke eats the rest of the week?" Richie said to Jesse, after they'd been lucky enough to find a parking spot on Boylston Street in front of the Capital Grille. "My father swears he has the guy's dining-out schedule. Says Roarke is a creature of habit."

"The way he's tracking the guy," Jesse said, "sounds like your old man is, too."

"Roarke prefers the Rubbed Bone-in Rib Eye, in case you were wondering," Richie said.

"By the way," Jesse said. "Are you sure *you* want to do this?"

"Biggest night out I've had in a while," Richie said.

Roarke was having his dinner in a private room. The maître d' was happy to share that information, more reluctant to tell them which private room. At that point Jesse badged him and told him he was here because of a murder investigation involving a policeman up in Paradise.

"And we promise not to bother the decent people," Jesse said.

"Mr. Roarke isn't going to be happy about this," the maître d', whose name tag read ELLIS, said.

"Yeah, if you think about it, who other than you really gives a shit?" Richie said.

LIAM ROARKE'S PRIVATE dining area was to the left of the main dining room. As they walked in, Richie nodded at the man with white-blond hair at the head of the table. Bright blue eyes Jesse could spot from where he stood. Jesse didn't feel the need to tell him that he would have been able to figure out who Roarke was on his own. There were two men, each seated on either side of Roarke. No food yet, just drinks. Martinis all around. One of Roarke's guests was black, the other white. Roarke was in a blazer, red pocket handkerchief, white shirt, no tie. There was a muscle guy standing at the other end of a table much too long for just three people. The muscle guy's suit appeared to be about two sizes too small. Or maybe he'd just grown out of it. He crossed his arms and glared at Jesse and Richie. Jesse tried to keep himself from fainting dead away.

The maître d' leaned down and said something to Liam Roarke.

"It's fine, Ellis," Roarke said. "I'm sure this won't take long."

Then Ellis was gone. Jesse admired the fact that he'd managed to keep himself from running out of the room, maybe to a new job.

"Ellis says you want to talk to me about a murder," Roarke said to Jesse. "You don't happen to have some ID I could look at?"

"Don't want to see mine?" Richie said.

"I know who you are," Roarke said to him. "The way you know who I am, Mr. Burke."

"Mr. Burke is my father," Richie said. "And you know who he is, too."

Jesse put his badge out in front of Roarke.

"You got a name, Chief?" Roarke said.

"Jesse Stone."

Roarke smiled. "So you're the guy from that shoot-out up in Paradise that I read about. I believe you took out one of Tony Marcus's former employees that night."

Jesse smiled at him. "And another angel got its wings."

Roarke stood up then, and just seemed to keep going once he did. Six-five or -six. Giving the impression that he was looking down from a great height at his two dinner companions. "Could you just take your drinks to the bar and give us the room for a few moments?"

The two men knew it wasn't a request, and wordlessly got up and left, almost as quickly as Ellis the maître d' had.

Jesse and Richie made no move to sit in the empty chairs.

To Richie Roarke said, "What are you doing hanging around with a cop?"

"Been asking myself that question all night."

Roarke sat back down and refocused his attention on Jesse. The muscle guy stayed where he was, unmoving. But staring down only Jesse now.

"Who's the dead cop you mentioned upon your arrival?" Roarke said.

"His name was Charlie Farrell," Jesse said, "and he was once the chief of police in Paradise."

"Now I do recall reading something about that," Roarke said.

Jesse quickly told him the rest of it, how Charlie died, Roarke saying he'd read about that, too, the death of Sam Waterfield, and the disappearance of Steve Marin.

"Marin used to work for you," Jesse said. "I believe in your headbanging division."

"You say."

"His arrest record says."

"A lot of people work for me," Roarke said.

He looked down, as if just remembering he had a martini in front of him, and drank some of it.

"My friend Charlie gets his head caved in," Jesse said. "Marin's roommate gets thrown off a cliff. It turns out Marin used to bounce people around for you. Or worse. I'm just trying to understand if there might be a connection."

"Go try to understand someplace else," Roarke said, "and not come down here from your precious little town and insult me in front of business associates."

"From what I hear," he said, "insulting you might not be even possible."

"*That* supposed to be an insult?"

"Kind of."

"Beat it before you make more trouble for yourself than you already have with this bullshit fishing expedition of yours."

"Not quite yet," Jesse said.

The muscle guy took a couple steps in their direction. Roarke held up a hand.

"Before my friend died," Jesse said, "he had taken a sudden interest in cryptocurrency. And I have recently heard you described as the crypto king of Boston. So stay with me here: I've got a guy who's called the crypto king and a guy who used to work for him disappearing from my precious little town. That's why I don't see this as making trouble for myself. Or you. Just solid police work."

"Your problems, not mine," Roarke said.

Roarke shifted slightly in his chair and looked back at Richie now.

"Make sure to tell your father there could be consequences for a breach of respect like this," Roarke said.

"Respect for whom?" Richie said. "Or from whom, that might be a better way of looking at it?"

No one said anything then. The muscle guy didn't move. Roarke stood up again. Definitely a big boy. He came around the table. He and Jesse were close enough Jesse could smell the gin. Even Jesse had never liked the taste of gin.

"You made a mistake coming here with nothing tonight," Roarke said. "So now I'm telling you not to make a bigger one and bother me ever again."

"Yikes," Jesse said.

"I'm old school, Stone," Roarke said in a quiet voice.

"I always wonder what that actually means," Jesse said.

Roarke smiled. "Maybe it means that it would be a terrible tragedy if one dead cop turned out to be just a start."

Jesse let Roarke have the last word and walked out first. Richie followed. He drove Richie back to where he'd parked at Tony and Elaine's, and thanked him for the ride-along.

"I really didn't do anything," Richie said.

"You did a lot you didn't have to do with no skin in the game," Jesse said. "I owe you one."

"You poked a bear tonight," Richie said. "I think even my father is afraid of this guy, even though he'd die before admitting that to me. And I've never known Desmond to be afraid of anyone."

"Did it occur to you that Roarke's response wasn't proportional to me showing up here?"

"Just watch your back," Richie said. "And maybe not just yours. That's coming from the son of an old-school guy."

They shook hands.

"You want me to tell Sunny you said hello," Richie said.

"Your call," Jesse said.

He was already thinking about making a call of his own, and did, as soon as he was on 93 heading north. He had a bad feeling about Liam Roarke.

Molly occasionally accused him of not being in touch with his feelings.

Not tonight.

FORTY-FIVE

Nellie slid in next to Hal Fortin. Molly sat across from him. "Mind if we join you, Coach?" she said.

"Yes, I do mind," Fortin said, "not that it seems to matter."

"Bitches," Nellie said, sadly shaking her head. "What *can* you do about them?"

"You're both out of line," Fortin said.

"Are you going to make us run some laps?" Nellie said.

"I'm expecting someone," Fortin said.

"No worries, this won't take long," Molly said.

Fortin was stuck and knew it, unless he decided to shove Nellie out of the booth, or climb over the table to escape.

Nellie had her chin in her left hand, and was smiling at the coach of the Paradise High baseball team.

"I've got nothing to say to you," Fortin said to Molly. When he turned just enough to look directly at Nellie he said, "And I never had anything to say to *you*."

"But you hid it so, *so* well," Nellie said.

A waitress came over, ready to take a drink order.

"I'll have a Sam Adams in a bottle," Fortin said. "The ladies are just leaving."

The waitress looked at Nellie and then Molly, somewhat uncertainly, then turned and walked away.

"We are leaving," Molly said. "Just not this second."

"You can't just accost somebody like this in a public place," Fortin said.

Molly grinned. "Want to call a cop?"

Fortin's face was starting to redden. "What the hell do you want?"

"Well, for starters," Molly said, "Chief Stone and I continue to be of the belief that we are not getting your full cooperation regarding the death of Jack Carlisle. So I have embraced this opportunity to ask you myself why that might be."

The waitress came back with Fortin's beer, and placed it in front of him. He ignored it, and her.

"I don't know what you're talking about," Fortin said.

"From the start you have gone out of your way to tell your players not to cooperate with our investigation," Molly said. "I find that odd."

"I would, too, if I'd done it. But I haven't."

"Coach," Nellie said, admonishing him. "We all know better than that."

"It is also our belief," Molly said, "that you are either hiding something about Jack or hiding something about your team. Frankly, nothing else makes sense."

"In your opinion," Fortin said.

"What promise to Jack or about Jack are your players keeping?" Nellie asked.

"News to me if they are."

"Is it?" Molly said.

"You calling me a liar?" Hal Fortin said.

"You tell me," Molly said.

Before Fortin could answer her, Nellie said, "I know you've heard this before, Hal, but we are eventually going to find out if you are hiding something. And when we do, it is probably going to burn your ass when I put it in the newspaper."

"All I am trying to do at the moment is try to win a state tournament for these kids, without the kid who might have been the best ballplayer his age in the whole goddamn Commonwealth of Massachusetts."

"I saw you slap one of those kids," Molly said. She grinned again. "I thought there weren't supposed to be any black eyes in *team*."

"Clever," Fortin said.

"Still thinking there might have been more to that slap than you've indicated," Molly said.

"I told you already," he said. "I lost my head for a second. Everybody's been under a lot of pressure lately, including me."

Now he drank some of his beer.

"What do you think happened to Jack?" Molly said.

Nellie was giving her room.

"I was under the impression that it's the police's job to find out," Fortin said. "Now, for the last time, will the two of you please leave me alone? My dinner guest is here."

Molly's back was to the front door. She turned now in the booth to see that Hillary More had just walked into the Gull.

But she wasn't there for long.

As soon as she saw who was sitting with Hal Fortin she turned and left.

FORTY-SIX

In Jesse's office the next morning Molly told Jesse about Hillary More being Hal Fortin's dinner date. Just then, the woman herself showed up, unannounced.

"What are the odds?" Molly said, then promptly excused herself, grabbing a donut out of the mixed Dunkin' box Jesse had brought for everybody before she left.

Hillary More was clearly dressed for work. Black pantsuit, white shirt underneath. Black leather sneakers with white soles. More and more, Jesse noticed that both men and women were wearing sneakers to work, not that he really gave a shit.

"We need to talk," Hillary said in what passed for a greeting, taking one of the visitor chairs.

"I agree," Jesse said. "You first."

"You were out of line yesterday," she said.

"Par for the course with me, some would say."

"You know I like you, Jesse. You *do* know that, right?"

Jesse resisted the impulse to tell her that if there were life on Mars, *they* knew that Hillary More liked him.

"I thought that went without saying" is what he did say.

"But what I do not like, not even a little bit, is you showing up at my house and trying to intimidate my son."

"Not my intent," he said. "Also not what I did."

He opened the box of donuts. "Help yourself, by the way."

"Are you trying to be funny?"

"Not when the subject is Dunkin' Donuts," he said.

"No, thank you."

"Your loss. I got extra Boston Kremes."

Hillary gave an exasperated shake of her head. "Kevin felt as if you treated him like some sort of suspect."

Jesse sipped some of the large coffee he'd brought with him, first of the day until he made some of his own.

"Hillary," he said, "we're going to have this conversation, the two of us, just this one time and never have it again. I'm going to give you a pass, just this one time, on your showing up in my office and trying to tell me how to do my job. Because I also like *you*, and I've clearly annoyed you. But I had legitimate questions to ask your son about Jack Carlisle. I asked them. I left. No harm, no foul."

"Says you."

"He paid a visit to Jack's room after Jack's death. Maybe you knew that, maybe you didn't, not my concern, or my problem. I wanted to know what he was doing there. I asked. He told me. End of story, at least for now."

"It's Kevin's feeling that you didn't believe him."

"Also not my problem. But I am sorry if he felt that way."

"Are you?"

This wasn't flirtatious Hillary now. This was the boss lady, in high gear. If not on fire, getting there.

"You could have given me the courtesy of a heads-up," she said.

"And granted you the consideration we haven't granted to other parents in the course of this investigation?"

He pointed at the donut box again. "Are you sure you don't want one before the rest of my staff attacks what's left in that box like a pack of hungry dogs? Donuts always take the edge right off for me."

"Perhaps another time," she said. "Will you at least assure me that you're done upsetting my son?"

"No, I won't make that assurance," Jesse said. "And by the way? He's a man now, Hillary, not a boy. I am genuinely sorry if I did upset him. And you. And if you have to apologize to his father for me, apologize to him."

"His father died a long time ago."

That stopped him.

"I'm sorry for that, too."

She pulled up the sleeve of her jacket, checked her Apple Watch.

"I need to get to work," she said.

"Work can wait for a few more minutes."

"I have a meeting."

"Meeting can wait," Jesse said. "We're not done talking."

"I am."

"I will be," he said, "when you explain to me why you neglected to mention that Steve Marin, wherever he is, happens to be a Mobbed-up ex-con."

"Because he's not."

"Bet you the whole box of donuts that he is," Jesse said.

FORTY-SEVEN

Jesse told Hillary More what Healy had learned from his friends at Organized Crime Control in Boston. And about his own visit to see Liam Roarke the previous evening, and the pleasantries they'd exchanged at the Capital Grille.

"You have to believe me when I tell you I had no idea," Hillary More said.

"When he filled out his job application and interviewed with HR, or however you do it, it never came up?"

"He was forthcoming about having been in juvenile detention," Hillary said. "But he was a kid. You're making it sound as if he's Al Capone. Now I have to apologize for not knowing all the players in the Boston Mob."

"I tend to look at aggravated assault as a grown-up-type thing," Jesse said.

"I talked to him about that part of his past myself," she said. "I just looked at him as having been disabled in a different way. Sam

Waterfield actually recommended him. It turns out they'd met each other when they were both in foster care."

"Now one of them is dead and the other one has disappeared."

Jesse told her about what Molly and Suit had found at the apartment in Marshport.

"I'm told that no one has yet been able to reach him by phone," she said.

"Have you tried to locate the phone?"

She sighed forcefully enough to rattle Jesse's window shades.

"Jesse," she said, stepping on his name pretty hard. "I'm genuinely concerned about where Steve might be, or what might have happened to him. But as I've pointed out before, and despite everything that is happening in our town, I am in the business of selling *chocolate*. I market our brand. As we speak, I have smart young people figuring out the best way, and best timing, to perhaps take More Chocolate public. Early stages, but we're having those conversations. That's what my meeting is about this morning, one for which I am now late. This is my area of expertise, or so I've been told, not finding missing persons."

She checked her watch again, either looking at the time or for messages.

"Any thoughts about where he might run to, if he still has the ability to do that?"

"Are you saying you think something might have happened to him, too? If he's dead, why would he have cleared out his part of the apartment?"

"He could have tried to run," Jesse said, "and then been caught by whomever killed Sam Waterfield."

She slumped back in her chair and stared at the ceiling.

"This is a nightmare. All I've been trying to do is give people a chance who might not otherwise get one."

"Has there been any kind of trouble with Marin since you hired him?"

She shook her head. "Model employee, same as Sam."

"So no indication that the trouble in his life might have followed him to Paradise."

"None. Far as I can tell, he kept to himself, the same as Sam did. I told you already that the only reason I found out that they even shared that apartment was by accident."

Jesse sipped his coffee. Almost cold by now. Still better than none.

"And Marin never mentioned that he'd been in Liam Roarke's crew?"

"Again: The name would have meant nothing to me even if he'd mentioned it. I was just going off my first impression, and him telling me that I'd never be sorry that I gave him a chance."

She crossed her legs, clasped her hands around the top knee, stared at him. "Don't you think people can change, Jesse? You did."

"I didn't change," he said. "I just stopped drinking, at least so far today."

"And you would like to drop that particular subject."

"If I wanted to talk more about it," he said, "I'd find an AA meeting. Or go see my shrink."

She smiled.

"I hear you," she said. "And now am I dismissed?"

"Go to your own meeting."

"I'm sorry we got off on the wrong foot this morning."

"Friends are allowed to have disagreements."

"I really do want us to be friends."

"I feel the same way."

He wasn't sure about that. But there was no point in saying otherwise.

She started to get up.

"One more thing," Jesse said.

She smiled again. "You sound like an old *Columbo*."

"Now there was a damned cop," Jesse said, "even if he was a made-up one."

"One more question for me?"

"More like an observation," he said. "I was surprised to hear that you were seeing Hal Fortin."

She put out her hands. She had beautiful hands. Went with the rest of her. "Whoa there, Chief," she said. "Not seeing. Was about to have dinner with. Big difference."

"But Molly said you just up and left when you saw her and Nellie sitting with him."

She shrugged. "I realized I didn't want to have the conversation he wanted to have, about Kevin maybe coming back to the baseball team. He was Jack's backup, you know that, right? Anyway, I told him that he needed to talk to Kevin about it, not me. And by then it had been a very long day." She sighed again. "Like this one is already shaping up to be."

Jesse came around the desk then and told her he'd walk her out. Before he could open the door, she turned suddenly and was quite close to him.

"I'm scared, Jesse," she said. "What the hell is going on around here?"

"Planning to find that out."

"You have a lot of belief in yourself, Chief."

"I've always found out what needed finding out in the past."

"You think we've already been through the worst of this?" she said.

"Sure," he said.

"You sure about that?"

"Could be wishful thinking," Jesse said.

FORTY-EIGHT

Jesse invited Nellie to dinner at his place. He said he'd cook. She insisted that she wanted to cook, in one of her occasional bursts of domesticity. Sunny would have them, too. Nellie just had them less frequently. When she did want to prepare dinner for the two of them, Jesse would reluctantly agree, and just hope she didn't try to punch above her weight in the kitchen.

Tonight she did not, going with a simple green salad and pasta with Rao's marinara sauce. Jesse didn't mention it to her, but even Nellie Shofner couldn't screw up pasta with Rao's.

She did allow Jesse to prepare the garlic bread.

When everything was ready, they both had iced tea with it. By now Jesse had made it abundantly clear to her that he didn't mind if she drank in his presence. But didn't fight her on that, either.

As they ate he told her about Hillary More's visit to his office.

"You believe that Fortin just wanted to talk to her about getting her kid back on the baseball team?" Nellie asked.

"If he thought you could help him win the state title," Jesse said, "I believe he'd try to recruit you. But if Kevin More was a good enough player, why didn't his coach find another position for him before Jack died?"

"You tell me," she said. "You're the old ballplayer."

"Just old."

They ate in silence for a few moments. Nellie was a talker, but had slowly come to realize that Jesse hated small talk the way he hated bad guys. He didn't mention that the pasta was slightly undercooked. But Rao's sauce, as always, saved the day. Jesse had long since stopped calling it gravy, what his Italian mother had called it when he was growing up, and it had so often been just the two of them eating like this at the kitchen table.

He sometimes thought that the only time he hadn't felt lonely in his life was when he *was* a shortstop, and had a team around him, even if he was the only one out there between second and third and in the batter's box. Didn't matter what team. It was the only family he really felt he had when he was growing up. The only thing that resembled a family for him until Molly and Suit.

Nellie finally said, "I'm not sure Kevin quit, by the way, even though that's the story everybody goes with."

"Fortin cut him?"

"It wasn't a big thing at the time, because the team was so good," Nellie said. "At the very least, it was a mutual parting of the ways. He didn't like the coach and the coach didn't like him."

"So his mother having a dinner date or meeting to talk about him rejoining the team doesn't make sense," Jesse said.

"Does anything these days?" Nellie asked him.

They cleaned up together. He had decided that he didn't want her to stay the night. Somehow he knew that she knew, without it having been discussed over dinner. Maybe Molly was right, and women really were smarter than men. They got a step or two ahead of you when you were young, and then you spent the rest of your life trying to catch up.

At least on stuff like this.

"I think I'm going to head home now, if you don't mind," Nellie said.

"You sure?"

She came over and kissed him almost chastely on the lips, pulled back, smiled. "No," she said. "But you are."

Jesse pulled her into him and kissed her now, with some follow-through.

"I hope you know how much I appreciate the way you've helped us out on Jack Carlisle," he said.

"Not doing it for you, old ballplayer guy," she said. "Doing it for me. Same as you're doing it for you." She smiled again. "Me being me. You being you. So far it seems to be working for us."

"We're doing it for Suit, too."

"Yes," she said. "We certainly are."

"Can I get a rain check on us hitting the sheets?" he said.

"'*Hitting the sheets*'?"

"What can I tell you. I'm a product of my times."

"Which times?"

He stood at his front window and watched her go out the front door of his building and make the walk up the street to where she'd parked her car, never wanting to park it right in front of his place.

He was about to stop watching her when he saw the van come up the street. It was going too fast and then stopped with a screech of tires. Then the van's side door was opening and a guy was jumping out and Nellie was turning in to him as he swung his right fist.

He knocked her to the ground before grabbing her by the hair and pulling her up, his other hand over her mouth.

Jesse was already running, hoping he wasn't going to be too late getting down there, grabbing his Glock off the table in the foyer, then out the door.

He was taking the stairs when he heard the shot.

FORTY-NINE

The thought flashed across his brain, there and gone, that he should call 911; his phone was in his back pocket. But even that would cost him seconds.

He didn't have the Glock pressed against his chest, the way you were taught. It was in his right hand as he came through the front door of the building now, at full speed.

When he was on the cobblestone front walk he took in the whole scene at once, like he was taking a picture of it.

The van, no back license plate, disappearing up the street, once again at too high a speed for a residential neighborhood like this.

Nellie sitting on the sidewalk, maybe fifty yards ahead of him, right where she'd been hit.

A man crouched over her, his back to Jesse.

"Police!" Jesse yelled. "Stay right the fuck where you are."

When the man straightened and turned, Jesse clearly saw who it was in the light of one of the old-fashioned streetlamps you could still find in some Paradise neighborhoods.

"No need for that kind of language in front of a lady," Crow said.

FIFTY

Jesse had called Crow the night before to find out as much as he could about Liam Roarke, his version of getting a second opinion after getting one from Richie Burke. Crow said he had found out as much as he could.

"And after I did," he said, "I decided that the best thing was to come straight up here."

He grinned.

"You're welcome."

They were in Jesse's living room. Jesse and Crow had driven Nellie to the hospital in Marshport to have her jaw x-rayed. It turned out there were no broken bones. Now they were back, one side of Nellie's face both bruised and swollen. She was holding an icepack to it, seated in the easy chair under Jesse's Ozzie Smith poster.

"Guy could pick it," Crow said, nodding at the poster.

"None better," Jesse said.

Crow sat next to Molly on the couch. Jesse had known enough

to call her on their way back from Marshport. If he didn't call, he knew he was only opening himself up to heartbreak in the morning.

Especially with Crow back in town.

"Jesse told me about this Roarke guy at dinner," Nellie said. "That was right before the afterparty."

Jesse had offered to make coffee. Nobody wanted any, especially not Nellie, who said she didn't know if she was going to get much sleep tonight, even with the pain pill she'd taken, but she was going to give it her very best shot.

"Wish we could have met under better circumstances," Nellie said to Crow.

"Now you got a story to last a lifetime," he said. "Look at it that way."

He wore a black Western shirt with gleaming pearl buttons. Black jeans. Black cowboy boots. Jesse knew it was an expensive brand of boot, he just couldn't remember which brand. Lucchese maybe? Even if it was a nice brand, Crow could afford it. He had a lot of money, almost all of which he'd once stolen from rich people in Paradise, Mass. Crow now said that was all from another lifetime. Every time he did, Jesse would remind him that it didn't work that way.

"After you called me the other night," Crow said, "I talked to a guy I knew who knows about where the bodies are buried, and who did the burying. Turns out this guy had come up with Roarke before Roarke pulled off his hostile takeover on Jackie DeMarco. Says that even though Roarke comes across like some kind of gentleman pirate, he's as badass as anybody my guy has ever come across. Crazy as Whitey Bulger. Just dresses better. And is taller."

"With all that," Jesse said, "Richie told me his father doesn't see Roarke as an imminent threat to his interests."

Crow shook his head. "If Desmond Burke believes that Liam Roarke isn't a threat to him," he said, "then his brain has turned to oatmeal. Roarke is a threat to everybody. Maybe even himself.

"By the way?" Crow said to Molly. "Nice for us to be working together again."

"Nice for whom?" Molly said.

At least she smiled when she said it, as a way of taking the edge off. The last time they'd all worked together, things had at least been civilized between Molly and Crow after a rough beginning. Jesse was hoping things were still good.

He'd have to wait to find out just how good.

If he actually wanted to find out.

"Either way," Crow said to Jesse, "here I am. When I was driving up from the Cape, I decided to surprise you. Glad I did."

"You, Wilson Cromartie, at Cape Cod?" Molly asked.

"Fishing," Crow said. "I brought my boat up from Florida last month. Striped bass come up in April."

Nellie spoke up then, from across the room.

"*Would it be all right if we talked about what just happened to me, for fuck's sake?*" she said, pointing her icepack at the rest of them.

Crow explained that it was pure luck that he'd just parked his rental car when he saw the van pull up and the guy jump out. Crow had no idea what the guy planned to do with Nellie. He didn't wait to find out, just fired a shot in the air, ran in their direction, gun pointed at the guy who'd hit Nellie, right before the mystery guy dove into the back and the driver took off before the sliding door was closed.

"This wasn't about taking Nellie," Jesse said. "This was about sending a message to me. In front of my home. Like they put up a goddamn billboard."

"You think these were Roarke's goons?" Molly asked.

"Put it this way," Jesse said. "I don't think they weren't. I go see Roarke, get under his skin."

"A gift you seem to have," Molly said.

"Now this happens," Jesse continued. "Anybody got a better theory?"

Molly grinned and shook her head and turned to Nellie.

Molly said to Nellie, "The *chief's* theories on the fallacy of coincidence are well established."

"Tell me about it," Nellie said.

"Somehow Roarke did some intel on me in a pretty short amount of time," Jesse said. "He was either watching you, Nellie, or watching me. Doesn't really matter. These guys were here and ready to move on you when you came out alone. If I'd walked you to your car, they probably would have followed you home. But I think they liked doing it here once I didn't walk you to your car."

"If they did want to send a message, what was it?" Nellie said.

"How easy it was for them to get to you," Jesse said. "And me."

FIFTY-ONE

Nellie said she was fine going home if somebody would drive her. Molly said there was no chance of that happening, none; Nellie was spending the night at her house if that was all right with everybody else. They all knew that "everybody else" meant Jesse, who said that he was all for Nellie having police protection tonight, and going forward, and that she could come back for her car in the morning.

"Thank you again," Nellie said to Crow before she left.

She leaned up and kissed him on the cheek.

"Trust me on something," Molly said. "He was a lot more interesting when he was the badass."

"Not was," Crow said. "*Is.* I just try to throw you off, time to time, depending on the situation on the ground."

When they were gone, it was just Jesse and Crow.

"I know I'm coming in late to the movie," Crow said to him. "But it doesn't seem to me as if your action with Roarke should have provoked this much of a *re*action."

"Doesn't seem that way to me, either," Jesse said. "And yet here we are."

Crow grinned. There wasn't much of a change to his face when he smiled. You had to be paying attention or you missed the slight shift in attitude. Jesse mostly saw the amusement in the darkest eyes he'd ever seen.

"Kemo sabe speakem the truth," Crow said.

Maybe more of a grin now. Almost a smile.

"That make me the Lone Ranger?" Jesse said.

"Fuck, yeah," Crow said.

Crow reached into the back pocket of his jeans and came out with a silver flask that looked only slightly thicker than a money clip.

He drank.

"I would have offered to share with the ladies," he said. "But I knew you probably wouldn't have anything, and I'd taken a few sips on the drive up."

"In a moving vehicle? That's against the law."

"Like I always said. Only if you get caught."

"Where's your gun?"

"I stuck it back in the glove compartment when I was parking at the hospital. I figured I was safe with you."

Crow took another sip. He looked the same as he did the first time Jesse had seen him. And the last time Jesse saw him. Maybe more wrinkles in the weathered face. Maybe the hairline had receded a little more. But not looking older. Just like Crow.

As always, he was as comfortable with silence as Jesse was. Maybe more comfortable. Jesse knew that *kemo sabe* meant "friend," whether he was using it ironically or not. He wondered if they were really friends. He supposed they were when you added it all up, with all that they'd been through together. Maybe it was more important that he knew he could trust Crow, even knowing that Crow would always have at least one of those boots over on the other side of the line, no matter how much he maintained he was now walking the straight and narrow.

"You told me you were worried that you'd gotten under Roarke's skin," Crow said. "What you didn't explain is about what."

"Not sure," Jesse said. "I was just asking him about some mutt used to work for him."

"You think he's hiding something?"

"Maybe the mutt."

Crow said, "You got any connection between him and Paradise other than the missing guy?"

"No," Jesse said. "Except the missing guy is connected to guy in the wheelchair who got thrown into the ocean. And there's the crypto thing, though I have no idea where that might fit, if it even does."

There was another silence, longer than the one before. Jesse asked what Crow was drinking. He said Irish whiskey. Crow sipped more of it, then screwed the cap back on. Maybe he was done, maybe not. The flask sat there on the table next to Crow. Jesse had always been fascinated by people who could stop whenever they wanted to. Never show any signs that they were even drinking. Sunny Randall could make a glass of wine, or her own late-night sipping whiskey, last for an hour. So could Molly.

When Jesse and Nellie would eat out, he had never seen her order a second glass of wine. In his drinking days, Jesse had already been thinking about his second one before he finished the first, he felt the ice on his teeth that quickly.

After that he was off to the races.

"Want some advice?" Crow said.

He stared at the flask as if remembering it was still there. Unscrewed the cap. Drank again. When he was done he put the cap back on, stood up enough to put the flask back in his pocket.

Jesse knew there had to be some whiskey left.

But he was done, at least for now.

Amazing.

Jesse was as impressed as he would have been if Crow had suddenly jumped up and done a handstand.

"Always looking for good advice, especially if it's about women."

"Got nothing for you on that particular subject," Crow said.

He took in some air through his nose, let it out slowly through his mouth.

"It was me," he said, "I wouldn't fuck with somebody like Roarke till I had something on him. Or till I absolutely had to."

"You think he might have done something worse to Nellie than clock her if you hadn't come along when you did?"

"Depends on what he knows that you don't know yet," Crow said. "But whatever intel he did get on you, he must have skipped over the part about how you're not somebody to fuck with, either."

"Don't make me blush."

"Just remember what I told you about my guy comparing him to Whitey Bulger," Crow said. "I saw that movie about Whitey. With the guy who played the pirate playing him."

Jesse felt himself grin.

"Johnny Depp," he said to Crow.

Crow said, "The point I'm making here is that Whitey killed people to stay in good killing shape. Or sometimes just when he got bored."

"You think Roarke came at me this hard just because I asked him a few questions?" Jesse asked.

Crow stretched out his legs, put his arms behind his head.

"Or because he didn't like the way you asked them. Or because he didn't like you asking them in the first place. Or because just by turning up at that restaurant, you showed him up in front of business associates. Never forget how important face is to guys like him."

Crow stood now, stretching his back.

"I'm thinking about hanging around for a few days," he said, "just to make sure you don't cock this thing up."

"Up to you."

Jesse stood, smiling at him fully now. "Admit it, you missed us."

Crow shrugged.

"You can only fish so much," he said.

FIFTY-TWO

I need to know a little more about the hunky Native American man," Nellie said to Molly in the morning.

"You think he's hunky?"

"Don't you?" Nellie said.

Nellie told Molly she wasn't going to look in a mirror the rest of the way unless she absolutely had to, saying it totally looked as if she'd lost the fight. When she pointed that out Molly said, "My dad was a boxing fan, and he'd probably point out that if you win the decision, it's worth it in the end."

"I had help," Nellie said.

"I know," Molly said. "The hunky Native American man."

Nellie had slept later than Molly expected her to. Before she'd awakened, Jesse had already called to give Molly a heads-up that Crow would be staying in town for the short term, and maybe longer than that. Both Molly and her boss knew by now, having occasionally learned the hard way in their working relationship, that "need to know" with Molly Crane meant she needed to know everything, at least when possible.

At the kitchen table now, Molly and Nellie were talking about Crow.

"Full name Wilson Cromartie," Molly said. "He has a bit of a checkered past."

"I got that vibe."

"Almost everybody does. Usually in the first minute or so after meeting him."

Molly's maternal instincts had now kicked in with a vengeance, nothing to do to stop them, as upsetting as it was to think of her mothering Jesse's current girlfriend. She'd ordered Nellie to eat the eggs and toast and bacon she cooked up for her before Nellie headed off to the *Crier* office on Broad Street, fully back to being an in-person operation, though still not a very big operation, after COVID. Molly would then head over to her own office, Jesse already there; he'd already checked in.

"How checkered, just out of curiosity?" Nellie asked.

Molly explained she would need a PowerPoint presentation to do justice—"the term *justice* used loosely," she said—to what she knew of Crow's résumé, and what Jesse knew.

"Holy crap," Nellie said. "I remember the Stiles Island thing, just none of the names. I was just a kid."

Still are, as far as I'm concerned.

"Holy crap indeed."

"He got away with all that money?" Nellie said.

"Apparently so."

"And now he and Jesse the Boy Scout are friends?"

"They are," Molly said, "sometimes behind each other's backs.

I am of the opinion that one would take a bullet for the other without hesitation."

"Or fire one, clearly."

"At least last night he didn't have to actually shoot anybody," Molly said.

"He really is kind of sexy in a bad-boy way."

Molly didn't reply, just got up to pour herself more coffee. She knew that she and Nellie were early in the process of becoming friends themselves, almost as if they were giving each other a battlefield commission.

Just not good enough girlfriends, at least not yet, to share secrets about boys.

Especially not a bad boy like Crow.

"C'mon, you have to see it," Nellie said.

"Of course I do," Molly said. "I'm married, not dead."

Nellie tilted her head to the side. She started to smile, but had already pointed out to Molly that even smiling made her face hurt.

"Is there more to this story?" she said.

"Is this an interview?"

"Such a strange couple," Nellie said.

Before Molly had to decide how she wanted to respond to that, Nellie added, "Jesse and Crow, I mean. I'm going to need to question the chief about his friend."

"Of course," Molly said. "You know how Jesse loves to share."

Then she told Nellie that she might notice Crow lurking in the background for the next few days. But only if Crow wanted her to notice him.

"I don't need a bodyguard," Nellie said. "I can take care of myself."

"How'd that work out last night?"

"Well," Nellie said, "you've got me there."

She stood up.

"Thanks for taking me in," she said to Molly.

"We think of ourselves as a full-service cop store," Molly said.

NELLIE'S CAR WAS still at Jesse's place. Molly drove her to it. If Crow was in the vicinity, even in a small town like Paradise, Molly didn't spot him. But then she really didn't expect to. He told her once that Apaches tracked, they didn't *get* tracked.

When Molly arrived at the PPD, she saw through Jesse's front window that he had two visitors.

She could see only the back of one man's head.

The other visitor was Mayor Gary Armistead.

From experience, Molly knew that hardly any good ever came of that.

FIFTY-THREE

When Jesse saw Molly on the other side of the window, he waved her in.

Gary Armistead was in one visitor chair, Scott Ford's father, Ted, was in the other.

Suit was standing next to Jesse, Jesse's side of the desk.

"I don't know if you two have met, Ted," Jesse said. "But this is Deputy Chief Molly Crane."

Ford turned his head just enough to nod at Molly.

"And of course you know our boss, Molly," Jesse said.

"Mr. Mayor," she said.

Somehow when Molly said it she always sounded to Jesse like she was making fun of Gary Armistead. Or his title. Or both.

"Okay," Armistead said, "you guys now have us outnumbered."

Jesse couldn't keep himself from smiling.

"Would have been that way if it was just me," he said to Armistead.

Armistead turned to Ford. "The chief is a noted wit."

"Wit*less,* as far as I can tell," Ford said.

Molly sighed.

"I was just explaining to Jesse," Armistead said to Molly, "that Ted here has filed an official complaint against the department."

Ford pointed at Suit.

"Not the department," he said. "That guy. For harassing my son."

No one spoke right away. Molly had moved over and was leaning against the file cabinet to Armistead's right.

"What I want to know," Ford said, leaning forward in his chair, jabbing a stubby little finger at Jesse now, "is what you have to say about that."

"For starters," Jesse said, "don't point your finger at me in my office."

"Please cut the shit, Jesse," Armistead said.

You first, Jesse thought.

Jesse turned and looked up at Suit.

"Have you been harassing Mr. Ford's son, Detective?" he asked.

"No, sir."

Jesse turned back to Armistead and Ford, clapping his hands together as he did.

"Okay, then," he said. "We're done here."

Armistead rubbed his temples as if he felt a migraine coming on.

"Let's not make this situation worse than it already is," he said. "Ted has lodged a serious complaint against this department, and I expect you to take it seriously."

Jesse looked back at Ford. He was already at the edge of his chair, like he was in attack-dog mode, straining at a leash. If he made another move forward, Jesse was worried he might end up under the desk, trying to bite his lower leg.

"Define *harass*," Jesse said.

"He accosted my son when he was coming out of Daisy's," Ford said. His face was now the color of beets. "Probably followed him there, for all I know. When Scott told him he had nothing to say, your guy prevented him from getting to his car."

"It didn't happen that way," Suit said.

"I'm not talking to you, hotshot," Ford snapped.

"Ted?" Jesse said, still keeping his voice level. "You are going to speak respectfully to members of this force, or I am going to lift you out of that chair by your ear."

Before Ford could say anything, Armistead put up his hand to stop him.

"What is your version of this event, Detective Simpson," he said. "Just for the record."

"I simply was there to ask Scott why he got into a fight with my nephew that night at the Bluff," Suit said. "And he told me what he'd told us before, that it was a jam-up about Ainsley Walsh. I then explained to him that I didn't find that a credible version of things, since Jack and Ainsley were no longer a couple at that point, and everybody at Paradise High except the custodian seemed to know that. Then Scott told me, and I quote, 'I don't give a rat's ass what you think.'"

"You didn't interfere with him leaving?" Jesse said.

"No, sir, I did not," Suit said. "But before he left I told him what I've been telling other kids when they've refused to talk to me."

"Which is what?" Jesse said.

"That I believe they are all withholding information relevant to the investigation of my nephew's death," Suit said. "And that *I* didn't give a rat's ass why they were doing it, but the truth is going to come out eventually whether they like it or not."

"Scott took that as a threat," Ted Ford said.

"The last time I threatened a high school boy," Suit said, "I *was* a high school boy."

They all let that settle until Ford said to Suit, "If your boss won't tell you this, or *his* boss won't, I *will*. Stay away from my son."

Suit came around the desk then, until he was standing over Ted Ford.

"Your son is alive," Suit said. "My nephew is dead. And until I see your son again, which I most likely will, you can give him a message for me: Whatever he's hiding, he's not going to be hiding it for much longer."

Suit headed for the door.

"We're not done here," Armistead said as Suit walked into the squad room.

"Yeah," Suit said over his shoulder, "we are."

My boy, Jesse thought.

FIFTY-FOUR

Jesse was having dinner with Crow at the Scupper later when Liam Roarke came walking in, big as life.

The place was crowded, customers half a dozen deep at the bar, just about every table in both the front and back rooms occupied. Jesse and Crow had a round table that could have seated four in a corner of the front room. Crow was facing the door. "Force of habit," he'd said to Jesse when he sat down.

Jesse saw something change in Crow's eyes as he looked across the room.

Jesse turned his head and there was Roarke, his own eyes searching the front room until he saw them. He had his muscle guy with him. The guy's suit looked as if it had shrunk even more since the Capital Grille, Jesse wondering how the button of the jacket remained in place.

"Of all the gin joints," Jesse said.

"Pretty sure you stole that," Crow said.

Roarke was in a three-piece suit that fit him so well it must have been made for him. A dark one. Blood-red tie. White shirt. He and his guy made their way through the bar crowd until they were standing over Jesse and Crow, Roarke's blue eyes fixed on Jesse as if he thought he was about to make a sudden move.

"We need to talk, just the two of us," Roarke said.

"Call my office and make an appointment," Jesse said.

"Don't get stupid with me again," Roarke said. "I came all the way up here to talk to you, not him."

Now he acknowledged Crow.

"My trusty companion stays," Jesse said.

"I know who he is," Roarke said.

"I'm impressed," Jesse said. "You impressed, Crow?"

Crow didn't respond. Just kept his eyes fixed on Roarke.

Jesse waited. So did Liam Roarke, until Jesse said, "So what's it going to be?"

Roarke turned to the muscle guy. "Wait in the car."

"You sure, Mr. Roarke?" the guy said. His voice was raspy. His nose had clearly been broken a few times. Jesse thought he might have been a boxer, or just somebody who'd been punched in the throat a few times. Jesse was sure it wasn't the man who'd put Nellie on the ground the other night. Wrong body type. The man the other night was taller, leaner.

If it had been the bruiser from the other night, Jesse or Crow would have already put *him* on the ground.

"If I wasn't sure," Roarke said to him, "I wouldn't have mentioned that I wanted you to go wait in the fucking car, Dennis."

No hesitation now from the guy, who turned and got out of the Scupper fast enough that it was like he thought Roarke was timing him.

Roarke sat down, Jesse to his left, Crow to his right.

"Are you here to apologize for beating up women?" Jesse asked evenly. "Asking for a friend."

Roarke's expression didn't change. But by now, Jesse knew it rarely did.

"I have no idea what you're talking about."

"My ass," Crow said now.

They knew he'd heard. He just didn't act as if he did. His eyes were still on Jesse. And Jesse's on him.

"So you hang out with the Burkes *and* Crow," Roarke said. "I thought your job was to enforce the law."

"As I've gotten older," Jesse said, "I've tried to open myself to differing points of view."

A waiter showed up and asked if Roarke wanted to order a drink. Roarke dismissed him with wave of a big hand.

"Why are you here?" Jesse asked.

"I told you. We need to talk and I decided to have it face-to-face and I knew you were here."

"How did you know I was here?"

"Don't worry about how."

"You have people watching me?" Jesse said.

"I made a couple calls and got a call, put it that way," Roarke said. "Irrelevant."

"Not to me it isn't," Jesse said.

"We're wasting time here," Roarke said.

"Yours maybe, not mine," Jesse said. "And to be clear? You didn't seem to enjoy our previous encounter all that much."

"I don't like surprises, especially from cops."

"I'll bet," Jesse said.

Crow had a scotch in front of him, neat. Jesse could taste it. Feel it going down. Sometimes he was sure he could smell it.

"I did some looking into you," Roarke said.

"You must have," Jesse said. "You sent somebody to take a

swing at my lady friend and do who knows what else before Crow showed up."

"Luck," Crow said.

"Residue of design," Jesse said.

"What the hell are you talking about?" Roarke said.

"Old baseball expression," Jesse said.

The air at the table was suddenly thick and heavy, the way air gets before a storm is about to hit, like water vapor condensing to form the storm's energy.

"I had nothing to do with what happened to Miss Shofner."

Jesse said, "But you know her name."

"I told you, I looked into you, Stone. It's why I came up here tonight, to tell you I don't want trouble from you any more than you should want to make trouble for yourself with me."

"Should I be flattered?"

Roarke closed his eyes. Kept them closed for a couple beats. When he opened them he said, "I have enough cops, local, federal, you name it, already trying to get into my business. I don't need one more. So I'm telling you, straight up, man to man, that I have no business going on in your town. I have no knowledge about the guy in the wheelchair ending up in the water. I have no idea where Steve Marin might be." He sighed. "And I only wish I was the king of goddamn crypto, because I could retire and no longer have to worry about small-timers like you."

"So, wait, I *shouldn't* be flattered?" Jesse said.

His head swiveled slightly, as if taking in the bar scene at the Scupper, almost like one of those scanning shots in the movies. For a moment Jesse thought Roarke might have recognized somebody up there.

Crow remained still.

"Here's how this should go," Roarke said to Jesse. "You stay out of my business, I stay out of yours."

"You just told me you had no business in Paradise."

"Going forward," Roarke said. "It's a good deal for both of us. You should take it."

Jesse studied his face more closely. There was something about him. Something Jesse thought he might be missing. Something familiar? He wasn't sure.

"What if I don't accept the deal?" Jesse said.

Roarke finally smiled. "Do you and your trusty companion really want to find that out?"

It was like a threat he'd absently tossed on the table like a tip.

"So *do* we have a deal?" Roarke said.

"Sure," Jesse said. "Should we shake on it?"

"No need."

Roarke stood up then and turned and walked out of the Scupper.

When he was out of earshot Crow said, "Liar, liar, pants on fire."

He drank some scotch and toasted Jesse with his glass. "Old Injun expression, kemo sabe," he said.

"I might point out that you didn't seem particularly frightened of the bad man," Jesse said.

"Nope," Crow said.

He held his glass up to the light now, and studied it, drank again.

"But he's sure as shit scared of you," Crow said to Jesse.

FIFTY-FIVE

When he got home, he knew the first thing he needed to do was get the taste of Crow's scotch out of his own mouth. Not that he'd taken a sip of Crow's when he got up to go to the men's room.

Just because it was the same as if he had.

It was *there*.

It happened this way sometimes, not that he talked about it with anybody except Dix. Or occasionally at a meeting. When he least expected it. Maybe tonight it was because of the way his senses had heightened, or sharpened, or both, with Roarke sitting that close to him. Threatening him without coming out and issuing the threat, even as he was trying to make a deal to leave Jesse alone as long as Jesse would do the same with him.

In the end Liam Roarke was lying his ass off the same as Jesse had been.

Jesse knew he would go after Roarke again, and again, if necessary. And if he did that, Roarke would come after him. It was Tony

Marcus who had once said to Jesse, "I'm no good and can prove it." Roarke was the same way, maybe on steroids.

But whatever the reason the taste of scotch was in his mouth now, it was there. *Right* there.

And a familiar thirst along with it, one that never really went away.

He never needed a specific trigger like Roarke. Sometimes it was when he was tired. Or jammed up on a case. Or jammed up on cases, plural, the way he was now, feeling as if he were trapped in a maze, trying to get out so he could *find* out, once and for all, what had happened to Charlie Farrell and Jack Carlisle.

Whatever the reason, the wolf was back at the door, just like that.

He tried to tell himself when it happened, the way it was happening right now, that he'd just dropped his guard. But Jesse knew that wouldn't fly, because he *never* dropped his guard. He never took his sobriety for granted, not one single day as he went one day at a time.

He never forgot that he was a drunk.

Just a dry one at this time, and for a good long time.

Whether he was happy or sad or tired or pissed off or angry about Charlie Farrell or pleased that he'd managed to crack another case, sometimes hanging on to his job like it was a lifeline, he was still a drunk.

There it was.

He knew he could call Dix at any time of the day or night, but he wasn't going to bother him with this. Nellie was with Molly again tonight. As tough as Nellie Shofner was—and she was tough enough to be a cop—what had happened on the street in front of Jesse's place the other night had scared her. Nothing like it had

ever happened to her before. Now it had rocked her world. The
way Molly's world was rocked when she had been shot last year,
for the first time.

It had been Jesse's suggestion that Nellie stay on with Molly for
a few days. To his surprise, she had readily taken Molly up on the
offer.

"It's win-win," Jesse told Molly. "You can look out for her when
Crow isn't. And she can act as a chaperone now that Crow is back."

"Jesse?" Molly had said. "You know how much I love you, right?"

"This is going to be bad, it's always bad after you tell me that."

"Blow it out your ear," Molly had said and hung up.

He got up now and walked over to his desk, to the bottom
drawer he always kept locked, as if that meant anything, opened
the drawer with the key he kept on his chain, and pulled out the
bottle of Johnnie Walker Blue.

FIFTY-SIX

He knew why the bottle was there.

Why he *told* himself it was there.

Not in case of an emergency, because there would be no emergency until, and unless, he uncapped the bottle.

Jesse told himself he kept it there as a reminder that no matter how hard you tried, you couldn't hide from your own boozing.

Or run from it.

So here was the whiskey he told everybody he didn't keep in the house. They told you in AA about people, places, things. But this bottle, *it* was the thing. The whole ballgame. He could hold the bottle up, the way he was now, the way Crow had held his glass up at the Scupper, and look at the amber liquid, and see through it all the way to the bad old days.

He couldn't remember how long ago he'd bought the bottle. A couple years ago? Back when the world was still in lockdown because of COVID, definitely, when the days and weeks and months ran together. Two hundred dollars for the good stuff. Better than he used to drink when he was still drinking.

What he always told himself, and told the bottle, was this:

You don't scare me anymore.

The hell it didn't.

The bottle was still sealed. It didn't matter, the way it hadn't mattered with Crow's drink. Jesse could taste it, and could smell it. Sensory memory.

On high alert.

He put the bottle down on the middle of his desk blotter and leaned back in his chair and stared at it.

It never mattered why he took it out, even if it had been a while since he *had* taken it out.

There it was, anyway, right in front of him.

He reached over and did hold it up now, in the light of the antique desk lamp that Sunny had bought for him at a shop in the Vineyard one time. The feel of the bottle in his right hand as familiar as if he were holding a baseball, or had both his hands on a bat.

He could hear the sound of his own breathing.

It was then that he felt his phone buzzing in his pocket, loud in the quiet of the moment.

Jesse put the bottle back down, and took out his phone, and looked at the screen.

Miss Emma

Let go, they also told you in AA, let God.

"You need to get over here," she said. "Please hurry."

"Are you all right, Emma?"

"Yes and no," she said.

FIFTY-SEVEN

Maybe Miss Emma really was an angel, sent to look out for Jesse in this moment by God Herself, which was the way Sunny referred to God.

She was pacing on her front porch when he pulled into her driveway, lit by an overhead light, wearing a powder-blue sweatshirt tonight, sneakers to match. Jesse wondered if she was always color-coordinated like this, or just when he happened to be in her presence.

"What's upset you?" Jesse said.

"What has upset me and royally pissed me off," she said, "is that I got another call from one of those punk-assed bitches Charlie was after."

She was leading him into the house now, Jesse behind her, which meant that there was no way for her to see him smiling at her language.

When they were in the living room, it was impossible for Jesse not to notice the Smith & Wesson revolver on her coffee table. He would have bet all the money in his wallet that it was a concealed-hammer 640.

"A gun, Emma?" Jesse said. "Were you planning to shoot somebody through the phone?"

"I'm not in the mood for any sass tonight, mister," she said.

"I can see that. But am I allowed to know if you have a license for this thing?"

"My boyfriend used to have your job," she snapped. "What do you think?"

She sat on the couch. Her sneakers barely touched the floor. Jesse sat across from what appeared to be a mahogany table. There was what appeared to be a glass of whiskey next to the revolver. *One of those nights,* he thought.

The wolf now chasing him over here, even if Emma Cleary was his designated angel.

"The call upset you that much?" Jesse asked.

"I'm a little edgy these days. And you may recall that I got scammed once before."

He said he sure did remember.

"Charlie wanted to catch just one of these punks so badly," she said.

Finally her face softened as her voice did. Maybe it was the mention of Charlie. She was his Miss Emma again.

"He still wanted to be a cop *so* much," she said.

"He was still a cop," Jesse said, then asked her to tell him about the call.

She said it would be easier for him to listen to it.

"You recorded it?" Jesse said.

"Fuckin' ay," she said. "My friend Doris, down in Newport, got ripped off to the tune of five thousand dollars last week on a fake charity call. They tried that one on me a couple weeks ago, on my landline, before I might have told them what I wanted them to do to theirselves."

"The other times they called on your cell?" Jesse said.

Miss Emma nodded. "The assholes do both," she said.

Jesse and Healy had done enough research by now to know that family-members-in-peril was just one of the scams. There were old reliables, threatening calls from the IRS. Warranty calls on cars. Lottery hustles. People saying they're from your bank, asking about a recent purchase they know hadn't occurred, saying they'd blocked it, but asking for the account number. Just before they cleaned you right out.

The list was longer than that.

On the call Miss Emma had just recorded, a man with the deep voice of a radio announcer explained that Emma was about to lose her health insurance if she didn't send money right away. Preferably by money order.

Somehow this person knew how old she was.

"Listen to me play along," Miss Emma said proudly.

Jesse put a finger to his lips.

The radio announcer was in the process of telling her the easiest way to send the money so as not to interrupt her insurance when Jesse heard a familiar sound in the background.

FIFTY-EIGHT

It's late," Molly said when she opened the front door.

"I know what time it is," Crow said.

"You couldn't call first?" she said.

"I was afraid you'd tell me not to come," he said. "And I was already in the neighborhood."

She made no move to invite him in, even though they both knew she was going to.

"You don't have to shadow Nellie when she's with me," Molly said.

"She still up?"

"Actually she went to bed over an hour ago," Molly said. "She's just now starting to decompress after what happened to her the other night."

"Do I have to ask you to ask me in? Or are you going to ask me in."

"Do I have a choice?"

Crow grinned. Which was really more of a squint. "Life's full of choices, right? Good ones. Bad ones. In-between ones."

She walked him past the living room, and the stairs leading up to the second floor, finally into the kitchen at the back of the house.

"May I offer you a drink?" Molly asked.

"You got whiskey?"

"What kind you looking for?"

"Any kind. I haven't had the chance to refill my flask."

She happened to have a bottle of Macallan, the single-malt Suit had given her last Christmas, one she'd barely touched.

She poured them each a glass. It occurred to her that they had been alone like this, in close quarters, only a handful of times since they'd slept together. She was trying to assess, in the moment, how she felt about that. Mostly it felt the same to her. Being this close to Crow did not make her dizzy or silly or light-headed. It wasn't like that.

Molly just felt slightly off-balance, the way you did on a boat rocking gently on the water.

"*Aho*," Crow said as he raised his glass and leaned across the table and touched hers.

"What does that mean?"

"Thank you," he said.

Molly raised her eyebrows. "For giving you firewater?"

"Just trying to remember my manners."

They drank.

"Why are you here?" Molly said.

"You always get right to it."

"I've found it saves time."

"You asking why I'm still in Paradise?"

"Asking why you came in the first place," she said. "You could have told Jesse what you found about Roarke on the phone."

"Good that I didn't."

"You haven't answered me."

"If you're asking me why I'm sitting here with you, I just wanted to see how you were doing."

Molly thought: *Could he possibly know about me and Michael? But how?*

Nobody else knew, unless Michael had told somebody at sea.

"I'm doing just fine, Wilson." She grinned and raised her glass again. *"Aho."*

"How's your husband?"

"I'm not talking about my husband with you," Molly said. "Now or ever."

"He in town?"

"Sailing the seven seas."

"Have you gotten around to telling him about us?"

"No," she lied.

"Change of subject?"

"Please."

"It going to bother you if I stick around to help out Jesse?"

"Just Jesse?"

"You're right," Crow said. "Takes a village. Especially in this one."

They sat in silence now, neither of them reaching for their glasses.

Nowhere for Molly to look except him.

Shit.

"I never want to make you feel uncomfortable," Crow said.

That actually got a smile out of her.

"*Now* you're worrying about that?"

"It's good to see you."

"Good to see you, too," Molly said. "Though having told you that, I now have to kill you."

"Easier said than done."

"So I've heard."

Molly wondered what Nellie would think if she came downstairs for a glass of water or hunting for a snack. Nellie Shofner was smart. Sometimes annoyingly smart. Molly was afraid she'd be able to read the room.

"Jesse needs me around whether he wants to come right out and ask me to stay or not," Crow said. "Roarke is a threat to him. And if he's a threat to him, he's a threat to everybody, not just Nellie."

Molly drank. She liked the taste of the scotch, liked the way it felt going down. Leveled her off, even if it was going to take more than one glass to do that. They were both keeping their voices low, neither of them wanting to wake Nellie. But it was the time of the night for quiet talk. Jesse said it was the hour when people told each other the truth.

Not bloody likely.

At least not to Wilson Cromartie.

He told her about what had happened at the Scupper.

"Nellie would probably suggest you should have had that higher up in the news story," Molly said.

"I get to things when I get to them."

"Well aware."

Another silence. Molly was the one to break it.

"Is there any chance that Roarke might be telling the truth, and he really doesn't have business in Paradise?" Molly asked him.

"Man's got no business being *in* Paradise, you ask me," Crow said. "But I have a feeling for things the way Jesse does. First Roarke gets sideways because Jesse pays him a visit. Now Roarke pays *him* a visit. Like the man's running interference for himself on something."

It was like a speech for Crow, as still as he was on the other side of the table. His background—his backstory—couldn't be more different from Jesse's. Yet there were similarities, too, simply no getting around that. They were both completely inner-directed. Comfortable in their own skin. Crow had been a hardened criminal when he first came to Paradise, and when he left Paradise with a boatful of money. Might still be a criminal, for all Molly knew. Jesse really was the last Boy Scout. But had also been a falling-down drunk. Sometimes a blackout drunk. Still telling Molly that he was always just one drink away.

Other than her husband, Jesse had been the most important man in her adult life.

What did that make Crow?

So glad Nellie's upstairs.

"You had a seat at the table tonight, so to speak," Molly said. "Did you get the feeling things might be about to, uh, escalate between them?"

"Jesse says that the high school kids are hiding something about Suit's nephew," he said. "Roarke's hiding something, too. Or lying out his ass. Or both."

"About what?"

"Two cases. Same question."

"Jesse wants to be the one to find out."

"Needs to find out, you mean," Crow said.

"And now you think we need to put the band back together?" Molly asked.

"Don't you?"

Molly said, "Has he come right out and asked you to stay?"

Crow grinned again. "Like you guys are always saying to each other. It was more an implied-type thing."

He'd already finished his drink. Now he casually reached across the table, picked up her glass, drained the last of her scotch.

"Nice talking to you," he said.

Before she could reply he was out the back door. She got up and watched him walk across the yard and around the corner of the house until he was out of sight.

Now she felt dizzy.

FIFTY-NINE

Jesse and Healy were back at Charlie Farrell's house the next morning. It had been Healy's idea. He said he needed to get out of what he called the broom closet at the PPD and move around.

"Maybe breathe real air for a change," Healy had said.

"It's not all that bad at your home away from home," Jesse said.

"Worse," Healy said. "I'm tired of chasing ghosts around on the Internet."

"Ghost numbers."

"Same difference."

Healy no longer wore a tie, even if he was back to work. But he was still in a blazer, gray pants, black penny loafers. White shirt that matched his hair perfectly. He was still all cop. Wanting to be in motion like the great cop he had been. The way Charlie had been.

"Somehow Charlie figured out where the calls from these shitheels were coming from," Healy said. "He found out who was doing it, or how, or some goddamn thing. Only thing I can figure. And set up a meeting."

They were standing in the living room.

"Now we have to do the same," Jesse said.

He told Healy what he'd heard on Miss Emma's recording, the sound of a train whistle.

"What's that got to do with my friend Charlie Farrell?" Healy said.

"He was looking into where the scam calls were coming from, and Miss Emma taped one of them, and there was a train whistle in the background."

"So what?"

"So I did the math," Jesse said. "That whistle lines right up with the nine-fifty to Boston. So let me give you a what-if: What if some of those calls are coming from Paradise?"

Healy snorted.

"Or some train out on the Fitchburg line. Or Lowell. Or Newark Freaking New Jersey. Or Mumbai, for all we know. Just because somebody came for Charlie doesn't automatically mean they came from across the street in your town."

"But what if it *did* basically come from across the street?" Jesse said. "What if the whole thing has been local from the start, even though I know calls like that can come from the freaking moon?"

"Would make our lives easier, I gotta admit."

"Wasn't it you who told me that if this shit was easy, anybody would do it?"

"I thought you were the one who told *me*," Healy said.

He looked around, closed his eyes, took in air, let it out, with great force.

"You feel Charlie here? His spirit or whatever?"

"How can you not?" Jesse said.

"If he's here, I wish to hell he'd tell us something."

"Now you're talking to the ghosts," Jesse said.

"Let me play along with you for a second," Healy said. "Say it was the nine-fifty. Say the call did come from Paradise. What do we do now, go door-to-door at every building you think is close enough to the tracks? Every office in town?"

Jesse grinned. "I'm game if you are."

"If nothing pans out, though," Healy said, "we're back to where we started, and trying to track just one of those numbers."

"To an IP address?" Jesse said.

"My heart just skipped a beat hearing you say that."

"Being an optimistic bastard keeps me young," Jesse said.

"You think that might work for me?"

"Too late," Jesse said.

Their plan was to search the house as if searching it for the first time. When Healy asked him why, Jesse said it was because he knew he'd missed something. Healy asked how he could know that. Jesse said it was because he always missed something.

"But you got no idea what it might be."

"None."

"Narrows things down considerably," Healy said.

He nodded at Jesse.

"You didn't have to bring me along, you know."

"Yeah, as a matter of fact I did. Makes me feel like I'm working with Charlie."

It was Healy's first time in the house since Charlie had died. Jesse knew full well that when Maisie had still been alive, the Healys and Farrells had a regular bridge game. Until the day that he died, Charlie maintained that Healy had finally quit the game because he and the missus never won.

When Jesse mentioned that to Healy now, Healy said, "Prove it."

He took the downstairs. Jesse went back upstairs. He was back under the sink in Charlie's bathroom when he heard Healy call up that he'd found something.

"I found this in the side pocket of Charlie's windbreaker, the one with the logo from Paradise Country Club on the front," Healy said. "Hanging on a hook in the kitchen."

You always miss something.

He was holding a phone bill.

"I already checked the last phone bill that Charlie got in the mail," Jesse said.

"Take a closer look," Healy said, handing it to Jesse. "It's not his. It's Miss Emma's."

Then Healy said, "There's a number circled near the bottom."

Jesse did take a closer look now.

"Son of a bitch," he said.

"What?" Healy said.

"I know that number," Jesse said.

SIXTY

Dix cocked his head to the side, as if to appear curious. Jesse knew that was bullshit. He wasn't curious. He already knew where they were going. It was Jesse's job to catch up with him. Or keep up. Either way.

Sometimes when he walked out of Dix's office he was as tired as if he'd been to the gym.

"So you'd rather talk about your case than about taking that bottle out of the drawer the other day?" Dix said.

"Cases. Plural." Jesse managed a grin. "Try to keep up."

"Got it," Dix said. "Cases. Plural. That changes everything."

He looked as he always did. Jesse wondered, not for the first time, if he had to shave his head every day. How many white shirts exactly like the one he was wearing were in his closet. Why his nails always seemed to shine like the top of his head. Trying to imagine, also not for the first time, how he ever could have been a sloppy-drunk cop who'd even considered eating his gun more than once.

"Sarcasm is unbecoming to a shrink," Jesse said.

"Wow. I never thought of that one."

"There, you just did it again."

"I'd rather start by talking about the bottle," Dix said. "You think you would have uncapped it if Miss Emma hadn't called when she did?"

Jesse lifted his shoulders and let them fall. "Sounds like another mystery I might not be able to solve. Why not? One more can't hurt."

Jesse looked at the desk, nothing on it, no pen or notebook, and pictured Dix getting them out when Jesse was gone, as if taking note were some sign of weakness.

The shit you thought about.

"But you didn't drink."

"No."

"The bottle stayed in the drawer when you came home?"

"Yes," Jesse said. "The urge had, ah, dissipated."

Dix put his hands on the desk and patted it a few times. The quiet in the room seemed to last even longer than usual. It got like this, as if one of them was waiting for the other to make the first move.

"Out of everything," Dix said, "what's bothering you the most right now? The dead kid? Charlie? Or is it Roarke who's got you off your game?"

"Who said anything about being off my game?"

"Your old friend Johnnie Walker?" Dix asked.

"I am trying to protect people I care about," Jesse said. "Like always. Even the ones who are fucking gone."

"You're pissed because you couldn't protect Nellie."

"Or Charlie. Or the shortstop."

"You are aware that there was no way for you to know that Charlie needed protecting, right?"

"Maybe I should have."

"And maybe beating yourself up over shit you can't control gets you opening a drawer that should permanently remain closed. Or empty."

Dix leaned forward, just slightly. "You mind if we jump around a little?"

"Like you've ever needed my permission to do that."

"You know that boy likely killed himself."

"Even if he did, I want to know why."

"But if you never do, you need to be willing to accept."

"The things I cannot change."

"There you go!"

Then he told Dix about the scam call to Miss Emma's phone bill and where it had come from.

"Miss Emma was sure about the date. She's got a better memory than me," Jesse said.

"So maybe you finally got a break."

"Wonders never cease."

"No chance that it was some kind of technical mistake?"

"It's a mistake," Jesse said. "But not by the phone company."

"You're convinced a scammer might have killed Charlie Farrell?"

"More than ever."

Dix smiled. Jesse got one an hour usually. Occasionally two.

"Mind if I think like a cop?" Dix asked.

"You always think like a cop."

"What about the dead guy in the wheelchair and the missing roommate?"

"Just because I don't mention them doesn't mean I've forgotten them."

"You think it might have been them running a scam operation."

"The thought has occurred," Jesse said. "But then who killed Waterfield?"

"Hey, you're the chief."

"Nice that you still notice."

"A regular crime wave you've got going."

"Wow," Jesse said. "I hadn't thought of it that way."

Dix shook his head. "Sarcasm."

"It's like Harry Bosch says in those books," Jesse said.

"One of the great cop characters ever devised by mortal mind," Dix said.

"Everybody matters or nobody matters."

"Ought to be on the wall of every police station in the country," Dix said.

Now Jesse was the one leaning forward, feeling his fists clenched, the back-and-forth ending, just like that.

"Charlie matters the most."

"So find out who killed him."

"What if I don't?"

The second smile.

"You'll probably drive yourself to drink," Dix said.

SIXTY-ONE

It hadn't taken much detective work for Molly to find out where Ainsley Walsh got her nails done. California Nails and Spa wasn't much of a spa, but it was where just about everybody went for nails in Paradise. Molly had been there herself the day before. She asked the college girl working on her, Fukiko, to see if she could find out when Ainsley Walsh's next appointment was. It turned out to be today, an hour after school let out. Mani and pedi both.

It was five o'clock when Ainsley came out of the place, holding her hands out in front of her as if to admire Fukiko's artistry. She was wearing flip-flops to protect her toenails.

There were few guilt-free girly pleasures that could beat nails.

They were at the opposite end of Main Street from More Chocolate. On the way over Molly had looked at her own rust-colored nails and noticed that one had tragically chipped.

"They look terrific," Molly said when she fell in next to Ainsley on the sidewalk.

Ainsley jumped.

"You can't sneak up on people like that," she said.

Molly gave her a homecoming queen smile.

"Just did!" she said.

"What do you want, Mrs. Crane?"

"I was hoping we could have a chat. Just us girls."

"Yeah . . . *no*."

"I'm not your enemy," Molly said. "We're actually on the same side."

"You're on your own side."

Ainsley kept walking, at an even brisker pace. Molly was starting to worry about the girl's pedicure.

Molly picked up her own pace, got in front of her, turned, and stopped. Ainsley had no choice but to do the same thing. There were people walking the sidewalks on both sides of Main. The last thing Molly wanted was a scene, especially in the world of social media.

The whole world, Jesse liked to say, had become one extended photo op.

"Are you going to push me around like Jack's uncle did with Scott?" Ainsley asked.

She hadn't made a move to go around Molly, at least not yet. Her hair was to her shoulders. She was wearing Lululemon exercise tights that looked to have been applied with the same brush that Fukiko had just used. The makeup she must have put on before school had stood the test of time. She didn't need it. Total knockout. Flawless complexion, body by God.

"Detective Simpson didn't do anything with Scott Ford besides his job," Molly said. "Which is what I'd very much like to do."

Ainsley Walsh's head suddenly swiveled around.

"I don't want to be seen talking to you," Ainsley said.

She started to turn and walk back toward the nail salon.

Molly gently placed a hand on her arm, hopeful that Ainsley wouldn't start yelling about police brutality.

"Just give me a few minutes, Ainsley, that's all, and I promise I will be permanently out of your really great hair."

The girl seemed to relax then, if just slightly. Hair was as much a common language as nails. Molly had raised all those teenage girls. And had been one herself. You could never go wrong complimenting someone on hair, not one single time.

"I need to get it cut," Ainsley said.

"Need to have it just right for graduation, right?"

"Totally."

"Five minutes," Molly said.

Ainsley looked around again.

"Where?"

"Where did you and Jack go when you wanted to talk?" Molly said.

Ainsley told her.

"Let's go there," Molly said.

SIXTY-TWO

Cameron Beach was about two miles from where Jesse lived. The two women stayed inside Molly's car in the small public parking lot instead of walking down near the water. Ainsley was still being vigilant about her pedicure.

So they sat in the front seat of the old Cherokee, windows down, letting in the smell and the sound of the ocean. Molly hadn't tired of it yet, likely never would.

"Jack and I used to come here and just talk," Ainsley said. "Jack used to say he did some of his best thinking up here."

"Even when you weren't with him?"

"He used to joke that it got better when I wasn't with him," she said. "He said that when he was alone he liked to come here and write."

Molly had decided to go slow, now that she'd gotten Ainsley this far.

"Who really broke it off?" she asked.

"I thought I already told you it was mutual."

"Ainsley," Molly said, "even though it might be difficult for you to believe, I was your age once. In addition to that, I have raised four daughters. It's never mutual, whether you're about to go off to college or not."

The girl stared straight ahead, at some distant point on the water. Or even beyond that.

"I loved him," she said. "I never loved anybody before."

"Do you love Scott Ford the way you loved Jack?"

"That's not just mean. It's one more thing that's none of your business."

"Sorry, I was out of line."

"Okay."

Molly angled herself enough to see her face a little better.

"I could have had any boy in school," Ainsley continued. "But I wanted Jack."

"So he broke it off."

Ainsley Walsh nodded, her face almost solemn. "It turned out he didn't love me the way I loved him."

"That's a hard thing to accept."

Now Ainsley turned to face Molly.

"Does it get easier?" she asked.

Molly smiled. "If you're lucky, you'll never have to find out again."

It was high tide by now, the crash of the waves below them getting louder with each break on the beach.

Molly had always loved this time of day on the water.

"Here's what I've learned," Molly said. "Or at least what I think I've learned about Jack. Everybody at school knew him, obviously. But I get the sense that hardly anybody *really* knew him."

"Not even me," Ainsley said.

The girl was different today from the first time they'd talked. Molly knew this age, what it was like, especially for girls, with college staring them in the face. Like they had to become women whether they were ready or not.

"So he let people in," Molly said, "but only so far?"

"Yes," Ainsley said. "That's a good way of putting it."

"Who's Pepsquad1234?" Molly asked her now.

"You know about that?"

"I'm old," Molly said, "but I can find my way around social media."

"I don't know who it is. None of us do."

"Are you sure?"

"Swear."

"So what's the promise you have to be reminded to keep?" Molly asked.

"To keep being Jack's friend even though he's gone."

"That's it?"

"And that's all."

The water got louder suddenly, a tremendous wave making more of the sand below them disappear.

"Was there another girl?" Molly said.

"No," Ainsley said.

"Could he possibly have been getting another girl pregnant, even if he really wasn't with her?"

"No!" the girl said. "For the love of fuck? Is that what you think this is about?"

"I had to ask."

"Well, asked and answered, okay?"

There was one more thing to ask now, something she or Jesse or Suit or somebody should have asked already. She knew why

FALLOUT   [259]

they hadn't. At least why Jesse and Suit hadn't. Jack Carlisle was the golden boy in Paradise. Big man on campus. Star jock. On his way to college on a scholarship. Maybe on his way to the major leagues after that, making it to The Show Jesse had talked about endlessly, for as long as Molly had known him.

Ask her.

"Was Jack gay?" Molly asked Ainsley Walsh.

SIXTY-THREE

The Paradise High baseball team had lost in the first round of the state tournament the day before, with a team meeting scheduled for today. Jesse told Suit to make another run at Coach Hal Fortin, if for no other reason than to piss him off. Molly'd said she was going to make a run at Ainsley Walsh, just not in a rousty way.

"If we're going to jam somebody up, let's make it the coach," Jesse said.

"It will be both an honor, and a pleasure," Suit said.

"Suit?" Jesse said before he left. "I promise you we'll find out what happened to that kid."

"You're the one always telling me that cops should never make promises they can't keep," Suit said.

"Not planning to start now, Luther," Jesse said. "No matter *what* we find out. Wherever the evidence takes us."

Suit grinned. "If we ever get any evidence."

After that Jesse walked the town for an hour or so. He did that sometimes. Wondering how many secrets there were behind all these doors, inside all these buildings, even in a small town like this. Wondering how well he really knew the people he was hired to protect. Molly he knew. Suit he knew. And Nellie. And Crow, for better or worse. He knew what Crow was capable of, all the trouble Jesse knew he still carried around inside him. But he knew where he stood with Crow. It mattered.

Charlie he had known. And he knew as much about Dix as Dix wanted him to know.

He had spent a lot of time over the last week wondering how well anybody knew Jack Carlisle, including his own uncle.

He walked to the ballfield and back, thinking that the next games to be played there would be in Paradise Men's Softball, Jesse still having not decided if he wanted to play one more year. If he wanted to still be a shortstop.

He looked into the window at Rocky's Ace Hardware when he was back on Main Street, and saw himself smiling.

As if you ever stopped being a shortstop.

It was nearly five o'clock by now. He walked up to More Chocolate. Closing time. People started to come through the front door. Jesse had thought about going inside, but decided to wait out here.

Hillary More came out about ten minutes later, phone to her ear, chattering away.

She put it away when she saw Jesse.

"Well," she said, "isn't this a pleasant surprise?"

"Is it?"

She sat down next to him on the bench. Another day when she looked like a million damn dollars. The woman who had done so much to build up the town's economy after COVID. Saying she was going to make More Chocolate the main plaza of Paradise.

"Something tells me that to my everlasting regret, this isn't a social visit."

"You know the scam calls I've told you about with Charlie Farrell?" Jesse said.

"You thought they might somehow have been connected to Charlie's death."

"Well, it turns out that Emma Cleary, Charlie's lady friend, right before Charlie died, never got off their list."

"I'm sorry for her; those calls are particularly cruel for the elderly," she said. "But what does any of this have to do with me?"

"One of those calls was placed from your office," Jesse said.

SIXTY-FOUR

That's impossible," Hillary More said.

"I read somewhere once," Jesse said, "I forget where, I wish I had Miss Emma's memory, that the impossible becomes possible with the discovery of a new truth."

He stood then.

"Walk with me," he said.

"So we can be in motion when you suggest that someone who works for me might have tried to con an old woman?" she said. "What if I don't want to?"

"No reason for you *not* to want to," Jesse said.

He was standing over her. She'd made no move to get up off the bench. More Chocolate workers kept walking past them, some calling out greetings. Hillary would put on a smile for them, or nod or wave.

"I'm sure there's an explanation for this," she said. "No one who works for me would do anything like that."

She was up then and they were walking up to the corner of Main and Elm and up Elm until they got to Marian Park, with its swings and slides and monkey bars and what looked to be a world-class sandbox. Empty now on a Friday night. The place was filled with mothers and small children in the mornings.

They sat on another bench now, across from the swings. Jesse handed Hillary More the phone bill.

"I recognized the number because it's popped up as Nicholas Farrell's work number on my phone," he said.

She handed the bill back to him.

"Obviously somebody spoofed our number," she said. "Isn't that what these people do? Or do they call it ghosting? My son explained it to me one time when we got one of those calls on our landline at home and it looked like a real number. That must be it."

"No," Jesse said.

"No, I didn't get a call like that?"

"This number wasn't ghosted," Jesse said. "I checked with your carrier, and finally got the answer I needed after threatening to subpoena everybody at the company in alphabetical order."

He asked her then if she understood how VoIP worked.

"Voice over Internet Protocol," she said. "I'm aware what it is, from when we put our phone system into place."

"So you know that your calls are placed over the Internet," he said. "Same as ours are at the PPD."

He folded the phone bill and put it back into the inside pocket of the blazer he kept in the office and had worn here. Sometimes he didn't want to look the part. Even if they both knew he was all cop today.

"Charlie, I'm guessing, recognized the number when he saw it on the bill for the same reason I did," Jesse said. "Because of Nicholas.

And maybe, just maybe, the old chief was smart enough to track down the IP address, same as I did. Even at his advanced age."

She sat with her hands in her lap. Not looking at him as she spoke. "Please tell me you don't think I had something to do with this."

"I don't."

"I still think that this is the modern-day version of wires getting crossed," she said.

"It's not. Sorry."

"Not as sorry as I am if this is actually true."

Jesse put some snap in his voice now.

"No more qualifiers," he said. "It's true. Somebody made that call. Using your Wi-Fi. Now I'm going to find out who."

She was still staring straight ahead.

"I sell chocolate," she said in a small, tired voice.

"Hillary," Jesse said quietly. "Look at me."

She did. Beige jacket today, black T-shirt underneath, black jeans, black ankle boots. Jesse had stopped commenting on women's appearances in front of Molly, and in general. When he would slip occasionally, she would remind him that verbalizing about a woman's looks was as old as he was. Maybe older.

"Sam Waterfield ended up in the water, a homicide to which I am about to pay much closer attention. His roommate, a former juvie guest of the state, is missing. I'm starting to wonder if they were the ones shaking people down over the telephone. And if the missing guy might be the same one who killed Charlie and went after his grandson until his grandson shot him."

She started to speak. Jesse held up a hand to stop her. "You always look for a nexus. The nexus in this case might be two of your former employees, thinking they could work their scam from your office without ever being caught, probably using burner phones. But they got sloppy, or lazy, or both. And made a call using your Wi-Fi."

"May I speak now?" Hillary asked.

He nodded.

"Just what do you expect me to do about it?"

"For starters, I'm going to want my best tech guy, Gabe, to take another look at Sam Waterfield's computer at work," Jesse said. "And then go through the other computers upstairs, one by one. The sooner the better."

"That whole section gets one Friday a month off," she said. "This happens to be it."

"Gabe will be there in the morning then," Jesse said. "You just have to help him with the log-ons and whatever else he needs rather than make everybody come in on a Saturday."

"We still don't know if any of this is tied to Sam, or to Steve, who didn't even work in Sam's section," she said. "That's just a theory of yours."

"You're right," Jesse said. "For now, that's exactly what it is. And if there's no proof that they were involved, we cross their names off my list and move on."

"Am I on your list?"

"Just the one of people helping me get to the truth."

"Okay," she said. "What else do you need?"

"I want to know who might have been in the office the other night just before ten," he said, and explained why.

"You really are making a series of assumptions here, Jesse," she said.

"Well, to be honest, I've done more with a lot less, Ms. More," he said.

"Clever. But not funny."

"Not trying to be," he said. "None of this shit is funny."

"If this gets out, just why you're looking into my company, this would be extremely hurtful," she said. "You know we're heroes in this town."

"And will likely be again once I find out who got sloppy when they called Miss Emma," Jesse said.

"Could it have been somebody in a neighboring building hijacking our Wi-Fi, or whatever they call it?"

"Not unless you were giving out your password with chocolate samples."

"You believe Charlie might have figured it out?" she said.

"Molly Crane, good Catholic girl, says faith is believing in what you can't see," Jesse told her.

"Are you religious?" Hillary More asked him.

"Not if I can help it."

When he got home, there was a black Lincoln Navigator, tinted windows, looking fully loaded, parked in front.

The rear window rolled down, and a familiar face smiled at him.

"What's happening, motherfucker?" Tony Marcus said.

SIXTY-FIVE

They were all in Jesse's living room: Jesse, Tony, his body man, Junior. And his shooter, Ty Bop.

Junior remained the general size of a battleship. Ty Bop, even standing still in his oversized David Ortiz jersey, still seemed twitchy as a hummingbird. Tony, as always, looked as if he'd just come from his tailor. Powder-blue suit today, white shirt, navy tie with polka dots, pocket handkerchief matching the color of his tie. He'd informed Jesse from the car that he was here to collect a favor Jesse owed him, but that they'd get to that.

"Just curious," Jesse asked Tony now. "Does Junior or Ty Bop drive the Navigator?"

"Ty," he said.

To Ty Bop Jesse said, "So you passed driver's ed and everything, Ty? Good for you."

Ty Bop just fixed him with a sleepy, dead-eyed look, as indifferent as a snake.

"You need to know that Ty here's where irony goes to die," Tony Marcus said. "If he hasn't shot it already."

"To bring this back to that favor you say I owe you," Jesse said. "It seems to me that when we last spoke, I suggested I might pay you back someday for the help you gave me on the whole land thing up here, but you told me that you didn't believe me. And we sort of left it there."

Marcus smiled. He looked a little thinner than he had when they'd met last year at Buddy's Fox, the bar and restaurant in downtown Boston that served as his office.

"Also I believe I told you not to appeal to my better angels, on account I got none," Marcus said. "But I know you got 'em, playing Eliot Ness up here for the Podunk PD."

Jesse smiled, couldn't help himself. As dangerous as he knew Tony Marcus was, he could be a funny bastard. Sunny used to say that all the time.

"So what kind of help are you looking for from *my* better angels?"

"By helping me get Liam Roarke out my shit once and for all," Marcus said.

"Sorry," Jesse said. "Can't help you with Roarke."

"The fuck you can't."

Marcus asked if Jesse had any tea. Jesse told him he had some English breakfast, which he kept in the house for Nellie. Tony said that would be fine, maybe a little cream and sugar if he had it.

When Jesse came back with the tea he said, "If I had something that could help me bust Roarke's ass, even outside of his, uh, jurisdiction, I'd use it. But I don't have it."

"What about what he did to your new Sunny?"

Jesse grinned. Of course he knew.

He watched Tony sip some tea.

High tea with Tony Marcus.

"Can't prove he was behind it."

"You know he was. Was me, I'd do something about that."

"I'm not you."

Tony sipped more of his tea. At least he didn't stick out a pinkie.

"Here's what I know about Roarke," Marcus said. "He's getting his nuts squeezed by the Feds."

"So let them finish the job."

"When?" Tony Marcus said. "On the twelfth of never?"

"I heard he's into crypto," Jesse said.

"Big-time," Marcus said. "Running as fast as he can before the Feds regulate that shit and take all the fun and profit out of it for guys who do it like Roarke and me do it."

"Is it worth it," Jesse said, "turning money over that way?"

"*Hell,* yeah, if you know what you doing."

"And he does."

"*Hell,* yeah."

"Why doesn't Roarke transition to doing it legally?"

Tony Marcus snorted. "Sunny didn't tell me how fucking funny you are."

"Tell me what you know," Jesse said.

"What I hear is that the big white boy is looking to cash out, settle as many scores as he can on his way out the door, then go someplace where the Feds can't get at him. They froze a lot of his assets already. But the boy ain't stupid, he began diversifying a few years ago. Farming his shit out, so to speak."

"He could see how the story was going to end."

"Everybody calls him the new Whitey Bulger? He didn't want to end *up* like Whitey, on the run till they caught him living in some shit place in Santa Monica."

"Is it worth asking what Roarke might have done?"

"Not might. *Did* get done. I got that part solid inside my own brain. Just can't prove it quite yet. You ever get one like that?"

"Right now. Maybe more than one before I'm through."

"Listen up here," Marcus said. "A few months ago, I beat him out of a building we was both after, the South End. I ended up with it. Till it got torched; somebody knew what he was doing. One of my troopers, over there checking it out, didn't *make* it out in time. Boy I was quite fond of, you must know. Up-and-comer."

He sipped more tea. "But I got to be sure, 'fore I start a Mob war with the wrong guy. There was some others in the bidding, so to speak. Coulda been them. I just don't think it was." He grinned. "Haven't concluded my investigation yet."

"So many gangsters, so little time."

"Tell me about it," Tony said.

"If you're just waiting to nail him yourself eventually, why do you need me?"

"He's in the way of a new thing I got going, another part of town. I'm thinking that if you can light him up, it might pre-cip-i-tate him getting out of the way, and I don't have to get my hands dirty if I don't have to. Or till I'm ready to."

"You live a complicated life, Tony."

"You got no idea."

"But I have to say it seems to be working for you."

"All's I'm saying is, you already lit Roarke up once, without hardly trying. What would it hurt you did it again?"

"It's a gift," Jesse said. "Something I try to be a force for good."

Marcus shook his head. "You talk the same kind of shit as Sunny. Care to tell me how you made a mess of that with her?"

"No."

Then Jesse said: "Why would you move on Roarke later rather than sooner?"

"Next time you talk to Sunny Randall, if you do, ask her what I told her one time about how you handle a damn grudge." He paused. "You wait."

Jesse waited. "But sounds like you want me to settle my grudge with him *sooner* rather than later."

Tony flashed him a big smile now. "You said it already. I'm one complicated motherfucker."

Marcus stood now and looked down at his suit, for possible wrinkles. Flicked what Jesse was sure was imaginary lint off a lapel for effect.

"And you do owe me," Marcus said.

"Sure," Jesse said. "Go with that."

"Just givin' you a heads-up, case you need it," Marcus said. "Roarke don't look crazy. But is all *kinds* of crazy. He don't believe in just getting even, you cross him. Ain't no even with him."

Ty Bop had already opened the door. Tony Marcus got there and turned.

"All's I'm asking you to do, even having laid out the risk, is what I hear comes naturally to you," Marcus said.

"And what might that be?"

"Fuck with him a little."

Marcus smiled again.

"Or a lot, as the situation warrants."

SIXTY-SIX

Jesse, Molly, and Nellie were at Molly's. Jesse had brought pizza. They'd finished it by now. One slice each for Molly and Nellie, then they said they were done. Jesse couldn't understand a person stopping after one slice of pizza any more than he ever understood one drink.

"Where's Crow?" Molly asked.

"He said he had some tracking to do," Jesse said. "It's in his blood, you know."

"I hadn't heard that," Molly said. "Tracking whom?"

"He told me it was need-to-know."

"*I* need to know," Molly said.

"You will when I do," Jesse said.

"I hate when you do this," she said.

"Join the club," Nellie said.

"I actually started this particular club," Molly said.

Jesse said he wanted to hear more about Molly's conversation with Ainsley Walsh. Molly asked why she needed to tell it again. Jesse said because he wanted to hear it again, especially the part where Ainsley had F-bombed her into outer space after Molly had questioned her about Jack's sexuality.

"Actually," Molly said, "I might have left out the part about her calling me a grandma bitch."

Nellie giggled. Molly gave her a look.

"I never heard those two words together before," Nellie said. "They're actually kind of funny."

"Did you get the feeling that her reaction was genuine when you asked the question about him being gay, or was she overreacting for show?" Jesse asked. "And by the way? I should have asked that question already."

Molly said, "No shit, Sherlock."

Nellie said, "Maybe you haven't evolved as much as you think you have."

"So what *do* you think about the way Ainsley went off on you?" Jesse said.

"I raised four girls," Molly said. "When they were too over-the-top, I didn't think they were overreacting. Just acting."

"Say he was gay," Nellie said. "How does it change the circumstances surrounding his death?"

"Maybe he was ripped up about the thought it might get out," Jesse said. "Or coming out. And killed himself because of that."

"Sadly," Nellie said, "he wouldn't be the first."

"The world's gotten more accepting," Molly said. "But that doesn't make it any easier if you're the one dealing with it, I don't care how much people love you. Or how much of a jock you are."

"What did finally make you ask the question?" Jesse said.

"I just kept asking *myself* just how many deep, dark secrets a high school senior boy might have, since we were all convinced there was some deep, dark secret going on," Molly said. "Then no recreational drugs turned up in his system."

"Or did he get a girl pregnant," Molly continued. "But unless Ainsley is lying about a lot of things, there was no other girl in his life."

"Doesn't mean there wasn't," Jesse said.

"On that one, I feel as if she was telling me the truth."

"Why?"

"Because I do."

Molly spread her arms out wide. "When Ainsley stopped cursing me out, she got out of my car, slammed the door, and told me she was going to Uber home."

They sat in silence. It was late. Jesse was hoping to have heard from Crow by now. There had been no talk of Nellie coming home with him tonight. Jesse wasn't exactly sure why. Or maybe he was. Maybe he was being reminded, being in the barrel like this, that all he really had room for in his life, at least right now, was the job.

And maybe not just right now.

Jesse put his eyes on Molly.

"I know you," he said. "You think it's true. That he was gay."

No one in the room spoke right away, until Molly finally did.

"Yes," she said. "I do."

She looked at Jesse.

"I asked Ainsley about another girlfriend," she said. "What I should have done is ask about a boyfriend."

Jesse said, "Maybe all the fights were about that."

SIXTY-SEVEN

People were dying again in Paradise. It had happened that way when Crow had first shown up there, working in Jimmy Macklin's crew; lucky Jesse hadn't shot him the way he ended up shooting Jimmy.

That time it had been about money, a lot of it, most of it ending up with Crow.

But was it only about money this time?

Three people dead so far. Maybe four if they ever found Steve Marin, which Crow didn't think anybody ever would. Two had ended up going over the side at that place the Bluff. The old police chief dead, Jesse thought, because he'd found out something about scam callers. One of the calls coming from the goddamn chocolate company.

Crow thought: *What the fuck, Willy Wonka?*

Two of the guys had lived together. One of them had worked for Roarke once. Roarke: who sent a couple of his goons after Jesse's girl. Then came looking for Jesse himself, a way of admitting he'd sent the goons, whether he came right out and said it or not.

That was either reckless shit. Or desperate shit. Or both.

But why?

Jesse always talked about looking for the nexus.

It sure looked to Crow as if Roarke might be it.

No one was sure what Roarke's primary residence was, or if he even had one. A lot of guys with whom Crow had done business, or been in business *with*, were the same way. Moving targets. Not Richie Burke's old man, Desmond. But where Crow knew he lived, in Charlestown, was like living behind the Guns of Navarone.

Crow had made a few calls on Roarke. Now he sat outside Davio's at the seaport. Crow had eaten at the Davio's on Arlington Street a couple times. Never here. Crow had given Richie Burke a call, Jesse having told him that Richie's old man was having Liam Roarke watched. And that when it came to eating out, he was a creature of habit. Tonight was his Davio's night. Two black Navigators out front, the parking valets simply working around them. Maybe there was some kind of Mob rate on Navigators that guys like Roarke got.

Crow knew himself well enough to know that this was why he had come up from his fishing. *This.* Getting ready to follow Liam Roarke.

Back in the game.

Just acting like a cop without a badge. Who would've ever thought?

But he also knew he wasn't just doing it for himself. Jesse, too. Probably the best friend he'd ever had.

Shit.

Maybe he was going soft.

Roarke's body men came out first. Two to a car. One of them was the fat guy from the Capital Grille, and from the Scupper. They all looked around. Roarke got in the second car. It was late. Maybe this was it for the night.

Or not.

Crow had nowhere to be.

He knew how to follow a car, even making the turns on the side streets that finally took them around to 93, and then the Mass Pike, heading west.

The Navigators finally got off at the Watertown exit, circling around, like this part of town was a roundabout, then heading toward Brighton.

They ended up on Market Street, went past a big church, made a couple more quick turns and were on Parsons, before pulling up in front of a big old three-story Victorian. If this was one of Roarke's residences, it wasn't Beacon Hill. Maybe to throw everybody off.

Crow wondered if Roarke might own the two smaller houses on either side.

Crow circled around and parked on a side street that gave him a good view of the Victorian. Roarke must have gone inside by now.

Crow sat.

Nowhere he needed to be. Story of his life.

Jesse was where he needed to be. And Molly. He knew how it was between the two of them, too. Something that would always be there. But she was never leaving her husband. She was who she was. And Crow was who he was, because as much as he'd changed, he knew he couldn't change who he used to be.

A woman getting to him this way.

Who would've thought?

He sat in the rental car and found a country station and listened to Jason Isbell. He was starting to think about calling it a night and heading back to Paradise and trying to fall asleep before three or four in the morning for a change, when the silver Mercedes pulled up in front of Roarke's house.

And a woman Crow recognized got out and nearly ran to the front door, which Roarke opened for her.

The woman Crow had seen sitting with Jesse in front of the chocolate company.

SIXTY-EIGHT

Molly was still bothered by her conversation with Ainsley Walsh when she woke up in the morning, Nellie still asleep. Molly had the impression that Nellie could sleep like a college girl.

At seven in the morning Molly was already on her second cup of coffee. Awake since five. She still had no evidence and no proof that Jack Carlisle had been gay. Only intuition. But to Molly that was a lot, as much of a cliché as feminine intuition was. Jesse had always told her to trust her gut, even if it might ultimately turn out to be nothing more than heartburn.

There was something else that Molly could not get out of her brain, something that had been scratching around at the edges of her consciousness since Jesse had recounted his conversation with Kevin More.

Why was he the only member of Jack Carlisle's inner circle, if there was such a thing, who had gone to his house?

She knew what Kevin had told Jesse. That he'd been looking to retrieve a note of friendship that he'd written to Jack. But why was he so worried about it?

Jesse, or Sunny—it was sometimes difficult to remember which one of them had said what when they were still together—had referenced MacGuffins more than once. From the old Hitchcock movies. A thing that drove the story. The plot. Sometimes a thing, sometimes a person, sometimes missing, sometimes hiding in plain sight.

Jesse thought the MacGuffin might be the play that Jack was supposed to have been working on, or maybe even had finished.

What if it was that note?

Maybe, Molly thought as she sat at her kitchen table in the quiet of the early morning, *that's where the secret was.*

What if?

She had already showered, was dressed for the day. She had plenty of time before she had to get to the office.

She knew the address.

Drove over there now, not entirely sure what she was going to say.

There was no car in the driveway. Molly peeked through one of the garage windows and saw a Cherokee that looked almost as old as her own.

After Molly rang the bell, Kevin More answered the door.

"Are you here about my mom?" he asked Molly before she could say anything.

"No. Why?"

"She didn't come home last night and I can't reach her."

"Maybe she had a date?"

"She always tells me if she's not coming home," the kid said.

White T-shirt. Jeans. Shoeless. Hair still wet from a shower.

"But then she hasn't had *that* kind of date for a long time," he added.

Not for lack of effort with the chief of police.

"I'm sure there's nothing to worry about," Molly said. "If you still haven't heard from her later, and you're still concerned, we can look into it."

"Thanks," he said.

"See," Molly said. "The police aren't so bad when you get to know them."

He cocked his head to the side, narrowing his eyes.

"Wait," he said. "Why are you here, then?"

"We need to talk about you and Jack," Molly said.

SIXTY-NINE

'm going to be late for tennis practice," Kevin said. "Coach needed to have it early today—he's got somewhere to be."

Big, good-looking high school boy. But one Molly wanted to crowd a little now. Trying to make something happen. Force the issue the way she had with Ainsley.

"I'll write you a note for the coach," Molly said. "Notes from cops are even better than ones from moms."

"First Chief Stone comes to my house," Kevin More said. "Now you. I thought my mom talked to you guys about that."

"She did," Molly said. "But even though a lot of people in this town work for her, we're not two of them."

"So now it's your turn to hassle me?"

They were in the living room by now. The kid had wanted to just shut the door. But he didn't, and had reluctantly let Molly into the room. He stretched his legs out in front of him. They just seemed to keep going.

"Or maybe just trying to get you to open up," Molly said.

"About what?"

"You and Jack," she said. "I told you already."

"We were friends," Kevin said.

"I'm starting to think you might have been more than that," Molly said, trying to make it sound like more of an observation than an accusation.

"Who told you that!"

He seemed to know immediately that the words had come out hot, and loud. Or defensive.

He tried to take a beat.

"I mean, who said that about us?"

"No one did," Molly said. "But I'm a cop, Kevin, remember? Sometimes we piece random things together, whether they're actual facts or not."

"Good luck with that," Kevin said. "Did you really come to my house to talk shit about Jack and me being some kind of couple? Seriously?"

"Seriously."

"We weren't."

"No shame if you were."

"No," he said.

The kid put his head down, and shook it slowly from side to side. Almost sadly. "No . . . no . . . *no.*"

He wasn't looking at her.

His breathing seemed to be the only discernible sound in the living room. The whole house.

"What was really in the note, Kevin?" Molly said.

"I already told Chief Stone."

"Tell me."

"Before he went off to college, before we *all* went off to college,

I just wanted him to know what a good friend he'd been to me, even though I wasn't a sports star the way he was."

"You write letters like that to any of your other classmates?"

"I'm going to, for sure."

"But why was it so important for you to get this one back?"

"It had been for Jack to see, nobody else."

He looked up now, perhaps tired of staring at the rug.

"Did the coach not want you around the team because he knew about you and Jack?"

"He didn't know because there wasn't anything *to* know," Kevin said. "And he didn't give me that as a reason when he basically cut me. But he at least suspected."

"You told Chief Stone that you didn't talk to Jack the night he died," Molly said.

"No," he said.

"No texts, no calls, no contact of any kind?"

"I wish I had!" he said. "Maybe things could have been different. But no!"

The kid leaned back, stared at the ceiling for a moment.

"Why are you doing this?" he said when he was looking at Molly again.

Molly told him then what she'd told Ainsley. What she'd been thinking. About secrets. High school secrets. And how the biggest she could think of, for a golden-boy Prince Charming jock like Jack Carlisle, was that he was using performance-enhancing drugs, which would have lost him his scholarship. But he wasn't. Or he'd gotten somebody pregnant. Which he hadn't. Or that he'd committed some kind of crime and covered it up.

Or that he had come to the realization, at the age of eighteen, that he was gay.

"Even though that should have been nobody's business but his own," Molly said in a gentle mom voice. Like Kevin was one of her kids.

Telling herself that in this moment, maybe he was.

"Even though it's nothing anybody should ever be ashamed of," Molly said. "Especially if you really love somebody."

"I want you to please leave now," Kevin More said. "And *please* leave me alone."

"It's true, isn't it?" Molly said in a voice almost she couldn't hear.

Kevin More looked at the ceiling again, for a long time. Then back at Molly.

It came out of him, just like that.

As if he couldn't keep it inside any longer, whether he was basically talking to a stranger—and a cop—or not.

"Yes," he said, his voice as soft as Molly's had been.

"It's true," he continued.

And began to cry.

"Are you happy now?" he asked. "Did you ever get anybody to come out to you before, Mrs. Crane?"

"None of this makes me happy," Molly said. "Not from the day we found Jack down on the rocks and it felt like this town got tipped over on its side."

Then she said, "Does your mom know?"

"I finally told her," he said.

"When?" Molly said.

"The day before Jack died," Kevin More said.

SEVENTY

Crow was waiting in Jesse's office. Jesse got there late today—he had stopped at the gym, to punish himself a little with weights. The urge to do that came and went. The guy who trained him sometimes, Gary, said you had to worry about muscle tone as you got older. Every time he said that Jesse suddenly would feel himself calcifying.

"I let myself in," Crow said.

Jesse wondered, not for the first time, just how many of the black Western shirts Crow owned, how many pairs of black jeans. He couldn't possibly have another pair of boots that worn in. As always, he looked like an Old West hero and Old West outlaw, all at the same time. Cowboy *and* Indian, from when you were still allowed to say that.

"I can see that," Jesse said.

"Made coffee."

"You think we're getting too domestic and people are starting to talk?"

"Fuck 'em," Crow said. "Molly and Suit not here yet?"

"I texted Molly and she said she was with Suit, as a matter of fact. Said she had something."

"So do I," Crow said.

Jesse walked over and fixed himself a cup of coffee, tasted it. Strong as his own. He brought his mug back to his desk. "Isn't this pretty early for you to be awake?"

"We never close," Crow said and then got to it, telling Jesse what he'd seen at Roarke's place.

He told it at his own pace, beginning with when he'd decided to drive into Boston, why he'd decided to go to Boston, following Roarke and the boys all the way to Brighton. He told how he finally decided to come back, because by two in the morning it was clear that Hillary More was staying. And that he'd learned enough for one night.

He left nothing out. Didn't add anything that didn't belong.

Telling it the way a cop would.

Just without notes.

"I gotta ask this," Jesse said.

"Am I sure it was her?"

Jesse grinned. "Took the words right out of my mouth."

"I saw you talking to her outside More Chocolate yesterday afternoon."

"You're even following me now?"

"I'd showed up here looking for Molly," Crow said. "She wasn't around. Neither were you. I knew Nellie was at her office. Nice day, so I decided to go for a walk."

"I didn't see you."

Now Crow grinned.

"Weren't supposed to see me. Would've hurt my feelings if you did."

Jesse grinned. "You have feelings?"

"They come and go."

Jesse told Crow about Hillary More's response to seeing Emma Cleary's phone bill when they were sitting in the park.

"What else was she going to say?" Crow asked him. "'You got me'?"

"Hillary More and Liam Roarke," Jesse said. "Odd couple."

"Even odder than us," Crow said.

"There are those who would disagree," Jesse said. "Starting with an old captain down the hall who still can't believe I'm working with you. And you with me."

"Maybe Roarke didn't come up here just to see you," Crow said. "Maybe combined it with a booty call. One way of looking at it."

"I get made fun for being old when I talk about booty calls."

"With age comes wisdom," Crow said.

"You don't know Hillary More, but I do," Jesse said. "I just can't see them together."

"You couldn't see Molly and me together."

"Still can't."

Crow let that one go.

"Maybe it's not about sex," Jesse said. "Maybe it's about money."

"Maybe you heard," Crow said. "They go hand in hand sometimes."

"Could be he's a silent partner in the company and she wisely elected not to share that with anybody," Jesse said. "For all the obvious reasons."

"Or he's more than a partner," Crow said, "and it's his money behind the whole thing, and he's the puppet master. Been thinking on that all night, that he might be the guy pulling the strings from behind a legit front. Didn't Tony Marcus tell you he was diversifying?"

"What the bad man said."

"Maybe chocolate is just part of his diversification," Crow said.

Jesse took out his phone and tried to call Hillary More. Went straight to voicemail. Then he called the main number at More Chocolate and got a recording, before he realized it was Saturday morning. Gabe was supposed to meet Hillary More there today and look at the computers on the second floor.

Jesse left a message, even though he knew he was probably wasting his time. If he didn't hear from her by this afternoon, maybe he'd take a run at her son. But he could wait, for the time being.

"You could call somebody with the cops in Boston and ask them to send a car, see if hers is still parked out front," Crow said.

"It still being there doesn't get us to where we need to get," Jesse said, "which is us knowing exactly *why* it's there. I could use a little time to consider the possibilities."

"Bullshit."

Crow said this with just the barest upturn of the corners of his mouth. Mr. Fun.

"I know you," he continued. "You've already considered all the possibilities while we've been sitting here drinking my excellent coffee." He nodded at Jesse's mug. "You want more?"

"You even had to ask? Maybe we're not as domestic as I thought."

Crow took Jesse's mug along with his own over to the pot, filled both mugs up, came back. Jesse was still fond of this pot because of

how hot it kept the coffee. He drank some. When he was still playing ball, they used to say that the first cup of clubhouse coffee for a
day game was when you started to feel good and caffeine-cocky.

Jesse was looking for some of that cocky now. He tried to picture the Hillary More he knew, the one who kept trying different
ways to come on to him, with Roarke. Could not, no matter how
hard he tried. But then he couldn't imagine any smart woman getting into bed with Liam Roarke.

Literally or figuratively.

It didn't change that they had been together last night, in some
form or fashion.

"Roarke and Hillary More," Jesse said.

"You said that before. Just in a different order."

"You think my conversation with her sent her running to
Roarke?" Jesse said.

"Every action, a reaction," Crow said.

"Okay, if you can only pick one," Jesse said, "is it money or sex?"

"With Roarke?" Crow said. "Money *is* sex."

Jesse saw Healy in his window. When Healy saw it was Crow in
one of the visitor chairs, he pointed at Crow and shook his head,
obviously disappointed. He and Crow hadn't been formally intro-
duced. But he knew Crow by reputation the same way Crow knew
Healy by reputation.

Jesse held up a finger, telling him to wait.

Crow turned around.

"Healy?"

"Himself," Jesse said.

Healy was still in the window. Crow stood and saluted, back
straight, form perfect, elbow forward, arm horizontal.

Healy gave him the finger in response.

"How much do you really know about Hillary More?" Crow asked now.

"What everybody knew when she got here. What she said, what we all read. I don't do a background check on everybody who opens a new business in Paradise."

"Maybe you could have the old Statie run one now."

"I was about to raise *that* possibility myself."

"Stop trying to take credit for my ideas," Crow said.

Molly came into Jesse's office then, shutting the door behind her, getting into the chair next to Crow, not greeting either one of them.

"Where's Suit?" Jesse said. "You said you were with him."

"I was," she said. "But he doesn't want to be with anybody except his sister at the moment."

She told them why.

"Gonna need a new pot," Jesse said to Crow.

SEVENTY-ONE

Jesse waited an hour. When Suit still hadn't shown up he tracked him on his phone, not surprised when he saw his location.

He was at O'Hara Field, sitting up in the same part of the bleachers where they'd watched Jack make the play that won his team the league championship.

"Hey," Jesse said.

His voice didn't startle Suit. He didn't seem surprised to see Jesse. He just smiled.

"Hey," Suit said.

Jesse would think of him as a kid today and always. The big, sweet, good-hearted kid who was almost as tough as he wanted to be. But then nobody was ever as tough as they wanted to be, if you really thought about it. Not Jesse. Not even Crow, though Crow came as close as anybody Jesse had ever known.

"Figured you'd eventually come find me," Suit said.

"Even if you didn't want to be found."

Jesse walked up the steps and sat down next to him.

"Can't believe how little time has passed since Jack won the big game," Suit said, "and how much has happened since."

"What they always say in sports," Jesse said. "Next moment can change everything."

"Like when you got hurt."

"Like then."

"Not just sports," Suit said.

Jesse stared out at the big patch of dirt between second base and third that had felt like his whole life once.

"You okay?" he said to Suit.

Jesse saw him swallow hard.

"He should have told me," Suit said. "Or I should have known. Either way. I could have helped him with it."

He was wearing the same outfit he pretty much always wore once Jesse promoted him to detective. Maybe the only nice blazer he owned. White shirt. Jeans. Dressing the way Jesse dressed a lot of the time. Getting out of uniform had been one of the happiest days of Suit's life. Which had been a mostly happy life. Until now.

Jesse said, "Maybe the best part of this, if there is a best part, is that the friends of his who did know seemed to have been cool with it. Which, by the way, they should have been."

"So why'd he get into a fight that night?"

"Kevin told Molly that Scott Ford wanted Jack to just come out with it," Jesse said. "No more sneaking around. They were about to graduate. Only idiots would really care. But according to what the Ford kid told Kevin later, that made Jack snap, and it escalated from there, and Jack threw the first punch. Ford was the one who'd had a few by then, and slugged him back, even though he thought he was trying to help."

"But then why did Ford catch a beating from Matt Loes?"

"To be determined, now that new information is rolling in," Jesse said. "How's your sis?"

"She's just sorry that she wasn't there for him," Suit said. "She talked about how hard it must have been for him, being a jock, to come to terms with it. But it was one more part of his life he kept bottled up."

Suit took out his phone. "While I was sitting up here by myself, I looked it up," he said. "You know how many openly gay players there are in the big leagues right now?"

Jesse said, "As many as there were on the Paradise High baseball team."

They went several moments without either one of them saying anything. Both of them staring out at the ballfield.

Suit turned to Jesse. "Don't you feel like we ought to be out there throwing a ball around?"

He had been a first baseman when he'd been at Paradise High, playing because his friends did, always more of a football player.

"I always feel that way," Jesse said, "even when I'm nowhere near a field."

Grass had just been cut. Infield dragged recently from the looks of it. New white lines for the softball season.

"You know, just because he was gay doesn't mean he killed himself," Suit said.

"*Hell* no."

"Somebody still could have done it."

"Still an open investigation, even with what Kevin More told Molly this morning."

He'd tell him about Hillary More's visit to Roarke when they were back at the office. Right now, just the two of them here, this was all about Suit's nephew. Athlete who'd died young.

"If his friends *were* cool with it," Suit said, "and they've only just been trying to protect him, I like them a lot more today than I did yesterday."

Suit sighed and leaned forward, elbows on his knees, eyes still fixed on the field.

"Maybe I owe the Ford kid an apology," he said.

"For doing your job?" Jesse said. "You looking to get busted down to desk duty, Detective?"

Suit turned to him. Not a kid. A grown-ass man, the way he kept reminding Jesse.

"So let me detect for a second," he said. "Did Molly ask Kevin More if he was with Jack after the party at the Bluff that night?"

"She did. He said he was not."

"Molly believe him?"

Jesse nodded.

"So I've still got a question we haven't answered," Suit said. "Where was Jack between his fight with Scott Ford and when he ended up in the water? And who might he have been with?"

SEVENTY-TWO

They were in the conference room in the middle of the afternoon, still no callback from Hillary More. Her son wasn't answering his phone.

Jesse sat at the table with Molly, Suit, Healy.

And Crow.

"Does he really need to be here?" Healy said, jerking his head at Crow.

Crow was at the far end of the table.

"I come in peace," he said.

"Maybe today you do," Healy said.

"We're having this meeting because of Crow," Jesse said. "He's the one who put Hillary More with Roarke."

"Doesn't mean I have to like it," Healy said.

"If it helps you at all," Molly said, "he does grow on you after a while."

"I do?" Crow said to her.

"I was talking about you growing on Jesse," she said.

Healy had spent the last several hours talking to his old friends at the State Police, the Boston PD, and any Fed who still owed him a favor, whether he was retired or not.

They were establishing one timeline for Hillary More and another for Liam Roarke, looking for periods when their lives, or business careers, or both, may have intersected.

Molly had already checked with Town Hall, and discovered that the only owner listed for More Chocolate was Hillary McConnell More.

"Now, that doesn't mean other people's money wasn't propping her up," Molly said.

"But if it's Roarke's money we're talking about," Jesse said, "I suspect we'd need an army of forensic accountants to trace it back to him."

"Good luck with that," Crow said.

"But we still don't know for sure if they *are* business associates," Suit said.

"What is verifiable for now," Healy said from his end of the table, next to the easel he'd set up, "is that she went running for Roarke the minute she thought Jesse might be squeezing her."

Molly said, "Just not the kind of squeezing she wanted from the chief, of course."

Healy had drawn a line down the middle of the oversized whiteboard. Hillary More's name at the top on one side, Roarke's on the other. Old school.

"Let's focus on her for a moment," Healy said. "She's forty-four years old. Born in Shaker Heights, Ohio. Graduated from Northwestern. The Medill School. Journalism."

"Speaking of which," Molly said to Jesse. "Why isn't Nellie here for our team meeting?"

"Not invited."

"She even know there's a team meeting?" Molly asked.

"Only if she found out with her own independent reporting," Jesse said.

"She's going to be pissed," Molly said.

"I expect," Jesse said. "Pissed off and better off." He made a gesture that took in all of them. "Everybody in this room can take care of themselves."

"Nellie can't?" Suit said.

"Not like we can," Crow said.

"Not saying it wasn't the case before," Jesse said. "But this shit is about to get real."

Healy cleared his throat.

"May I continue?" he said.

"Least he asked," Crow said to Jesse.

"Please stop talking," Healy said to Crow.

Most of what Healy told them about Hillary More matched up with what Jesse had read in pieces written about her when she arrived in Paradise. Brief career on the air with the CBS affiliate in Chicago after she graduated. Still Hillary McConnell at that point. Both parents deceased by then. Ended up going into marketing at the same station. Moved from there to a VP position with Hershey. Next thing she was in Boston, working PR for a small chocolate company based in Cambridge. Married a lawyer. Justin More. They had a son.

"She told me she had a husband who died," Jesse said.

"She mention how?" Healy asked.

"No."

"Single-car accident, as it turns out," Healy said. "Falmouth. You ever been down there?"

"To the Cape," Jesse said. "Not there."

"We used to rent there," Healy said. "Justin More was driving too fast on Central Ave., blew through a stop sign, crossed over Menauhant Beach and down into the ocean."

"Was he drunk?" Molly said.

"Nope," Healy said. "No alcohol in his system. No sign of foul play. Cops convinced themselves he fell asleep at the wheel and closed it."

"How long ago?" Jesse said.

"Fifteen years?"

"What did the Widow More do after that?" Jesse said.

"Went off the grid," Healy said, "at least as a professional-type woman. Far as we can tell, she stayed in the house that she and the dead husband and the kid lived in, in Needham. Finally, a lot of time passes and she ends up here."

"How'd she support herself?" Crow asked.

Healy gave him a long cop stare. "Still talking."

"I love you," Jesse said to Healy. "So I say this with love: Cut the shit with Crow."

Then he said: "The period when she was off the grid, where was Liam Roarke?"

"He'd made his way to Boston," Healy said. "Building a brand-new empire off what was left of Jackie DeMarco's operation the old-fashioned way."

Healy paused. "Mostly by taking out anybody who got in his way. Sometimes for the sheer enjoyment of it, from what I hear."

It was much later, middle of the night, Jesse asleep next to Nellie, the two of them finally having made up, when he got the call about the fire.

SEVENTY-THREE

Jesse stood in front of More Chocolate, the place burning up in front of his eyes, listening to the roar he knew a fire like this made, amazed that somehow the Paradise Fire Department and the trucks that were already on the scene from Marshport had contained it, at least so far, to just this one building.

He thought about the night when the old theater, rebuilt now, had burned like this, afraid that time that half of Main Street or more was about to go, too. But they had contained that one and were in the process of doing the same with the chocolate company, even though this part of Paradise looked as bright as the middle of the day.

The members of Jesse's department who weren't on the scene when he arrived had shown up by now, Molly and Suit and Gabe and everybody. They were containing the crowd that had formed at four in the morning.

Jesse saw Nicholas Farrell on the civilian side of the police ropes that had already been set up, his eyes fixed on flames still trying to reach to the sky even as the nozzle teams were hitting them hard with water, which only made the night louder.

In the distance, there was the sound of another siren, maybe one more truck from Marshport, whose fire department was bigger than the one they had here.

He didn't know how they'd classify this one, how many alarms. But two departments.

One candy company.

One big-ass fire.

Jesse walked over to Nicholas.

"I mean, what in the holy fuck, Jesse?" Nicholas said.

He stared up at the fire, transfixed, maybe wondering what was happening to his own life, right in front of his eyes.

"This has to be an accident, right?" Nicholas said.

"Not necessarily," Jesse said, and told him they could talk later, and walked away.

Up the block Jesse managed to smile as he saw that Nellie was inside the ropes, pen and notebook out, talking to Bob Fishman, the fire chief in Paradise. Captain Gus Morello was as close to the building as he could get, barking out orders. Jesse knew the drill. Fishman was the chief, but Morello was the one in charge.

When Morello stepped back, Jesse walked over to him.

"Anybody inside?" Jesse said.

"Imaging says no," Morello said, eyes watching the second floor.

"Any of your people inside?"

"If there's nobody in there," Morello said, "nobody *goes* in there."

And went back to work.

Fishman stepped away from Nellie. When she started to follow, he turned and motioned with his hand for her to stop. Just then one of the windows suddenly blew out, and the roar of the fire got a little louder.

Bob Fishman shook his head.

"Oxygen," he said.

"Feeding the beast," Jesse said.

"It was a couple kids who called it in. They were walking through town, overserved, all the way from the Swap," Fishman said.

He was tall, rope-thin, white hair, buzz-cut. He reminded Jesse more of a Marine. He had been working in the department since Jesse had arrived from Los Angeles.

"They heard it before they saw the flames and the smoke," he said.

Just then there was what sounded like an explosion, and the second floor began to collapse on the first.

"Do you think this might have been set intentionally?" they heard from behind them.

Nellie.

Jesse put a hand on Fishman's arm and walked him away.

"Hey," Nellie said.

"Church and state," Jesse said.

"*Could* this be arson?" Jesse asked Fishman when they were out of her earshot.

"If it is," he told Jesse, "somebody knew what the hell they were doing."

Nobody's going to search the computers now.

Convenient, Jesse thought, at least if you had something to hide.

Jesse told Molly and Suit to fan out, ask people in the crowd if they'd seen or heard anything before the fire started, even at this time of morning.

Then he stared at the flames again, feeling the heat of them on his face, remembering the day that the makeover of the old firehouse was complete, and More Chocolate was ready to open for business, and Hillary More and Mayor Gary Armistead did the ribbon-cutting and smiled for the cameras.

"Paradise is open for business again," Armistead said that day, even though Jesse knew it had never really been closed, even at the height of COVID, when most of the world had been forced indoors, and even the cop work felt as if it were somehow being done remotely. In Paradise, the money had held. But then it almost always did.

Something about the subject of arson was nagging Jesse, something he knew he knew. Just too much going on for him to come up with it right in middle of Main Street, middle of the night.

"*Take your hands off me!*"

A woman's voice.

One Jesse knew.

He turned around and saw Hillary More, eyes wild, on this side of the ropes, having broken away from Gabe, who knew enough to let her go.

She came running for Jesse.

Now he was the one stopping her as she tried to get too close to the fire.

"*My God!*" she said. "*My God!*"

She shook free of Jesse, didn't make any move to get closer, looking at what used to be More Chocolate.

Then she turned back to Jesse and said, "He did this."

SEVENTY-FOUR

The crowd was beginning to disperse as Jesse walked Hillary More back to the station. Fishman and Morello said it might be a couple hours before it was safe enough to begin sifting through the rubble, but that they would call when, and if, they found any kind of evidence of how the fire had started. Jesse told Gabe and Suit to stay with them, telling Molly she could try to go get some sleep, it was going to be a long goddamn day.

"I always knew he liked her best," Gabe said to Suit.

Nellie had tried to get a comment from Jesse and Hillary as they were leaving.

"Not now," Jesse said.

"Wasn't asking you, Chief Stone," she said.

"Must have heard you wrong," Jesse said, and walked Hillary through what was left of the crowd and back down Main Street to the station.

Then it was just Jesse and Hillary in his office, the sun still not up. No more sirens now. But Jesse could still smell the smoke, even in here.

"I can't do this right now, Jesse," Hillary said. "I need some space and some time to process this."

"We actually are going to do this right now," Jesse said, making it sound as if she had no choice, even though she did. "There are things we need to discuss, and there is no point in putting them off."

She said she had gotten a call from one of her top managers and driven up from Boston. Jesse didn't ask her where she'd been. He knew where she had been.

Due time.

She sat back in her chair, resigned if not relaxed.

"My face must be a fright."

"It's not."

"Thank you for that, at least."

He asked if she wanted something to drink. She said no, let's get this over with.

"You said 'He did this,'" Jesse said. "Who's 'he'?"

"You'll figure it out eventually," she said. "Maybe you already have."

Jesse waited.

Nobody better at waiting.

"Liam Roarke," she said.

"Why would Liam Roarke burn down your company?" Jesse asked her. "The part of it that's here, anyway."

He tried to read her face and could not. In the moment, he believed that what she was really trying to process wasn't just the fire down the street, but how much to tell him. And how much he knew.

"It's not my company," she said.

Boom.

"It's his," she said.

Hillary More paused and then said, "Or was."

SEVENTY-FIVE

Jesse felt his phone buzzing a couple times, ignored it. For now, even with the fire, Hillary More was the main event.

Charlie had been murdered. It had something to do with scam calls, Jesse had been sure of that, almost from the start. At least one of those calls had come from More Chocolate. The money man for which, she had just told him, was none other than Liam Roarke.

A small light went on at the very back of his brain.

Steve Marin. Worked for Roarke when he was a kid. And one of the things Marin had gone down for was arson, when he wasn't busting heads.

Jesse sat at his desk, across from Hillary, and wondered if Marin had busted in Charlie Farrell's head.

"I swear I didn't know what Liam did when I first started going around with him," she said.

Going around with.

Maybe not the dumbest expression for what she was really talking about.

But one of them.

"You have to believe me," she said, as earnest as if she were on a sales call.

"About that? Sure, why not."

"I'm not going to sit here and lie to you," she said.

"Let's hope not." Then he added, "For both of our sakes."

He let her tell it.

She had been thinking about starting her own chocolate company for years after her husband died, she said. It was because of a happy experience at Hershey. She'd made some money there, invested it well, then made more from insurance when her husband died in the accident. A few years ago, everything in place, she made the decision to buy the old firehouse at a very fair price from the town, bought a factory in New Hampshire that had shut down back in the nineties.

"Were you and Roarke still a couple then?"

"No."

She rubbed the back of her neck.

"I was going to be one of those small-business success stories," she said. "Then came COVID."

"And you went to Roarke for help."

"We'd stayed in touch."

Jesse smiled. "But by now you had to be aware that he was a fucking gangster, right?"

She flinched, almost involuntarily.

"I swear, I didn't know the extent of his business," she said. "I knew a lot of it was outside the law. Maybe I didn't know how far outside because I chose not to know." She took in air through her nose, out through her mouth. Calming exercise. Probably learned it when she was killing it at yoga. "But he had never been anything other than kind to me."

"And he offered to front you the money you needed."

"A lot of money," she said. "Like an interest-free loan, he told me at the time. He said I could pay it back over time, if the business became as profitable as I told him it was going to be."

"No strings attached?"

"One," she said. "I was never to say anything about where the money was coming from."

"And you never questioned why someone like him would want to be in business with someone like you."

"Not until it was too late," she said, "when I realized that they were selling more than chocolate on the second floor."

"Who hired those people?"

"He did," she said. "He told me he was an expert at that as he diversified into legitimate businesses."

"And you are now sitting here and telling me that you didn't know what was going on up there."

She leaned back in the chair. Looked up at the ceiling.

"It always seemed quite normal when I would go up and visit the troops," she said. "I think they had some system, one I found out about later, when I'd check up there. But our profits were steady. The business was thriving. Supply was meeting demand up in New Hampshire. And, as I said, the second-floor people reported to Liam."

"Madoff's investors never seemed to question why their profits were so steady," Jesse said. "And while all this was going on, what were you focusing on?"

"National branding," she said. "I told Liam I wanted to go public, and he told me if I thought it was best. But it turned out *that* was never going to happen. He was just waiting to close everything down, the way he'd begun to close down his other businesses."

"Because of the Feds."

"He portrayed himself as a victim," Hillary More said. "Said he was being persecuted."

"More like prosecuted," Jesse said. "But you were still going along to get along." He shook his head. "Because he'd always been so kind."

"You're mocking me."

"Or just being shocked at how naïve you were," Jesse said. "Or maybe just being a fool who couldn't see past her own ambition."

"I guess I deserve that."

"Fuck, yes."

He leaned forward and clasped his hands together.

"When exactly did you realize you were just a tool?"

"When Sam Waterfield died," she said. "I told Liam what you said, that it was like somebody was sending a message."

"What did he say to that?"

"He said the boy probably killed himself, he was so overcome with grief."

"Grief about what?"

"He smiled at me and said, 'Stealing.'

"I asked him, 'Stealing from whom?'

"'Me,'" he said. "Then he told me about the scam calls, some of them coming from up there, some of them farmed out remotely. He said I wasn't going to tell anybody, because nothing that was going on up there would ever be traced back to anybody but me.

And he was right about that, of course. Then he told me that Waterfield had gotten careless, trying to make money on the side, and called the wrong guy."

"The wrong guy being Charlie Farrell?"

"He didn't mention a name."

Now Jesse took in a lot of air, and let it out. Because he was the one trying to calm himself.

"Maybe he didn't have to," he said. "Waterfield and Marin were probably in it together, making some on the side. You ever ask him what happened to Steve Marin?"

"I did," she said. "Liam told me he still had some use, or maybe he would have been overcome with grief and killed *him*self."

"Are you aware that Marin once made himself useful to your friend Liam by burning down buildings?"

"*No!*" she said. "His records were sealed, and he just told me he'd done things he was ashamed of, and been punished for them."

"And you bought that?"

"Are you saying that I had some idea that Liam was going to do this?"

Jesse studied her. It was impossible in that moment to remember the woman who would sit in that same chair and flirt with him.

"Why are you so sure he did it now?"

She didn't hesitate. "I was with him earlier tonight. And told him about the call to Emma Cleary coming from our Wi-Fi. He took that very calmly, I thought, and said there was nothing for me to worry about."

"Apparently not."

Jesse was the one who needed coffee now.

Or a drink.

"You'll never tie him to this," she said.

"Probably not," Jesse said. "Probably can't draw a line from him to Charlie, either."

"You think Steve Marin killed Charlie?"

"Well, Hillary," Jesse said, "Charlie sure as shit didn't kill himself. And he was onto them."

She said, "What are you going to do about Liam?"

"Like he told you," Jesse said. "Nothing for you to worry about." He nodded at her. "Where do you go from here?"

"To New Hampshire, to close the plant down," she said. "Set in motion a plan to pay my legitimate people with whatever money I can put my hands on. And then I am leaving here, first chance I get after Kevin's graduation. Get as far away from Liam Roarke and from Paradise, Mass., as I can."

She was rubbing the back of her neck again, hard.

"May I leave now?" she said.

"No," he said. "We haven't talked about something else you could have told me about and didn't."

"Such as?"

"Such as Kevin and Jack Carlisle," Jesse said.

SEVENTY-SIX

They talked for another hour.

"I think I might have always known about Kevin," she said. "But as trite as this sounds, he was a young man and I was his mom, and there were places I just chose not to go. And probably should have."

"He had girlfriends?"

"Some," Hillary said. "Never serious. Never for long. I asked him once why he couldn't get a girl like Ainsley, the way Jack had. And he gave me one of those withering looks you get from your children and said, 'Mom, you don't know what you're talking about.' And then I just left it alone, though it turned out I didn't know what I was talking about."

"And left him alone," Jesse said.

She looked down at her hands and then back up at Jesse.

"Maybe I didn't want to know what I didn't want to know."

"And you never suspected that he and Jack were more than just good friends?"

"I'm telling you that I didn't," she said. "I'm not absolving my-self. I'm not avoiding the fact that I should have been more present as a mom, more focused on my son than on being a titan of indus-try. But no. Or yes. I thought they were just friends."

Jesse watched her and listened and wondered if she was trying to fool him. Or herself. Or might even be telling the truth.

"Please leave this alone, and leave Kevin alone now," she said. "This is his business going forward, not yours and not even mine. And you can only hurt him if you *don't* leave him alone."

"If we've reached the point where you think you're another per-son who can come into this office and tell me how to do my job," he said, "then you *can* go now."

When she was gone, he called Crow and told him to meet him at Daisy's. Crow told him he was already there.

He was at a window table by the time Jesse arrived and hadn't waited to order. He had a plate of scrambled eggs in front of him, well-done bacon next to it, English muffin, another plate for the pancakes.

"I'm sorry," Jesse said when he slid into the booth across from him. "I didn't know you were about to go to the chair."

"Daisy calls this particular combination her Triple Bypass Special."

"Only a triple?"

"I could order you the same, you want."

Daisy appeared then with a mug of coffee for Jesse. Her hair today was violet. She wore a T-shirt with the flag of Ukraine on the front.

"I won't have what he's having," Jesse said.

"Pussy," she said, and walked away, as if Jesse'd insulted her.

Jesse told Crow about his conversation with Hillary More,

everything she'd told him about Roarke, including how they'd gotten together in the first place.

"So she says she didn't know what was going on upstairs until she did," Crow said.

"Her story and she's sticking to it."

"You believe her?"

"Some of what she told me, not all."

"People telling their version of the truth, and trying to get by with it." Crow broke off a piece of bacon and ate it. "You probably never run into anything like that, your line of work."

Daisy came back. "Last chance to order breakfast."

Jesse grinned. "Stop badgering me."

"No."

"No more name-calling," Jesse said.

She grinned now, before walking away. "Why can't you be a real man like me?"

Jesse reached over and grabbed some of Crow's bacon.

"She makes it sound as if Roarke is about to disappear," he said.

Crow said, "By the way, and even though you might not want to hear this? It's not as if Roarke ordered a hit on Charlie."

"I don't give a shit," Jesse said. "They were his people. If it happened the way we both think it did, it's on him."

"The old man must have turned himself into a target without knowing it."

Jesse said, "His gun was on the floor. Whoever came to his house that night, I swear Charlie thought he still had the chops to arrest him."

Crow pushed away his plate.

"You have to know you can't prove much of this, as sure as you are," he said. "Maybe not any of it. And just because Hillary says Roarke had the fire set doesn't mean you can prove that, either."

"Stop sugarcoating it."

"Just keeping it real."

"I went past what's left of More Chocolate on my way over here," Jesse said. "Fishman and Morello told me they hadn't found any sign of accelerants. They were able to go inside now, without worrying about the ceiling falling on them, because it already collapsed."

"But they think it's arson?"

"They do."

They sat in silence, both looking out the window. Finally Crow said, "You're going after Roarke."

"You know I am."

"Even though you took an oath to uphold the law, and even tried to uphold it with me occasionally, I gotta ask you something."

Jesse was reading Crow's mind. It was happening more frequently.

"I am going to do whatever it takes to nail that son of a bitch," he said to Crow.

"I could just kill him, you want."

"Maybe short of that."

"Felt like I had to make the offer."

"I can't let him just walk away, go somewhere where even the Feds can't find him."

"I could find him." Crow shrugged. "Apache deal."

"I got the sense from Hillary More that I don't have a lot of time to roll this up."

"We need to burn down his house." Crow shrugged again. "Figuratively speaking."

"I've got to make something happen."

"*We* need to make something happen."

"Have it your way," Jesse said.

He told Crow then what he wanted him to do. Crow agreed, and said he would call him later. Jesse told him that he was going home for a couple hours, he needed to be alone and think. He'd thought about calling Dix. He knew Dix would make time for him even if he didn't have it. Jesse was well aware he often did some of his best thinking in that room with Dix, occasionally when he least expected it.

He wasn't going to let Roarke get away.

Vanish the way Whitey Bulger did.

The chocolate company had been a front. What had it been for Tony Soprano, somebody he'd actually watched back in the day? A pork store? Molly told him one time that in one of *her* favorite shows, *Better Call Saul,* the front was a nail spa.

Roarke was hiding behind More Chocolate. Hiding the phone scam and maybe turning the profits from it into crypto before the Feds squeezed him there. Hiding behind his old girlfriend.

And I can't tag him with any of it.

Jesse sat at his kitchen table and made one of his world-class lists, page after page on his yellow legal pad, establishing a timeline of what he knew and what he didn't.

And getting nowhere fast.

He was about to go back to the office when the call came in on his cell.

He was surprised to see her name on his screen.

"I wasn't expecting to hear from you," he said.

"I may have something that can help you," she said. "Are you free right this minute?"

"Now I am," he said to Sunny Randall.

SEVENTY-SEVEN

He valet-parked his car at the Four Seasons, walked up Boylston and around the corner and then up the stairs of her building. They had still been together when she had moved into this office, the first she'd ever had. Jesse had even helped move things around, including the desk behind which she was sitting when he walked in.

As always in her presence, he felt something contract inside him, like his air passage had suddenly narrowed, or there simply wasn't enough oxygen in the room.

She wore what he once would have called a fisherman-knit sweater, maybe a peach color. Somehow she still looked glamorous enough for a photo shoot. Boston's hottest female private eye. But part of Sunny's beauty, at least for him, was that she never appeared to have tried too hard to look the way she did.

Spike was on the couch.

Jesse sat down in a client chair.

"I'm happy to see you both," he said to Sunny. "But you could have told me whatever you want to tell me on the phone."

"True," she said.

"Or you could have told Spike and Spike could have told me."

She was still smiling. It did hardly anything to calm Jesse's breathing, as relaxed as he tried to look and sound.

"Or," Sunny said, "I could have passed Spike a note and he could have passed it to you before Chem class."

"Always goes back to high school," Jesse said. "Got a high school case still ongoing up in Paradise."

"I heard," Sunny said.

"Is this a meet-cute," Spike said, "or reacquainted-cute? I'm confused."

"Spike is why we're here," Sunny said.

"Just so you don't get the idea that it was destiny that brought you two together," Spike said.

Spike looked as if he'd just come from the gym. All in black, head to toe, even his Bruins cap.

"Before we get started," Sunny said, "how's the girl reporter?"

Now Jesse smiled. "How's the boy reporter?"

"He's hardly a boy," she said.

"Nellie would likely be resistant at still being classified as a girl," Jesse said.

"Oh, no," Spike said. "Mom and Dad are fighting again."

Jesse told them they needed to get to it.

"Richie told me that you had managed to get yourself sideways with Liam Roarke," Sunny said. "Spike, being my man on the ground in Paradise, told me the same thing."

Jesse said, "I don't recall mentioning that to Spike."

"You didn't," Spike said. "But let's move on."

Sunny asked Spike to tell it. He did, getting up off the couch and walking around the room, describing a phone call he'd gotten from a friend of his. Jared. Jared had gone to work for an escort service after COVID, when he lost his job as a software engineer, and was making such good money now he'd stayed with it.

You had to let Spike tell his stories his way.

"Jared's roommate also works at the same service," Spike said. "Exclusively male clients for him. Tayshawn Leonard is his name. Part-time model, part-time escort. Had a drink one time with him and started to feel light-headed. That kind of gorgeous."

"Focus," Sunny said.

"Right," Spike said. "Anyway, Tayshawn didn't come back from his last date a few nights ago, and Jared is worried as shit."

"Are we talking about a date where money changed hands?" Jesse asked.

"Jared says that sometimes it does, sometimes it doesn't," Spike said. "Lately the john hasn't been going through the service, and is dealing with Tayshawn directly. So it does feel more like a date."

"Did Jared try to find him on his phone?"

"According to him, the phone is gone, goodbye," Spike said. "Something else that's worrying him."

"Why hasn't Jared called the police?" Jesse said.

"And tell them that he's managed to misplace a missing male-escort-type guy?" Spike said. "You see them dropping everything to get right on that? Because I don't."

"Listen, I'm sorry about your friend's missing friend," Jesse said. "But what does this have to do with me? Or Liam Roarke?"

Spike sat back down.

"You want to tell him, or should I?" he said to Sunny.

"You're doing so well," she said, "though I might have tightened the presentation in the middle."

He made a face at her.

"Tayshawn's last date, his last *several* dates, were with Mr. Liam Roarke himself," Spike said to Jesse.

No one in Sunny's office spoke.

"Roarke is gay," Jesse said.

"Or at least bi," Sunny said.

"Everything's supposed to be anonymous, as you can imagine," Spike said. "At the service, I mean. All sorts of NDAs the boys have to sign. Lots of layers to it. But very high-end. But it was definitely Roarke. And his preference, according to Jared, is definitely for young African American men. Prettier the better. Another thing bothering Jared is that the last time they spoke, Tayshawn said that he might have messed up."

"How?"

"Jared says it was something vague about how he'd said something he shouldn't have," Spike said.

He sat back down on the couch.

"Roarke makes people disappear," Jesse said. "You know that, right? It's practically part of his job description."

"You think Tayshawn might have tried to squeeze more money out of him?" Sunny asked.

"Hoping not," Spike said. "Thinking maybe."

"Jared still could file a Missing Persons," Jesse said.

"He won't out him that way, like I said," Spike said. "And by the way? Jared doesn't think Tayshawn is just missing. Jared thinks that Roarke *did* make him disappear. He's worried that Tayshawn might have said something about the two of them being together, as much as they're together, and somehow it got back to Roarke."

Jesse quickly caught Sunny up on as much as he could. He told her about the phone call from More Chocolate to Emma Cleary, about Roarke and More Chocolate, about Sam Waterfield and

Steve Marin and what he was sure had happened to Charlie Farrell.

Spike had already told her about the fire last night. What Spike didn't know, until now, was that Hillary More believed Roarke had been the one to set it.

"So you believe it all goes back to Roarke?" Sunny said.

"Very much so."

"You going to nail his ass?" Spike asked.

"Very much so," Jesse said again.

He thanked Spike and Sunny, telling them he had work to do. Lot of it. He came around the desk and leaned down close to Sunny, into the scent of her, and kissed her softly on the cheek.

When he got to the door, he turned back around.

"Take care of yourself," he said.

"That's my line," Sunny said.

SEVENTY-EIGHT

Jesse called Molly from the car and filled her in on what Hillary had told him about Roarke and his conversation with Spike.

And he let her know that he'd seen Sunny.

"How did that go?" she said.

"Nothing to see here," he said. "Move along."

"Don't make me beat the details out of you when you get back."

"Deal."

"How did she look?"

"Like the Sunny you remember. Just older."

"May I quote you?"

"May I bust you back to overnights?"

"No, you may not."

"Hey, Mols? I haven't spoken to Nellie since the fire. But if you talk to her before I do, don't tell her about Roarke. Let's keep the circle on that tight for the time being."

Molly didn't tell Jesse that she had asked Nellie to stop by the station. She felt Nellie had a right to know what Molly had learned about Kevin More and Jack. Molly trusted her. On top of that, Nellie had gone out of her way to help them. Had even taken a punch along the way, and nearly been abducted. Molly was going to make clear that what she was telling Nellie Shofner was off the record. Molly was convinced that telling Nellie about Kevin and Jack was the decent thing to do.

If Jesse got angry with her later about telling Nellie, Molly would deal with it. She didn't always need the chief to tell her the right thing to do.

"Where are you headed right now?" Molly asked Jesse.

"I need to talk to somebody smarter than me."

"You are."

"I meant Dix."

NELLIE ARRIVED AT the station predictably out of breath, informing Molly that her story about the fire was up on the *Crier* website, when they went into Jesse's office.

"The principal's not going to like this," Nellie said.

And you're not going to like that Jesse saw Sunny today, provided he even tells you.

Molly knew she wasn't going to fill Nellie in. Or she'd be looking at the overnight shift.

"What I'm about to tell you is off the record," Molly said.

"We're past that."

"Jesse says cops and reporters never are," Molly said. "Past that, I mean."

"Jesse's not here."

"The rules don't change whether he is or not. Off the record?"

"Of course," Nellie said.

Molly told her about her visit to Kevin More, about his relationship with Jack. Nellie listened without interrupting. It was another of Jesse's theories. Sometimes interviewers did their best work when they were listening and not talking.

"Why are you telling me this if I can't write it?" Nellie said when Molly finished.

"Because as transactional as things can be between cops and reporters, I just thought you had a right to know," Molly said. "And because I consider you a friend now."

"Wow," Nellie said.

"Imagine my surprise after the way things started out between us," Molly said.

"You're still acting like I'm one of you," Nellie said. "But I'm really not."

Molly grinned.

"Sometimes you are."

"Yeah," Nellie said, "when it suits the chief of police."

"It's one of the many perks of *being* chief," Molly said. She grinned. "Notice I didn't say 'benefits.'"

Suit knocked on the door, and came in.

He had a printout in his hand.

"What you got?" Molly said.

"We finally got Jack's phone records, praise Jesus," Suit said. "I was actually starting to think Jesus would come back before we did."

They had gotten Charlie's phone records right away, because Charlie's death was labeled a homicide from the start, with very little resistance from the DA at the time. Emma Cleary's phone bill for her landline had simply come in the mail, like always; that streamlined finding out about the More Chocolate Wi-Fi. It had been different with Jack Carlisle's cell phone. No sign of foul play with him. No suicide note. So the whole process of a subpoena, once put in motion, had plodded through the system, to the point where they had all forgotten about it.

Nellie tried to grab the paper out of Suit's hand as he went past her. He snatched it back and handed it to Molly.

"She's deputy chief, remember," Suit said to Nellie.

"Should count for something," Molly said.

She looked at the numbers on the page, the times next to them. In the margin, Suit had written down names next to the numbers in Magic Marker.

"These are just from the night Jack died," Suit said, "the missed calls from ten o'clock on, which is about the time we figure he had his fight with Scott Ford. You can see there's a bunch from Scott, from Ainsley, from Matt Loes."

Molly reached into Jesse's desk and came out with reading glasses. Usually she was too vain to wear her own when anybody was around.

"There are some texts, too," she said.

"Yup," Suit said. "One each from the Ford kid, the Loes kid, and the girl."

Molly ran her finger down the page and stopped at a text that came in at eleven-thirty-two.

"Wait a second," she said.

"What?" Nellie said.

"This one came from Kevin More's number," she said. "I asked him for it yesterday and he gave it to me and I put it in my phone."

"So?" Suit said.

Molly took off the glasses and set them down on the printout.

"Kevin More told Jesse, and he told me, that he didn't try to contact Jack that night," she said. "He was pretty emphatic about it with me. Said he wished he had reached out, maybe he could have changed things somehow, he'd obviously been beating himself up on that. Jesse told me he asked him twice. There was no reason for him to lie. None. Somebody else sent that text. Faked his number the way they fake spam calls."

She handed the paper to Nellie, who looked at it, nodded, and handed it back. Then Molly asked Suit to do her a favor.

"Is this a request?" he said. "Or is it an order?"

"Request," Molly said. "I'm only *deputy* chief."

SEVENTY-NINE

After his allotted time with Dix, Jesse stopped back at the office long enough for Suit to tell him what he'd learned from Verizon.

Then Jesse told the team he needed to get back to Boston.

"Where are you going?" she said.

"I need to get with Sunny and Spike again," he said.

"Are you telling me the truth?" she said.

"Might be," he said.

He wasn't.

HE WAS BACK on 93 headed south, when he called Crow.

"Are you still following Hillary?" Jesse said.

"Did you tell me to stay with her?" Crow said.

"Any sign of Roarke?"

"No. Did you think there'd be?"

"No," Jesse said. "But I had to make sure they weren't together on this, and she was just handing me a load of happy horseshit."

Crow had followed Hillary More to New Hampshire, her plant up there.

"She was inside the factory for a while," Crow said. "There's a Hampton Inn close by. Looks like she's spending the night."

"You mind spending the night, too?"

"They say you get a fresh duvet every day," Crow said. "Sounds like too good a deal to pass up."

Then he asked Jesse where he was.

"On my way to Boston," Jesse said.

"Tell me you're not going alone to see Roarke?"

"Okay, I won't tell you."

He ended the call. He was crossing over the Charles on the Zakim Bridge when he had another incoming call. He thought at first it might be Crow calling him back.

It wasn't.

"Turns out our interests coincided more than you thought, homey," Tony Marcus said. "Guy set my fire turns out to be the guy set yours. And did worse than that."

"Marin," Jesse said.

"His own self."

"Where are you?" Jesse said. "I'm nearly in town. I can come to you."

"Ain't gonna be no none of that," Tony said. "Boy's mine. But he sure can talk, once you put him with Junior."

Then Tony Marcus told Jesse what Marin had told him.

"So turns out I do need to settle my grudge with Roarke sooner rather than later," Tony said.

"Me first," Jesse said.

EIGHTY

Richie Burke helped him out again. Pretty soon they'd be organizing their own poker night.

Technically it was Richie's father who'd helped him. As secretive, and elusive, as Liam Roarke wanted to be as he moved from house to house, Desmond Burke had come to know that Roarke's primary residence was at Monument Square in Charlestown.

Not all that far, Richie told Jesse on the phone, from where Desmond himself lived.

"You're really planning to show up there alone?" Richie asked.

"I want to tell him what I know."

"How much of what you know can you prove?"

"Hardly any without a full confession."

"Anticipating one out of Liam Roarke?"

"Not in my lifetime, or his," Jesse said. "Maybe I can make it a race to see whose lasts longer."

"But you know things."

"Lots."

The red-brick town house, three stories, was at the end of the block. Biggest in the neighborhood, but not looking terribly different from the other town houses in the row. There was no signage letting the neighbors know that there was a career scumbag in their midst.

But there was.

Desmond had assured Richie that Roarke was home tonight.

"How does he know for sure?" Jesse asked.

"Because he's Desmond and because he is," Richie said.

One last time he asked Jesse if he was sure he knew what he was doing.

"This isn't the Old West," Richie said.

"Crow says everything is in the end," Jesse said, and ended the call then.

He drove past Roarke's house once, saw two black Navigators parked in front. He kept going and went around the block, found a parking place, left his Glock and his phone in the glove compartment. They weren't going to let him in without patting him down.

The Old West, maybe, just minus a shoot-out.

At least that was what Jesse was hoping.

Maybe this would be more of a high school stare-down, to see who backed up first.

High school again.

When he walked up the block and turned to head up the front steps, the door to the front Navigator opened and two guys in black suits got out. One blew right past Jesse on the steps, turned around at the door. The other got ahead and stopped Jesse with a forearm.

"Before you do something you're going to regret, I'm a cop," Jesse said.

"The one who's going to have regrets if you don't get your ass out of here is you," the taller of the black suits said.

Jesse was wearing his old Red Sox hat, jeans, running shoes, and a lightweight black leather jacket that was possibly the nicest article of clothing he owned, a gift from Sunny.

"Beat it," the guy guarding the door said.

"Not just yet."

The guy closest to Jesse said, "You want to get in our car, maybe?"

"I don't get in cars with strangers," Jesse said.

The man patted him down.

"Now that we've got the preliminaries out of the way," Jesse told them, "one of you ferocious guys go inside and tell your boss that Jesse Stone is here, and that he wants to talk about Tayshawn Leonard. And about the aria Steve Marin just sang for Tony Marcus."

Nobody said anything until Jesse said, "It's a solo number at the opera."

Five minutes later he was inside.

EIGHTY-ONE

The two bruisers walked him up a stairway in the front hall. A room that looked to be a combination den and study was in the back, on the second floor. When Jesse stepped into the room, the bruiser Dennis he recognized from the Capital Grille and from the Scupper patted him down again. Obviously the top bruiser. Jesse wondered if he had better benefits.

"If I wanted to shoot you," Jesse said, "you'd be shot already." He grinned. "I know a guy."

"The Indian," Roarke said from where he sat on the other side of the room.

"Well, yeah," Jesse said. "But the man can shoot a long gun like Buffalo Bill."

Roarke was in a big leather chair that barely contained him. Lemon-colored V-neck sweater, what looked like a polo shirt of the same color underneath. Jeans that Jesse was certain were a lot more expensive than his own. Loafers, no socks. The loafers looked softer than the sweater.

Gangster in repose.

Like he was ready if somebody else burst in the door for a photo shoot.

Dennis stood just inside the door, leaning against the wall, arms crossed in front of him. Jesse managed not to look terrified.

There was an antique desk set against the back wall. One chair on each side. Also antique.

"Grab that chair," Roarke said, nodding at the desk. "Not that you're going to be here for long. But then neither am I."

"Running?" Jesse said. "I would. Tony's got Marin. And Marin told him just who it was who ordered him to burn down some building of Tony's in Southie and kill one of his guys." Jesse shook his head. "You bad, bad boy."

"I'll be gone in an hour."

"To a non-extraditable country?" Jesse said.

Jesse sat down so that he and Roarke were facing each other.

"Dennis needs to leave," Jesse said.

"You don't tell people what to do in my house."

"But, see, that's the thing. I *am* in your house, Liam. And if you want Dennis to hear what I came here to tell you about your private life, well, that's your call. Makes no difference to me."

Now it was a stare-down.

Roarke finally said, "Give us the room, Dennis."

He likes saying that.

All big guys do.

Before Dennis left Jesse said, "No listening at the door."

"Fuck off," Dennis said.

Roarke told Dennis to send men outside to see if Jesse had brought anybody with him.

When it was just the two of them Roarke said, "Now who's this Tayshawn Leonard?"

He really was a very big man. Somehow bigger in here, in this setting, than he'd seemed the other two times Jesse had been in his presence. The highball glass in his hand looked as small as a shot glass.

"Are we really gonna do this?" Jesse said.

"Do what?"

"Fuck around, Liam," Jesse said. "I know. Okay? I *know*. And something *you* need to know? I don't give a shit about your sexual preferences. But I know you had a thing going on with Tayshawn, a side deal away from the escort service on the occasion when love wasn't for sale. What I don't know is why he had to go away. And go away permanently would be my guess. But that's just one more thing about which I don't give a shit."

Roarke smiled. It reminded Jesse of a large dog baring its teeth.

"You only know what you think you know," he said. "It's why I'm frankly not quite sure why you're here. What gave you the idea that I was going to get scared off by some small-town asshole ex-drunk of a cop?"

He drank whatever it was he was drinking. There was a bottle of Hennessy on a tray next to the desk. That had to be it. Jesse had never been a brandy guy, unless it was all that was handy.

"Because I need you to listen to what I know," Jesse said, "whether I can prove it or not. And not to make too fine a point of things, but I must scare you, or you wouldn't have come to Paradise and tried to cut a deal with me."

"I'm listening. But make it fast. I've got a private plane to catch."

He told Roarke that Marin should have been smart enough to

be on the run himself, except he was never very smart. A friend of his had given him up by now for the fire set at Tony's property. Tony had tracked down Marin at a strip club near Chinatown.

"Marin told Tony about the side game he and Sam Waterfield had going with scam calls of their own, and how you found out about it. Then how Marin went to my friend Charlie Farrell's house after Charlie convinced him he was some feeble old man so scared of the IRS coming after him that he'd drawn out twenty thousand in cash. When Marin got there Charlie put a gun on him and Marin panicked and killed him. When you found out about all *that*, Waterfield and his wheelchair went into the ocean."

"That's some story. I just don't happen to know anything about it."

Jesse ignored him. "What I don't understand is why Waterfield had to die and Marin got to live." Jesse shrugged. "At least until tonight."

"Maybe, since we're just speaking hypothetically, I needed a fire-starter one last time. For old times' sake, maybe?"

Roarke crossed his long legs.

"Not that it matters to you, Stone. But I had nothing to do with that old man dying. I never had anything to do with killing a cop in my life." The bared-teeth smile again. "I mean, maybe until now."

"But you set it all in motion, you son of a bitch."

Roarke drank.

"I thought you said you came here to talk about Tayshawn, by the way."

"That just got me in the door," Jesse said. "You can never go wrong breaking the ice with sex."

"Had a feeling this had to be about more than some missing queer."

Jesse was still hopeful that he could goad Roarke into making a mistake, or an admission, that could actually be used against him. Jesse had palmed the micro-recorder he'd brought when they'd patted him down outside, then again when Dennis went through the drill. Now it was inside his jacket. If Roarke did say something stupid, the recorder would be even better than a Glock.

Roarke hadn't done it yet. He really hadn't told Jesse anything Jesse didn't know when he walked through the door.

"You know what I really think, Roarke?" Jesse said. "I think that wherever you go on the *fucking* earth, I'm going to find you. I don't know if the confession I'm going to get out of Marin will be enough to nail your ass, but I'm going to try like hell to make it so. Maybe even after you have run like the dog that you are."

"And maybe when we're done here," Roarke said, "just think-ing out loud, my guys could hold you down and pour a bottle of whiskey down your throat and you could have a tragic drunk-driving accident."

Roarke drank again.

He let the threat linger in the air.

"Where's Tayshawn?" Jesse said.

Roarke sighed. "Tayshawn got greedy and threatened to tell on us. Then, as far as I know, he chose to go on a long, unplanned vacation." He paused. "*Now* are we done here?"

Jesse reached into his jacket, slowly, came out with a copy of Jack Carlisle's phone records, the one Suit had printed out for him before he'd left Paradise.

"Just one more thing," Jesse said. "For the life of me, what I can't understand is why somebody using the More Chocolate

Wi-Fi—again, the dumb bastard must have gotten careless—ghosted the phone of Hillary More's son, and sent a text to another kid named Jack Carlisle, telling Jack to come meet him at the Bluff the night Jack died."

Before Roarke could respond, they heard voices arguing outside the room, and then the door was opening.

"Boss," Dennis said, "I didn't know how to stop him without having to hurt him."

Kevin More stepped in behind Dennis.

"Dad," he said, "is it true what Mom said, that you burned down her fucking company?"

He noticed Jesse then.

"Wait," Kevin More said. "What's going on here?"

Jesse stared at the kid, processing what he'd just heard.

"Even more than I knew," he finally said.

EIGHTY-TWO

Roarke tried to remain calm. In command. Still the big boss, still in control of the room. But Jesse could see it was a struggle for him now with his son in the scene.

"You know you're not supposed to interrupt business meetings," Roarke said.

"I spoke with Mom," Kevin said. "She told me you're behind the fire. And that she told Chief Stone the same thing."

"She's lying, Kevin," Roarke said.

Kevin barked out a harsh laugh. "Like she hasn't been lying to people my whole life about who my father really is?"

In a quiet voice Roarke said, "You have no idea just how much your mother lied to herself about me. And about what."

He's got that right.

Jesse wondered when Hillary More knew about Roarke being gay. Or if she knew.

Or cared.

Kevin turned to Jesse now.

"Is that why you're here?"

"Partially."

"Not another goddamn word!" Roarke shouted at Jesse.

He jerked his head at Dennis and said, "Get this asshole out of my sight. *Now.*"

"You get the fuck out of here, Dennis," Kevin said. *"Now."*

As if he was the one in charge now.

As if he had the room.

Dennis looked at Roarke, who nodded, almost imperceptibly. Dennis said he'd be on the other side of the door if Roarke needed him.

Roarke was stuck. Jesse knew it. So did he. Dennis wasn't going to come back in and put a gun on a cop, not in front of Roarke's son.

Kevin was Roarke's son.

There was a slight resemblance, but not one Jesse would have ever noticed. The boy was more his mother. Her dark hair. But Roarke's blue, blue eyes. Tall, almost as tall as his old man.

"Before you walked in," Jesse said to Kevin, "I had just asked your father if he happened to know why a text message had been sent from your phone to Jack Carlisle the night Jack died. A text sent off the More Chocolate Wi-Fi."

"Now he's lying," Roarke said. "He's just trying to turn you against me."

To Roarke, Jesse said, "And why would I be looking to do that, having just now discovered that he's your son?"

To Kevin he said, "Apparently, kid, everybody lies except your criminal of an old man. Go figure."

Roarke started to get out of the chair. Stopped himself. Still in a very bad place.

This place.

"Kevin," he said, "I don't know anything about Wi-Fi or a text message or any of that."

"I could tell you what was in the text," Jesse said. "Whoever was impersonating you told Jack how much he loved him, and that the two of you needed to talk."

Nobody spoke until Kevin did. Jesse watched him, the kid frowning, as if he were starting to put things together. Or at least trying to.

"I had told Mom about being gay the day before Jack died. I told her about Jack and me. I wasn't ready to tell you myself, so she said she would. I figured that might soften the blow or whatever."

Jesse said, "It was his people making scam calls. So they'd been ghosting numbers for months. Easy to ghost yours if he wanted them to—Lord knows they knew how to do it."

Kevin was staring at his father.

"Did you have one of your men ghost *my* number?"

"Don't listen to him," Roarke said.

"Did you, Dad?"

"No," Roarke said.

Not looking at him. Staring out the window.

"Did you get Jack to meet you?"

Kevin was shouting now.

And in that moment, Liam Roarke seemed to collapse into himself, as if the fight had gone out of him, at least for now. Jesse thinking: *They're all tough until they're caught.* What Roarke said next came out in a harsh whisper.

"I couldn't let you be like me," he said.

"Like you?" Kevin said. "You mean a criminal?"

Roarke shook his head. Still whispering. "I didn't want you to be gay."

Kevin opened his mouth and closed it. "*You?*" he said. "You're . . . ?"

Roarke nodded. Then nodded at me. "You might as well hear it from me. Stone would have told you, anyway."

Then Roarke said, "I didn't want you to end up hating yourself the way I hate *my*self."

"*What are you talking about?*" Kevin was shouting again. "I was *happy*. I loved Jack. He loved me. What was there to hate about that?"

He was standing over his father then. He was the one who looked like the bigger man, Jesse thought.

"So how did it work, Dad?" he said. "You killed Jack because you couldn't kill me to keep me from being gay?"

"You need to leave, Kevin," Roarke said. "I'm done talking about this for now."

"Got it," Kevin said. "I'm leaving now, and won't be back, not ever again, you son of a bitch."

He turned and walked out of the room and maybe half a minute later the front door slammed.

Just Roarke and Jesse now.

"You got a death wish, Stone?" Roarke said.

"I thought I'd given it up when I gave up drinking," Jesse said. "Maybe not."

"Because you act like you have one."

"Why did that boy have to die?"

"Fuck you."

Roarke finished his drink, slammed the glass down hard.

Jesse thought: *I should have waited to come here with Crow.*

Everything had changed when Kevin More came through the

door, not in a good way for Jesse. Now Roarke was back to being a gangster, in full. Self-hating or otherwise.

Jesse reviewed his options, limited as they were. He was wondering if he could make a move on Dennis when he came back in here, because that might be his only chance to leave this house alive.

"You're a fucking dead man now," Roarke said. "You might not have been before Kevin showed up. But you are now."

"People know that I came here."

"Tell them to try and find you in about an hour."

"If Crow doesn't hear from me, he'll come for you."

"Tell him to try and find *me*. Him and Marcus both."

At some point Jesse was going to have to make a move, maybe on Roarke, knowing that there were guns on the other side of the door. He just didn't know when. Or if the moment had already come and gone when Kevin was still there as distraction.

"Dennis!" Roarke yelled finally.

This time when Dennis came through the door, he had his gun out.

"It's time for Chief Stone to have that accident we talked about a week ago," Roarke said. "Take a bottle from the cabinet downstairs. No reason to waste the good stuff on a drunk."

Dennis motioned for Jesse to walk out ahead of him, and start down the stairs.

Roarke was right behind them.

"You and the boys tie him to a chair in the kitchen," Roarke said. "I want to watch him start drinking again."

"You'll have to kill me first," said Jesse.

"Have it your way," Roarke said.

They had just gotten to the foot of the stairs when the front door opened and Kevin More, gun in his own hand, yelled for Jesse to get down and fired his first shot into his father's chest, and then two more in rapid succession after that, all of the shots sounding like explosions in the small area.

Dennis was raising his own gun, but Jesse wheeled and knocked it out of his hand before punching him in the neck. Then he had Dennis's gun in his hands as the black suits from outside were coming through the door, Jesse yelling at Kevin to get down now.

The taller black suit got off a shot before Jesse put him down. The second guy put his gun on the ground, and his hands up. Jesse told Kevin to now use his phone to call 911, and then let Jesse do the talking when the cavalry arrived.

Even before Jesse heard the first siren, and had established that Liam Roarke was dead, he wondered whether Kevin had shot Roarke to save Jesse.

Or if he had shot him and kept shooting for Jack Carlisle.

EIGHTY-THREE

Two weeks later.

Nellie Shofner had made headlines just about everywhere, and put herself on the national map, with her story headlined "To a Gay Athlete Dying Young."

She had written the piece with the permission of Jack's mother, and also with permission from Kevin More. It turned out he'd had a copy of Jack's one-act play all along, which he'd written on a computer at the Paradise High library. He'd shown it to Kevin the day before he died, because he said it was finally ready to be seen.

Nellie didn't use all of the play. But she used a lot of it, primarily the speeches from the main character.

"The world is going to care about my story," the main character, called Ben, says at one point. "I just hope it cares for the right reasons."

From the responses Jesse had seen, that they'd all seen, the world had embraced the story of Jack Carlisle, who'd finally come out.

Kevin More hadn't been charged in the shooting death of Liam Roarke. Jesse had told Lieutenant Frank Belson, the first cop to the house on Monument Square—Jesse imagined it being a race once they found out who the victim was—that the kid was actually a hero for saving a policeman's life.

His.

When Belson had arrived, Jesse was the only witness still on the scene, Roarke's men having run like the dogs *they* were, same as their boss had been about to do.

"Kid put four in him," Belson said, chewing on an unlit cigar. "He must have *really* wanted to save you."

"He's a kid, Frank," Jesse said. "He'd never shot anybody before. He clearly panicked. Probably couldn't even tell you right now how many times he fired."

"Unless it was an execution," Belson said.

"Of his dad?"

"Well," Belson said, "maybe this dad."

JESSE WAS SITTING across from Kevin More at the Gull, having just finished lunch. He told Jesse his mom, last he heard, was somewhere in Southern California, sorting out the shuttering of the company and the payouts remotely.

"She told me she wanted to move near Stanford so she could be close to you," Jesse said.

"She lied," he said. "She does that."

"Noticed."

Jesse had spent a lot of lunch telling Kevin what Dix had told him, and how being a self-loathing gay man had made a violent man even more violent, especially someone as obsessed with power and appearances as Liam Roarke was. A few days after Monument Square a badly beaten and horribly bloated body, Tayshawn Leonard's, had been found floating in the water near Castle Rock, in Marblehead.

One more body in the water because of Liam Roarke.

"There was no way the guy was going to kill his own kid," Jesse told Kevin, repeating what Dix had said to him. "He wasn't going to kill himself. But somehow in that moment, without knowing what went on that night, the object of his anger, and his self-loathing, became his son's lover.

"We'll never know whether he went there to kill Jack or tell him to stay away from you," Jesse said. "But something must have snapped."

"I'm just relieved Jack didn't kill himself because of us," Kevin said.

"From my reading of that play," Jesse said, "he sounded like somebody who couldn't wait to get on with his life. Openly."

After a pause, Jesse said, "Molly wanted me to ask you if you had any idea who that Pepsquad1234 was on social media."

"It was Scott Ford," Kevin said. He grinned. "I think Scott may have had more feelings for Jack than he did for Ainsley, if you want to know the truth."

"I'll take any I can get."

"Why did Matt Loes beat him up?" Jesse said. "Scott, I mean."

"Because Scott wanted to tell," Kevin said. "He said Jack had nothing to be ashamed of and so we shouldn't be ashamed of him even though he was gone. Pretty much what he told Jack before *their* fight. They were both drunk. Matt was drunker. And bigger."

Kevin had told Jesse he wasn't sticking around for graduation, the school would mail him his diploma. He was on his way this afternoon to another of his father's houses, one that really was a safe house, on Martha's Vineyard. He said he was going to stay there awhile, probably look for a summer job coaching tennis.

When they were outside the Gull, Kevin said, "Thank you for everything."

"Not sure what I did, other than be too goddamn slow on the uptake, all over town."

Kevin smiled. "But in the end you didn't just find out about my truth, and Jack's. You pretty much found everybody else's, too."

"How old were you when you found out who your father was?"

"It was only a few years ago."

"And you were able to have a relationship with him after that?"

"I knew he existed in a violent world." He exhaled loudly, shook his head. "But he was my dad. I never got to know the man who I thought was my dad. For better or worse, I thought I'd gotten a second chance."

"And he was good to you."

"And to mom. Until he wasn't, with either one of us."

They walked down Main Street, past where More Chocolate used to be, the cleanup of the remains almost complete.

"What do you think happened to Steve Marin?" Kevin More asked.

"Another gangster, this one named Tony Marcus, happened," Jesse said.

"You think Marin is still alive somewhere?"

"Not so anybody would notice," Jesse said. "Tony settles grudges. And sometimes not just his own."

"You okay with that?"

"Charlie Farrell might not have been okay with it," Jesse said. "But he was a better man than I am."

EIGHTY-FOUR

In the late afternoon, Jesse met Crow at O'Hara Field, where there was a Babe Ruth League game going on. Twelve-year-olds and up. Jesse remembered what it was like when he was that age, the first year he got to play on the big field.

But then he remembered just about all of it.

"Game goes faster when kids are playing it," Crow said.

"No shit," Jesse said.

The game was in the second inning when they got there, tied 2–2. It looked to Jesse like the happiest place in the world.

"You think Hillary More might have been in on more than she let on?" Crow said. "And was just lying that tight ass of hers off?"

"Bet *your* ass."

"So she gets away with it."

"Think about what her life is going to be like going forward," Jesse said. "And then tell me just exactly *what* she got away with."

"You think Tony took out Marin for himself, or for you?"

"I keep asking myself the same question about Kevin shooting his father."

"Only difference," Crow says, "is that Tony gets away with murder all the time."

Jesse turned as he heard the crack of the aluminum bat, knowing before he picked up the flight of the ball that it was going to be splitting the outfielders. It wasn't the same sweet sound as wood. But he still knew what a solid hit sounded like.

They watched in silence for a full inning. It was the beauty of bringing Crow to a game. He didn't think he was there to provide commentary.

Eventually, eyes on the action in front of them, Crow said, "Fixing to head back to the Cape tonight."

"Figured, now that your work here's done," Jesse said. "You tell Molly?"

"She bravely hid her disappointment," Crow said.

He turned to face Jesse. "You break it off with Nellie like you told me you were going to?"

"I let her think it was her idea," Jesse said. "And she's probably on her way to *The New York Times* or *The Washington Post* after her big scoop."

Jesse grinned. "She was too old for me, anyway."

The blue team finally beat the red team, 6–4. The kids in blue celebrated on the field as if they were the ones who'd now won the championship of the world.

Jesse and Crow started walking back toward town.

As they did, Jesse felt his phone buzzing in his pocket. He took it out and looked at the screen:

Spam Risk.

ACKNOWLEDGMENTS

Once again, my gratitude to David and Daniel Parker for allowing me to continue characters created by their giant of a father.

The same goes for Ivan Held, the boss of all bosses at Putnam, and my wonderful editor, Danielle Dieterich.

Big thanks, as always, to Esther Newberg, who treats the literary estate of Robert B. Parker like the trust that it is.

And finally, a shout-out to the members of the band—David Koepp, Peter Gethers, Ziggy and Nancy Alderman, Capt. John Fisher—who are never too busy to spitball.

TURN THE PAGE FOR AN EXCERPT

The beautiful wife of one of the world's richest men comes to Spenser hoping that he can find out what skeletons lurk in her husband's closet. Though he is a generous philanthropist and loving family man, she is concerned—he has recently become secretive, bordering on paranoid, and she wants Spenser to find out why. As Spenser digs into the billionaire's past, he realizes that the man may have done terrible things on his rise to the top—but he also may have had good reason to.

What Spenser discovers will cause him to question his own views on morality—and place him in grave danger.

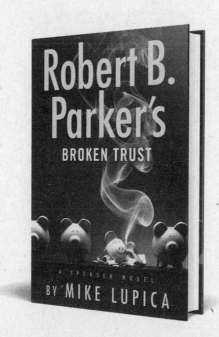

ONE

I was sitting at my desk drinking my third cup of coffee of the morning. I was doing this guilt-free, having read that two to five cups a day not only prevented a long list of diseases, but also helped you live a longer, if more caffeinated, life. But then you can always find somewhere on the Internet that tells you what you want to hear, about almost anything.

I was certain that if I looked long enough, I could find a site promising a reasonably priced way for me to look like Bradley Cooper.

By now I had already made short work of the second Boston Kreme I'd picked up at the Dunkin' just down Boylston from my office, the one near the Public Library. Two blocks down, two blocks back. But I had walked briskly, telling myself it was exercise, even if the prize had been the donuts, which didn't extend your life, just made it more worth living.

Dunkin' Donuts had long since rebranded and was just calling itself Dunkin' now. I had considered doing something similar, but knew it was too late for that. And when it came to branding your-self with just one name, I had frankly been way ahead of the game.

Carol Sloane's voice was coming out of the tiny speaker near the Keurig machine and I was methodically making my way through the print edition of *The Globe*, as I still did every morn-ing, front to back, section by section, saving sports for last. The man who owned *The Globe* also owned the Red Sox. The paper was having a far better September than his baseball team was.

But then just about everybody was. It had reached the point where I was no longer certain that the two guys who were sup-posed to be our top starting pitchers were actually still right-handed.

"Maybe you should think about finding a new hobby," Hawk had said the other day after listening to me bitching again about the local nine.

"I've got too much time invested in them," I said. "It's the same reason I'm still with you."

"You're with me," Hawk said, "because I don't have no bad years."

We had just finished moving the last of my furniture that we could carry ourselves into my new apartment, which just hap-pened to be a few doors down from the one I'd been burned out of a few years ago. It was the event that had prompted my move away from Marlborough Street and all the way to the Charleston Navy Yard.

At the time Susan Silverman, trying to mitigate my loss, had said that while it had been the equivalent of a forced eviction, it might have been time for a change, even though she knew better than anyone that I liked change about as much as I liked TikTok.

"Most people do move sooner or later," Susan said.

"The Red Sox haven't," I said.

She had promised that I would embrace the new place once I was in it, and proceeded to move in and decorate it like an invading ground force. And eventually I had grown both fond and familiar with my new surroundings, the neighborhood, the proximity to the Navy Yard, even the younger vibe over there, as if I were the one who was young and had moved to Boston all over again.

But recently I'd done some work for a man named Kevin Boles, who owned great big chunks of property in Back Bay, getting Boles's son out of a jam with Tony Marcus that involved substantial gambling losses that Tony had decided required more than just money in payment. Tony wanted real estate favors from Kevin Boles, specifically involving a particular building he hoped to use for a new escort service on Charles Street now that COVID was over and the sex trade was booming again.

Boles had come to me and I had gone to Tony, reminding him that he owed me a favor. Tony told me that he didn't owe me shit and get the fuck out of his office. But being as transactional as he'd always been, an accommodation had been reached and he got the building he wanted. Kevin Boles considered it a small price to pay to get his son clear of Tony, and even after he'd generously settled up with me, he said that he was the one who now owed me a favor.

ABOUT A WEEK later he'd called and told me that an apartment on Marlborough near the corner of Arlington had opened up, having remembered me mentioning that I'd lived on the same part of that street before what I called the Great Boston Fire. Boles said that the apartment hadn't yet gone on the market, and asked if I might be interested in moving back to the old neighborhood. I surprised myself at how quickly I said that I was. He said he could give me a break on the rent. I told him that wasn't necessary. He insisted. A month away from the end of my lease in Charlestown, I signed the lease that day, put down a deposit, and just like that Daddy was home.

"Do you know how much I've missed walking to work?" I said to Susan the first time we stepped into the empty apartment.

"At this point, people in outer space know that."

She asked me just how much Kevin Boles had paid for my services, and how much of a break he was giving me on the rent. I told her. At which point she had smiled, wickedly. Susan has a lot of smiles, most of which make me feel light-headed and oxygen-deprived when directed at me.

This one, I knew from experience, was going to cost me money.

"I know that look," I said.

"What look is that?" she asked innocently.

"The one where you can't wait for the stores to open."

She'd kissed me then and said, "Don't you worry your pretty little head about it."

The new apartment, about the same size as the old one, didn't actually feel like home yet. But I was getting there. Pearl the Wonder Dog had already settled in quite nicely when she and Susan would be there for sleepovers. Pearl hadn't come right out and said how much she liked it that she could walk to work with me, too, when Susan would leave her with me. It was more something I had intuited.

Now I just needed work, as there hadn't been any since I'd saved Kevin Boles's son.

"If you can walk to work but there ain't no work," Hawk had said, "answer me something: What's the fucking point?"

I was pondering that, and whether I should walk back down to Dunkin' for more donuts before I got too close to lunch, when there was a knock on my door and the wife of the sixth-richest man in America came walking in.

TWO

Laura Crain was a friend of Susan's from a couple charity boards they both served on in Boston, one of which—the Jimmy Fund—was as famous a charity as there was in the city, aligned with the Dana-Farber Cancer Institute, and deeply connected to the Red Sox all the way back to when Ted Williams had first gotten involved.

Susan and Laura Crain shared a Pure Barre class a couple times a week and would meet occasionally for lunch. I knew that Susan liked her very much, as rich and famous as Laura and her husband were, and not just in Boston.

Laura had met Andrew Crain when they were both students at Harvard. Laura was an English major. He was a full-fledged, card-carrying Division of Science nerd, along with his best friend, Ethan Lowe. I knew the general outline of their shared biography, because by now most people in America knew it. Five years after Lowe and Andrew Crain graduated, working out of a small rented lab in Dorchester, they had invented a synthetic form of lithium that had reimagined the world of batteries forever.

Susan had mentioned in passing a few weeks earlier that I might be hearing from her friend Laura about a problem she was having, one she'd shared in confidence with Susan.

"Are you treating her now?"

"Not professionally. Just hearing her out as a friend and offering advice when she's asked for it."

"And she has a problem that you can't solve?" I said. "What is it, the melting of the ice caps?"

"She'll tell you when the two of you meet," Susan said, "if she doesn't lose her nerve."

"Couldn't she buy some nerve?" I'd asked. "I assume she can afford it."

"Let's just wait and see," Susan said. "She should be the one to tell you what's happening in her life. But I told *her* that if anybody could help her, it's my cutie."

Now Laura Crain sat across my desk from me. Tall. Honey-colored hair hanging to her shoulders. Blazer, white jeans that fit her the way God intended jeans to fit women with legs as long as hers, ankle boots. Whatever her actual age was, I had already decided she looked younger. She reminded me of a slightly younger version of Julia Roberts, not that I would ever say that to Julia.

A knockout by any measure. It was something I knew I couldn't verbalize without sounding as if I were objectifying her, and being on my way to Weinstein Island.

But Andrew Crain, I could see, hadn't just gotten stupidly rich. He had even gotten the girl.

"So you're Spenser," she said, crossing one long leg over the other.

"I am he," I said.

I had come around the desk to greet her when she'd arrived. In the post-pandemic world I'd first asked if she wanted to shake hands before extending mine. She'd said she'd risk it if I would.

"People often say 'I am him,'" I said. "But that's ignoring the fact that 'he' is actually supposed to be a predicate nominative renaming the subject."

She smiled. It was, by any measure, a high-wattage dazzler, if not of Susan quality, at least in the conversation. Susan had prepared me for how lovely Laura Crain was. I was certain I would be cross-questioned later about just *how* lovely *I* thought she was.

"Susan told me about you," she said.

I ducked my head in false modesty.

"The rugged good looks?" I said. "Or devilish charm?"

She shook her head slowly from side to side, as if in the presence of a precocious child.

Which, all things considered, she was.

"She actually told me how hard you'd try, almost immediately, to show me what a literate detective you are," she said. "And that if I didn't acknowledge that fact you might get the bends."

"I can also diagram some sentences if you want," I said.

"Maybe when we know each other better."

Now I smiled at her.

"Want to can the small talk?"

"I'd be willing to pay you," she said.

I asked if she wanted coffee. She said thank you, but she'd pass, she was trying to quit caffeine. I told her I didn't want to live in that world. She managed to contain her laughter, but I sensed it was difficult for her.

"Might I offer just one last tiny bit of small talk?" she said.

"Okay, but *just* one."

"You really are as big as Susan said you were."

"Well, sure, but I come by it naturally."

We sat there in silence for a few moments, as if each of us were waiting for the other to make the next move. It often went this way with potential clients, like an awkward first date, and just how much they wanted to drop their guard.

"So how can I help you, Mrs. Crain?"

"Please. *Laura*."

"So how can I help you, Laura."

Her blue eyes were so pale as to be as clear as glass.

"That's the thing," she said. "You probably can't."

Robert B. Parker was the author of seventy books, including the legendary Spenser detective series, the novels featuring Jesse Stone, and the acclaimed Virgil Cole/Everett Hitch westerns, as well as the Sunny Randall novels. Winner of the Mystery Writers of America Grand Master Award and long considered the undisputed dean of American crime fiction, he died in January 2010.

Mike Lupica is a prominent sports journalist and the *New York Times* bestselling author of more than forty works of fiction and nonfiction. A longtime friend to Robert B. Parker, he was selected by the Parker estate to continue the Spenser, Sunny Randall, and Jesse Stone series.

VISIT ROBERT B. PARKER AND MIKE LUPICA ONLINE

robertbparker.net
 RobertBParkerAuthor
mikelupicabooks.com
 MikeLupica

The Dean of American
Crime Fiction

Robert B. Parker

To learn more about the author,
please visit robertbparker.net